chapter **1**

THE T

JANUARY 22, 1975
MONASTERY OF THE HOLY MARTYRS, LENINGRAD, U.S.S.R.

YURI TUCKED HIS chin under his coat collar, trying to ward off the stabbing wind that gusted across the frozen Neva River. The street slithered with white rivulets of snow as Yuri and his young daughter stepped around an old man struggling to shovel a narrow pathway up the monastery steps. Fat snowflakes churning in the raw evening wind accumulated faster than the old man could scoop them away with his one good arm. A pinned-over coat sleeve covered the stump of his other arm. A row of ribbons and war medals hung from his chest.

As Yuri and his daughter approached, the man paused, squinted against an icy gust and leaned on the broken end of his shovel. "The monks have bread for the hungry," he said, then bent over again and scraped his flat, rusted spade over the hard-packed ice that covered the path.

Yuri and Tanya moved up the steps and arrived at a pair of locked, cedar-plank doors. Yuri pounded the wood with a leather-gloved hand. A few moments later, the door creaked open, exposing bone-thin fingers that held a thick chunk of brown bread.

"We are not here for food," Yuri said.

A voice wafted from behind the door. "Then why do you come here?"

"I bring the girl. She has the gift."

"Gift?"

"The gift of the Pravda legend." Yuri waited for a response.

The thin fingers unfurled and the brown bread tumbled to the floor. The monastery door moved, widening the gap between it and the jamb.

Yuri and his young daughter stepped inside. A gray-bearded priest wearing a brown floor-length cassock, a black Byzantine klobuk perched upon his head, watched them with sunken eyes. A large, ornate, silver cross dangled from his neck. He lifted a flickering paraffin lamp and bowed in silent greeting. He then turned and pushed the heavy door shut against the invading blast of cold, and latched it with a large sliding bolt.

"I am sorry, but I usually tend to the welfare of men's souls—not the digging up of their bodies, as we are about to do." His words flowed over blue lips and lingered in a vaporous mist.

Yuri had no desire for small talk. "We must hurry. The KGB is looking for the girl. We must conduct our business and leave quickly. I will take the girl across the border to Finland and escape the madness of this vile government."

The priest nodded, then waved for them to follow in the flickering glow of his light.

Two rats nibbled at the fallen chunk of bread on the floor, unconcerned as the priest limped past. Yuri and Tanya followed the priest's lamplight and descended a steep set of stone stairs. The cold seemed to follow, pushing from behind.

At the bottom of the stairs was an arched stone chamber, its floor covered in a thin veneer of frozen scum that crackled with each footfall. Green water dripped from the ceiling.

The priest pointed to a dark corner, where a large gray granite sarcophagus rested.

Yuri felt Tanya pull his coat sleeve as she released a muffled sob from under her woolen neck scarf. Chiseled on the face of the crypt, in old Russian Cyrillic, was the moss-encrusted name of *Feodor Kuzmich*, with the date of 1864 carved below.

A monk, head bowed and hooded canopy shielding his face, stood on each side of the stone coffin, murmuring somnolent prayers.

The old priest bent to the girl. "You are the awaited one of the legend . . . the girl with the Pravda." His lamplight reflected in her small, troubled eyes. Tanya took a step back and brushed away a tear. The old cleric spoke slowly, his lips slipping over tarnished brown teeth. "The man entombed here has a message for you."

Yuri stared at the smooth granite casket. "I bring my daughter at the request of my wife, Natalia."

"Where is your wife?" the priest asked.

"She has died. Three weeks ago."

The priest closed his eyes in a moment of reverent reflection. "You have done well to bring her." Placing his hand upon Tanya's black hair, the priest asked, "So it is true? I must know for certain. You can hear when a voice speaks an untruth? Do you truly have the Pravda?"

Tanya looked at her father, whose eyes relayed his approval. She then turned back to the priest, and nodded.

The priest sighed. "At long last the legend breathes."

Yuri asked, "How did you know that the girl and I would come?"

"Your wife knew the legend. It tells of a girl born with the Pravda—a girl who should be brought here and given a message from the tomb."

"My wife would have brought the girl, but she was gravely ill for some time." The memory of his wife's passing drove a hot blade through Yuri's heart.

The priest gave a comforting smile. "Do not mourn. She awaits your arrival in Heaven, and Heaven is never far away. Her ears will be able to hear, and her lips able to speak words of love for you." He returned his attention to the girl. "It is a mystery why your daughter was born with the Pravda gift when her mother lived her entire life stone deaf."

Yuri studied the priest for a moment, long enough to remember the day his wife told him that when their daughter was old enough, they would visit the monastery. That was seven years ago. At the time Yuri hadn't understood his wife's words. Now he did.

The old priest clapped his weathered hands. The two monks standing by the stone coffin stepped forward, and, in unison, curled their fingers under the edge of the stone lid. They slid it slightly to one side. The scraping sound broke the chamber's silence. The lid refused to move easily. With a few more muscle-straining pushes, the heavy slab scooted a few more inches.

The priest turned his wizened face to the girl. "Remember this night well, child. Remember the legend. There is no secret in this world that time and Heaven does not unlock."

Stepping to the sarcophagus, he held the glowing paraffin lamp over the narrow gap between the grave's lid and stone side, and peered into the coffin's cavity.

Yuri moved to the priest's side and craned his neck to see what lay within. He saw a skull topped with a coarse, tangled tuft of gray hair. The tomb's occupant stared back with black, empty sockets. The skull had no jaw. His head, a stub of a spine, and a pair of arms was all Yuri could see. A full-length peasant chemise blackened with aged fungus covered the skeleton. In the naked bones of the right hand rested an old, golden snuff box.

The priest pulled back the sleeve of his cassock, then slid his arm through the space between the lid and side of the sarcophagus, until his searching fingers found the golden object. It was fused to brown, curdled skin. He pulled again and the relic came free, the connected dry sinew disintegrating into gritty granules. The priest drew the box slowly from the coffin and held it close to his light for a moment. Despite a layer of dust, it glinted in the light. He held it out to Tanya.

Tanya looked at Yuri. He nodded. Her hands trembled as she took the box. "What is it?"

The priest spoke softly, as if muttering a prayer. "It is a snuff box, child—a gold snuff box. Inside is a message from long ago—a message for you."

"Message?" Yuri asked.

"Yes, a message and a small glass vial of bread from Heaven— the manna of God."

Yuri took the box and examined it. It was heavier than he expected and ornately crafted. Delicate filigree edged the golden lid and a double-headed eagle decorated the middle: the imperial seal of the royal Romanov family.

"What's a snuff box?" Tanya asked. She looked confused and frightened.

The priest explained. "Long ago, men ground tobacco into powder. The wealthy kept their powder in a golden snuff box."

Yuri gazed at the box resting in his gloved hand, his mind whirling with questions. "Who is the man in the grave? What does he have to do with us?"

The priest stepped away from the sarcophagus. "He once lived as a czar, his soul lost to the wind, but he died a monk saved by the cross of Jesus."

"The czar?" Yuri said. The words drained him of strength.

"Yes—"

A loud pounding on the upstairs vestibule door rumbled down the stone steps. They froze in silence; the only sound Yuri could hear was the gulping breaths of his daughter.

They heard more pounding, followed by a muffled, harsh voice. "KGB. Open the door, priest."

The priest's forehead creased. He motioned for the two attending monks to go up the stairs and tend to the visitor. As they turned to go, the priest spoke in a reassuring tone. "In Christ, to die is gain." The hooded monks nodded, but said nothing. Their dark forms ascended the stone steps.

The priest turned to Yuri. "Bring the girl."

Without waiting for a reply, the priest turned and started down a narrow, low-arched tunnel that snaked into darkness. He was old and bent over, but he moved with urgency. The passageway's floor and walls felt slick. Yuri assumed the tunnel also served as drainage for the wet tomb. He gripped Tanya's hand.

Light from the priest's lantern reflected eerily off stone cavities cut in the walls. Stacked skeletons in various stages of decomposition plugged each cavity. A sour, pungent odor hung in the air. Yuri saw Tanya pulled her scarf over her face to keep from retching.

After a minute of shuffling and slipping in the icy maze of darkness, they reached the end. Yuri saw the faint blue hue of falling snow through the tunnel's exterior opening. A moment later, they stood in the monastery's courtyard.

The priest gulped for air—more from exertion, Yuri assumed,

than fear. The old man pointed to a dark clump of trees at the edge of the courtyard. "The evil one comes to take the child, so run; run with Godspeed."

Yuri led Tanya by the hand and had made fifty trudging strides in the snow when he heard a shot split the howling wind. Yuri turned and caught sight of a flashlight beam scanning the courtyard. The beam silhouetted the old priest as he held out his arms in a desperate attempt to stop the man's advance. The man easily shoved the old cleric aside, his frail form crumpling to the snow.

Yuri heard the crack of another gunshot, and something whistled past his ear. He began to turn when another gun blast parted the cold air, and a searing pain knifed through his leg. He collapsed into the snow. Warm blood seeped from his thigh and wafted steam, visible in the flashlight beam that fell upon his body. The gold box lay in the snow by Yuri's side. Tanya sank to her knees next to her father and wrapped her arms around his shoulders. He heard sobbing.

Yuri waited. He waited for the bullet that would strike him in the heart or in the head. More than anything he wanted to tell Tanya to run, to flee into the dark forest and hide from the monster with the flashlight and gun, but he knew she would never make more than a few meters before the KGB man caught her or shot her.

As he raised a hand to shield his eyes from the light, he saw the glint of the man's smile—and his silver teeth. A second later he heard a thud. The beam from the flashlight jerked to the side and dropped to the snow. The man standing over Yuri and Tanya had released the light. A half-second later, Yuri watched his pursuer fall face down, still clutching the gun in his hand. The man fell on the flashlight; its beam now shone upward.

Yuri saw a wide flap of pink scalp hanging from the back of the man's stump of a head. Thick blood matted his greasy hair.

Yuri turned his gaze to the one-armed man they had passed when entering the monastery. He held the same shovel, now caked with red snow. The caretaker's chest heaved from the shock and effort of his actions, making the medals on his chest clink like chimes. As he gazed upon the still form below him, he said, "The way of the wicked is death."

He then let the shovel slip from his hand and helped Yuri to his feet. The pain from the wound raced up Yuri's leg and into his back, as if someone had set fire to every nerve. Despite the support of the one-armed man, Yuri winced and swayed.

Yuri forced himself to speak. "We owe you a great debt of thanks. Thank you."

"My name is Sergey."

"The old priest? How is he?"

A voice came from the darkness. "I do not believe I am dead just yet." The priest hobbled through the snow to Sergey and patted his back. "One good arm from a righteous man can triumph over an army of two-armed men allied with the devil."

Yuri looked at the KGB man lying in the snow and wondered if he was dead or just unconscious. Yuri decided he did not care. All he wanted was to get his daughter away from this place.

"I fear more KGB will come soon," the priest said. "Sergey, take this man to the abbey; he is unable to travel very far. The monks there will tend to his wounds. As for the girl, she needs to be taken far from here. If the KGB knows of her gift, they will take her away, and God only knows what will happen then."

"Papa, what is happening?"

Yuri struggled to maintain his balance. "I am trying to understand that myself, Tanya." The snow below Yuri was slushy with dark blood. "You must go with the priest, Tanya. He will know what to do."

"I don't want to go, Papa. I want to stay with you."

A new pain coursed through Yuri, not from a wound to the body, but one to the heart. "Tanya, you are in danger. You must go with the priest."

"But Papa—"

"No arguments. You will do as I say."

"Yes, Papa." She lowered her head. He could hear her broken heart with every breath she took.

He pulled her close and ran a hand over her dark hair. "You are all I have left. I see your mother in every twinkle of your eye, hear her in every giggle. I . . . must do everything I can to make certain you are safe."

She turned her face up. Tears had left moist tracks on her cheeks. "When will I see you again?"

"We will see each other again. I don't know how long. However long it is, know this: our time apart can only make my love for you grow. Be strong, little one. Be wise. Will you do that, little one?" Yuri asked.

"Yes, Papa. I will."

Despite the pain, Yuri lowered himself and kissed his daughter on the top of her head. He prayed it would not be the last time he did so.

Yuri, with the help of the caretaker, limped down a nearby path. He glanced over his shoulder and saw his daughter trailing behind the priest. A stinging gust of ice particles swirled around them, and Tanya wrapped her scarf about her face.

The trail of their steps parted in the dark woods.

chapter **2**

THE BRIEFCASE

THE PRIVATE JET roared down the runway at Phoenix Sky Harbor Airport, rose gracefully and banked east. The rapid acceleration pushed Carolyn Dawson back in her richly padded leather seat near the rear of the aircraft. She had ridden in her employer's business jet many times but still found takeoffs exhilarating.

An object—black and small—blurred faintly past Carolyn's window. She surmised it must have been a small bird of some kind—what else could it be?

Outside her window, the sprawling grids of rooftops scrolled past at increasing speed, melding quickly into a sea of mesquite-dotted sand. It was as if Earth itself was attempting to put distance between it and the aircraft.

In the jet's path, dark clumps of rain clouds waited, ready to pour their cargo of water on the Sonoran Desert below. Such clouds meant a few moments of bumpy ride as the craft slid through turbulent air.

Carolyn leaned against the window to increase her view. The jet leveled from its bank but kept its nose up, climbing to its cruising altitude. She could see the white starboard wing glinting from the few sunbeams that managed to push through the billowing thunderheads.

Minutes later, the jet leveled off at thirty-five thousand feet.

Carolyn gazed at shadowless craggy mountains that bore no sign of human life, other than a lonely vein of asphalt road vanishing into the thirsty horizon.

The trip to Phoenix had been mercifully short. She had flown in early that day to conduct her business. Carolyn had come to acquire a book—a *Bible*—very old and very expensive. She made the purchase on behalf of an anxious, dying old man. Her boss, billionaire R. C. Cooper, had given her orders and authority to spend whatever she needed to get the book. Without so much as a handshake, she forfeited a fortune for possession of the Bible and packed it carefully in a camel-skin-covered titanium briefcase. Like a Kansas twister cutting through a cornfield, the deal was done minutes after negotiations began. The rare book was now hers, or, more accurately, R. C. Cooper's.

Now she was beginning her long flight to New York. After refueling there, she would endure a nighttime transatlantic crossover, putting her back in the verdant hills of England by morning's first light.

Her prize safely balanced on her lap, she allowed herself to relish the efficient way she had closed the transaction. She smiled at what the affable college grad must be thinking. He was probably shaking in his shoes at the thought of so much money changing hands in the last hour. Now, with some favorable tailwinds, she would be back home soon to enjoy, in all likelihood, the kind of raw English drizzle that kept her garden green all winter.

Since they had leveled off, Carolyn felt free to rise from her seat, step to the onboard bar and pour a glass of chardonnay. She returned to her seat, set the drink in a holder and searched in her over-stuffed purse. She found her bottle of sleeping pills and swallowed two small white capsules with a long sip of the wine. Snuggling the briefcase securely under her right arm, she thought it almost comical. Who would try to steal a briefcase when she was the only passenger? She tilted her seat back, satisfied with a mission that was all but complete.

Back home in England, she knew, Sir Richard Cooper eagerly awaited the treasure she had in her possession. Carolyn had been his personal secretary for over forty years, and—due in part to the attrition of bothersome family members, and in part to her persistent loyalty—she had become the only person the old man trusted; certainly the only one he trusted to courier this particular Bible, this priceless treasure, back to Britain.

In the cockpit, the pilot leaned forward, flipping switches with an extended knuckle, double-checking the instruments. With a quick flourish of finger strokes, he uploaded the navigational settings and engaged the jet's autopilot. He felt sluggish and exhausted. These emergency flights across the Atlantic depleted him. The day before, his bedside phone had awakened him at 3 a.m., and he received orders from R. C. Cooper himself to fly an emergency haul to Phoenix. It was rare that anyone heard directly from Sir Richard, much less a late-breaking request of this nature, so there could be no doubt that whatever the reason, it was more than important.

He stifled a yawn and glanced at his young copilot. "Rest your eyes a few. I'll turn her over in an hour or so."

The copilot, a young man in his twenties, newly hired out of flight school in Manchester, nodded and leaned forward in his seat. "I'm really not tired," he said, scribbling a few notes in the log for the mechanics back at Heathrow.

The pilot grinned, recognizing in the young man the same restless enthusiasm he'd felt on his first overseas flight. He checked the course once more on the computer.

"Do you feel that?" the copilot asked.

"Feel what?"

"I think I feel a vibration."

"I think you're more tired than you realize." He glanced over the gauges. "Instruments read normal."

"I guess you're right. Probably my imagination."

"You're new to this airplane. She's a good one, but like every aircraft, she has her own feel. You'll get used to it."

"Check," he said, then adjusted the flight path to slice over southern Colorado.

Carolyn felt a sudden need to take another peek at the rare Bible. She knew well the stories of how it had supposedly saved lives over the years through one miracle or another, and she thought perhaps by looking at it she might glean some clue to its powers.

Her boss certainly had no doubts. Two days earlier, Carolyn Dawson had been awakened at 3 a.m. to come to the old man's bedside. With a quaking voice, he'd told her the rare and sought-after book had been found, and that she was to fly to Phoenix immediately to retrieve it. She'd been given authority to pay whatever was needed. She understood his urgency. Time was short: his aged, emaciated body was shutting down.

With Carolyn leaning close to hear, R. C. Cooper had wrestled for air, fighting desperately to sip another breath into failing lungs. With bony fingers he had held her hand. "I will pay all I have to get that Bible."

In Phoenix, the young seller, a recent college grad named Gary Brandon, had only minutes before he handed the Bible over to Carolyn. *Seller* wasn't the right word: the young man claimed no ownership, having received the Bible through a set of complicated circumstances. He felt it was not his to have and sought only to give the book back to the rightful owner. He couldn't have known how priceless the tattered Bible was to one of the world's wealthiest men, or that he would have paid a fortune to have the old book.

Carolyn had to give the young man credit; he seemed uninterested in getting any money for the Bible. But she also felt that a handsome payment was warranted.

Gary had been bowled over with the unexpected amount of five million dollars that Carolyn had offered to him. But he said he believed all things came from God's hand, and if it was God's will that he have all that money, he would use it to create a foundation to fund the restart of a mission in San Francisco, an orphanage in Egypt and many other worthy needs that flooded his mind. After all, five million dollars could do much for Kingdom work. At least, that was what he had told her.

Carolyn was used to dealing with greedy men; a caring and giving man like Gary Brandon threw her. So they struck a deal, and the world, she believed, would be a better place for it. She knew well that five million dollars, from a wealth-laden man like R. C. Cooper, was a mere pittance.

chapter 3

COOPER

COOPER HALL, ISLE OF WIGHT, ENGLAND

SIR RICHARD COOPER struggled to sleep in his cavernous bedroom at Cooper Hall, a rambling Tudor estate on the Isle of Wight. The Bible he craved to hold again was scheduled to arrive sometime before dawn, and dawn seemed a forever away.

His immense wealth had never brought him much patience. When he was a younger man, in a situation such as this, he would have spent long hours pacing the floor, smoking one cigarette after another, drinking one Scotch after another. But now, at almost eighty-five years old, frail with age and disease, he remained in his bed, tethered by a clear plastic tube of oxygen.

He had not prayed much in his life, if at all, until doctors told him his heart was betraying him: that same heart that once drove him day and night to build an empire; that same cold heart that left him caring for no one but himself. He was crossing over unsure ground toward an uncharted horizon that was filled with long, cold shadows cast from a place called the Valley of Death. All day he murmured with dry lips, "Please let the Bible save me."

As the minutes strode by like a line of slow-marching soldiers, he hovered just above the threshold of sleep. Outside, the rain misted the dark hills around him.

His bedroom was large, with a high ceiling and bookshelves filled with musty relics of the past. Most of the artifacts had been hastily bought after he was told of his impending death. Cooper thought of the relics as holy talismans that might somehow make him healthy once again, or, if not, then at least provide some kind of a connection with God. He had acquired them at a dear price. As time passed, he learned that some were replicas or outright fakes. It really didn't matter to him now.

The bedroom also held display cases choked with acquired pottery, manuscripts, scrolls and old codex Bibles. One of the recently procured Bibles was from the Reformation period, and was stained with the blood of a martyr who held it as he was beheaded by orders of Mary, Queen of Scots. To Cooper's failing mind, all the artifacts, and there were over a hundred of them, were like a divine handhold with an unseen God—a God he would soon meet face-to-face. But none of the artifacts surrounding him compared in importance to the Bible now being couriered to England on his jet. His family thought him crazy, but he saw it as the indulgence of an old man who could afford anything and didn't need to explain his actions to anyone.

The Bible—that Bible—was not new to Cooper. He had carried it into battle as a young soldier fighting in France and Belgium during World War I. After a worldwide search, it came to Cooper by happenstance. The uncle of recent college graduate Gary Brandon had bought the old book from a store in Dubai and given it to his nephew as a graduation gift. Young Gary had seen R. C. Cooper's name in the Bible and felt compelled to find the real owner. A simple fax from the young American had resulted in Cooper's offer of millions of dollars for the old book.

R. C. Cooper had often reminisced with Carolyn Dawson about the special Bible and its unique nature. His stories and memories of the Bible were always of a rain-soaked day in 1917, when the Bible had saved his life on a battlefield in Belgium.

Even after all these years, while lying silent in his bed at night, he could often hear the distant sounds of war and feel the driving rain drumming against his helmet as he crouched low in a water-filled, hand-dug trench. His mind's eye could still see the contorted white corpses lying around him on a greasy swale of mud, their bodies twisted in the last agonizing throes of death. His nose could not rid itself of the rancid smell of putrefying flesh. Every recollection led to the awful moment when the enemy charged: so many of them; so much gunfire and shouting; so much death.

The German soldiers came at him in a long line, their shadowy, determined forms pressing forward like deadly predators. They ran across a mud-cratered expanse, dodging coiled barbed wire. They had superior numbers. Their hard faces showed anger and fear as they aimed and fired rifles fixed with long bayonets. The mingled sounds of screaming men and bullets snapping past his ears like cracking whips continued to haunt him in frightful nightmares, leaving him tossing and turning on sweat-soaked sheets.

He often awoke from those dreams just at the moment a bayonet came plunging toward him. His arms were raised in a futile attempt to stop the cold steel before it entered his organs, but the deadly thrust never came. In those dreams, as it had happened in real life, a young German soldier saw the Bible sewn in Cooper's tunic and could not make the easy kill. The German was a Christian.

That same Bible he had once carried into battle was at last returning to him. Cooper believed God supernaturally brought the Bible back into his life and that the book would somehow halt the imminent swing of Death's sickle.

High above Colorado in the cabin of Com Jet 125

The copilot returned to his seat and harnessed himself in. He looked at the pilot, his eyes telling the story of what he had seen in the rear of the plane.

The pilot switched the radio to frequency 121.5 MHz and depressed the mike key hard with his thumb. From behind his oxygen mask he pushed out the words, "Mayday, mayday, mayday, this is Com Jet 125 Bravo—declaring an emergency."

"Com Jet One-two-five Bravo," crackled in his headset, "this is Colorado Springs approach. What is your location, and what is the nature of your emergency?"

"We have an engine fire and pressure malfunctions . . . descending to sixteen thousand feet."

"Com Jet One-two-five Bravo, squawk seven-seven-zero-zero."

"Roger that approach. Squawking seven-seven-zero-zero." The pilot kept his voice steady.

The air traffic controller's voice sounded as if he did fifteen crash landings a day. "I have radar contact fifty-four miles west of Colorado Springs. Fly heading one-four-zero, descend and maintain one-six thousand, over."

The pilot repeated the orders.

Paul Lester had just started his shift. People around the tower referred to him by his call sign Papa Lima. For twenty-three years he had worked the tower, making him the old-timer among the controllers. He should have retired sooner; most did. The job of moving hurtling pieces of metal all day takes a toll on mind and nerves, but Paul Lester, whom younger controllers accused of having ice water in his veins, still loved it. He never thought of the passengers, never visualized mothers safety-belted in their seats holding babies, or the many fathers on business trips. He couldn't do that and do his job; he only saw blips on a green radar screen.

He was by far the best one in the tower to handle the situation. He had been an air-traffic controller in Vietnam and had heard the voices of fighter pilots when they knew they would soon be dead—the pilot on Com Jet 125 sounded the same to him. It was a voice of calm acceptance.

Paul Lester switched to the Pueblo frequency. "Pueblo approach, this is Colorado Springs. We may have an emergency coming your way. We have a twin-engine jet fifty miles west and we are trying to vector him south for a runway three-five landing. Let me know if you get visual."

"Roger that, Papa Lima. Good luck."

"Colorado Spring, this is One-two-five Bravo, and we can't stop our descent."

"Roger, Com Jet One-two-five Bravo, you should have the airport in sight at your ten o'clock and thirty-four miles."

"Approach, roger that, we have the field in sight."

"Com Jet One-two-five Bravo, you are clear to land runway three-five left."

There was a long pause, then chilling words. "We won't have a landing."

Paul Lester moaned quietly as he watched the radar's tracking sweep rotate around the green screen; the jet's flashing blip was traversing from the west-southwest. The plane's track made it clear that the pilot had lost control. The craft would crash somewhere around the Pueblo or the south Colorado Springs area. He shot a glance at two other controllers standing over his right shoulder, one grimacing as he said, "I'll alert Barnes Crossing Fire and Rescue."

Paul ticked off the altitude reading. "Two thousand . . . one thousand . . ." Gravity sucked the jet to the earth. Black, angry-looking smoke curled up from the horizon. Impact was thirty-five miles south of the Colorado Springs control tower. It looked like a stationary funnel cloud from a black, tilting tornado.

Paul Lester hung his head. "For the love of . . ." He lifted his face again to the radar screen as if it were all just a dream. His eyes reflected back in an eerie green.

SANDY CREEK ROAD, PUEBLO, COLORADO

In a blue dusk, Jimmy Orr drove his rattling Dodge pickup down County Line Road and headed out of the small town of Barnes Crossing, Colorado. He steered the old truck around a bend, and just past a picket line of piñon pines that sagged from a fresh load of snow, Jimmy saw black, tumbling smoke. At first he thought it was a grass fire, but with the snow he knew it couldn't be that. What would cause so much smoke? *Perhaps a farmer burning stumps or a pile of trash,* he thought. He couldn't remember seeing such a black, mushrooming cloud like this since he'd seen a Huey crash in Vietnam.

From behind him came the faint sound of sirens. He looked in his rearview mirror and saw twirling and flashing red and blue emergency lights. For a split second, he thought it was the sheriff's department stopping him for drunk driving again. He twisted his steering wheel to the right, but was traveling too fast for the turn. The pickup slid into a snowbank piled along the side of the road, evidence of a recently passing snowplow.

A line of fire trucks, police cars, and ambulances rumbled past. He pressed the accelerator, but the wheels just spun. He jammed the gear into reverse and tried again, but only got more wheel spinning.

He pounded the steering wheel with his left fist, then continued to rock the car back and forth as he ground the gears from drive to reverse and back to drive again. The worn tires would not bite into the wet, polished snow and ice. He rolled down his window and looked at the rear wheel. The snow was black from the friction of the spinning tires.

Jimmy exited the truck. The thick, dark smoke had begun to settle. Acrid and foul, the smoke stung his eyes and burned his throat. He raised his jacket collar against the biting cold and almost stepped on a shard of twisted aluminum. The torn metal was blackened by a sooty film. He then saw a ripped cover from a magazine slithering in a gust of wind. It tumbled across the packed snow and came to stop at his feet. The cover read *London Daily Business Journal*.

Just to his left he saw a yellow strap draped over a strand of barbed-wire fence, and beyond that a dark blue blanket almost torn in half. He caught sight of a seat cushion with white foam spilling from its gored side.

Walking up the long swale of the snowbank, he could see the burning remains of JP jet fuel and the splintered black carcass of what had been, only minutes ago, a multimillion-dollar aircraft. A hundred feet in front of him was a ruptured wheel, hanging almost comically from landing gear that stuck straight up from the snow like a small metal tree.

He walked a little farther down the road, found a break in the rusted barbed wire fencing and stepped through the gap. Each footfall punched through the thin crust of snow. He could hear men shouting and the echoes of fire trucks blaring loud radio messages. The chorus was a cacophony of frantic, unintelligible numbers and commands crackling through the early evening air. Fire hoses spewed white frothy foam on the steaming wreckage, wreckage that looked to Jimmy like a pile of burned bones of some ancient monster. A dark haze hung over the ground.

A woman's black high-heeled shoe sat a few feet in front of him, resting upright on the snow as if someone had just set it there. He then saw the edge of something burrowed into a mound of snow by the shoe. Jimmy took the tip of his wet cowboy boot and nudged the boxy object. He flicked away the ice and saw the edge of something that looked like wet leather. He bent and wiped away more snow and saw a briefcase, battered and scraped but intact.

His mind raced. The case must have belonged to someone on the plane. He started to pull it free, then stood to see if anyone was watching. The firefighters were hauling hoses, and the police were stepping through the tangle of charred wreckage, perhaps looking for survivors, but he doubted they would find more than mangled metal, oil, fuel and body parts.

He returned his gaze to the case and wondered what it held. No passenger would have use for it now. Jimmy stiffened at his macabre reasoning. He felt woozy with the idea of taking it. The five beers he'd had in the last two hours didn't help. His stomach tightened. Could the briefcase contain money? Expensive jewelry?

It was a special-looking briefcase, one that obviously belonged to someone of wealth. Maybe this was a lucky day to offset all the bad ones he had experienced.

He swiveled his head around again; no one was looking his way. More sirens cut the air, announcing the approach of additional emergency personnel. He pulled the valise free of the snow, shoved the wet object under his Levi's coat and started back. Jimmy stumbled as he hurried; his heart rattled. He made it to the road and then to his truck.

Another car was approaching. Jimmy yanked the driver's door open, making its rusted hinges squeak in protest. He then reached under his coat to toss the briefcase onto the front seat, but dropped the case onto the icy road. Before he could reach the case, Sheriff Powell and his deputy pulled up behind him. Jimmy looked back: they were both staring at the plane crash, and the sheriff was barking orders into a black microphone pressed to his lips.

Jimmy knelt, snatched up the case and tossed it onto the seat of the truck. He heard the sheriff's car door open and close. "Be cool," Jimmy whispered to himself as he slipped behind the wheel.

As the sheriff approached, Jimmy heard him shouting over the noise of firefighters and deputies. "Set some traffic cones out to keep all these gawkers from causing any more traffic problems." He aimed his words back at the patrol car.

"Ten-four, Sheriff," the portly deputy snapped back.

Jimmy turned away as the lawman walked by; the sheriff took no notice of him. The tragedy in the field a short distance away was the worst disaster the town had seen since a bus carrying the local high school football team went into the river fifteen years ago. No one was killed then, but ten boys landed in the hospital that night. This was much bigger. The sheriff's and deputy's eyes were riveted on the foam-smothered carcass of the jet.

Jimmy's hand shook uncontrollably. He couldn't get the key in the ignition to crank the engine. He stopped to take a breath and pleaded with his alcohol-fogged mind to cooperate. He needed to think fast, but all he could do was fumble with the keys as he repeatedly jabbed at the steering column.

Finally the key found its mark and the truck engine rattled to life. He jammed the gear shift into reverse and slammed his boot on the accelerator, spinning the wheels in the slick snow. The tires released a wisp of white smoke, and after a few seconds, dug through the slush underneath and into hard, frozen ground. The bare tires grabbed enough gravel to pull free. The truck lurched back, almost hitting the sheriff's patrol car. Jimmy then eased his pickup slowly forward, pulling onto the pavement, and drove down the road.

chapter 4

NEW ORDERS

NURSE NANCY JILES walked quietly into the dark room. Despite her attempt at stealth, Cooper knew she was there. A green glow from an oxygen monitor next to the bed provided the only illumination, but it was enough. For the last few years, sound sleep had become a rare commodity. Most nights, Cooper would doze off and on in random blocks of time, often awakened from fragile slumber by disturbing dreams. Minutes later, if he was lucky, he would nod off again.

"What is it, Nancy?"

Nancy had served Cooper for the last ten years. "Sir Richard, I'm afraid it's frightful news."

"News? What news?"

"I am sorry, sir, but there is a phone call for you." Nancy placed her hand gently on the old man's shoulder.

Cooper opened his lids and moved his eyes in the direction of the nurse. "Who would call at this hour?"

"It seems most urgent, sir. It is your attorney in Phoenix, and she wants to talk to you."

"I don't want to speak now. Have them call tomorrow."

"I understand, sir, but I am afraid it's bad news."

"Of course it's bad news; in the middle of the night it's never good."

"Sir, there has been a plane crash. The jet that was bringing you the Bible has gone down."

R.C. gathered a breath and held it in his chest, then released a moan. "Are there any survivors?"

"I'm sorry to say no, sir."

"Carolyn . . . Carolyn Dawson?"

"She's gone, sir."

He paused a long moment, struggling to focus his mind. "The Bible . . . what of my Bible?"

The nurse shook her head.

"Lord help me." He coughed and raised a hand to his brow. "Bring the phone."

Nancy lifted the phone and placed it in Cooper's shaking hand.

"This is Sir Richard Cooper."

"Sir, my name is Shannon Reed—"

"I had a Bible on that plane. Is there any news of it?"

"No sir, but I was there when it was purchased in Phoenix. Carolyn Dawson retained me to handle the legal documents on the purchase."

"I didn't expect a woman attorney."

"Sir?"

"I am too old and too weak to spend time explaining my comments. It is most important for me to get that Bible. Go to where the jet crashed and find it."

"I doubt it would survive the plane's impact, sir. I hear everything was burned up, destroyed."

"The briefcase with the Bible inside . . . it will survive." Cooper's breathing grew labored.

"In a jet crash?"

Cooper grunted. "Yes, that case is bulletproof and fireproof; it would survive almost any catastrophe. I had it made to protect my most important documents. The case contains the most important document in the world to me. Do you understand? It *must* be found."

"Yes, sir. I'll go to Colorado in the morning and see what I can find."

"You will go now. There is no time to waste. What time is it there?"

"About seven in the evening."

"Hire a private jet, a plane, a helicopter . . . whatever it takes, just go now. Do you hear me? I want you to go this instant! I will pay you well for the inconvenience, now just go."

There was a pause on the line. "Very well, sir, I'll get on it now."

"Just get me the Bible. Offer a reward if need be." Cooper handed the phone back to his nurse. "Leave me now, Nancy. I want to be alone."

"Very well, sir."

UTE TRAILER PARK, SLIP 23

Jimmy slid his truck to a stop in the cold twilight and flung open the door. His dog, a black Lab mix, waited for him at the base of the steps. He stumbled to his mobile home, turned the doorknob and shoved the tight-fitting aluminum door open with a shoulder push. He hurried to the kitchen where he tossed the briefcase on a table, marched to the refrigerator and retrieved the first of a twelve-pack of Coors. He flicked the can open and chugged three big swallows. Walking to his small black-and-white television set, he switched it on and fiddled with the coat-hanger antenna until the picture morphed from a fuzzy blur to something closer to an image of reality.

He wiped suds from his chin and watched a pretty blond anchorwoman stare into the camera. " . . . reports continue to come in. We're doing our best to get an interview with the fire chief and . . . hold on a moment . . ." She touched her ear. "I'm being told that we have a reporter on scene with a video link and . . . yes, we're going to him now."

The image of a man replaced that of the woman. He cleared his throat and said, "News Eight, Colorado Springs, Pueblo. I'm Hector Velázquez, coming to you live from the site of a private jet crash. We have unconfirmed information that all three people on board were killed. The plane is registered in the name of the Golden Well Drilling Company, an organization owned by famed British billionaire Sir Richard Cooper. The jet was on its way to an unknown destination after taking off from Phoenix Sky Harbor Airport late this afternoon." The newsman made a shivering gesture for effect. "We will have more updates later from this snowy pasture of death and disaster."

Jimmy turned and looked at the case on his small wooden kitchen table. It was still wet and covered in soot and mud. Returning to the kitchen, he skimmed his hand over the face of the case and discovered the mud-smeared logo of the Golden Well Drilling Company, London, England. He almost hyperventilated as he tried opening the valise. The clasps were locked. What could be in a briefcase on a billionaire's jet? His mind raced; his body surged with excitement.

"The drawer," he said aloud. He yanked open the drawer next to the sink. The sink was piled with brown-crusted pots and pans floating in water that looked as if it had been drained from a sewer.

He pushed away some white candles and an assortment of nails and screws before gripping the wood handle of a hammer. He returned to the briefcase and set it on edge. Jimmy then inhaled deeply, raised the hammer and brought it down on the locked clasps. The hammer's head deflected off the case. Jimmy swung the hammer again and again, with short choppy swings, but without effect. It protested each assault with a loud metal ping but refused to open. Jimmy began to swear and swing the hammer harder. Still nothing. No wonder the thing survived the crash.

Jimmy returned to the drawer and retrieved a large flathead screwdriver. Placing the head of the tool between the metal clasp and the case, he began to pound on the tool, driving it deeper and deeper. He did the same to the other clasp, but the case would not yield. For the next half hour he pounded on the case, the clasps and even the hinges. Sweat dripped from his forehead. Again he assaulted the clasps and lock. Finally, he heard it.

Snap!

The latch sprung open. Another dozen well-aimed strikes and the other locked clasp surrendered its grip.

Jimmy dropped the hammer and screwdriver on the table, and paused to stare at the briefcase. A trail of perspiration wound down his right cheek, and he licked at the salty glob as it found the corner of his lips. He took several deep, gathering breaths. Setting the case flat on the table, he curled his fingertips under the edge of the lid and slowly opened it. Inside, he saw something wrapped in white linen. Gently, he peeled back the cloth and found a Bible inside—a frayed and very old-looking Bible. He lowered himself onto one of the wood chairs.

"A Bible. All this for a Bible." Jimmy couldn't believe it. "What am I going to do with an old Bible?"

Ten minutes later, as the moon reflected off azure-tinted snow, Jimmy walked behind the trailer park. His skinny frame staggered down to the creek bed, where he flung the book off into a tangle of snow-powdered bushes next to the skeletal remains of a rusty '32 Ford and an old, doorless refrigerator. Then he trudged back to his mobile home, spewing profanities at his rotten luck.

chapter 5

WAKE-UP CALL

SHERIFF POWELL SAT up in bed and looked at the alarm clock on his nightstand. "Who's calling at 4:30 in the stinking morning?" He flipped on the light and snatched the cordless phone from its base. "What in the—"

A hurried voice cut in. "Sheriff, there's a woman down here who wants to see you right now. She's a lawyer from Phoenix and says it's urgent."

"You woke me for that? Tell her to see me in the morning. And the next time you wake me at this hour, it had better be for something more pressing than an impatient lawyer. You got that, Deputy?"

"Yes sir, but I think you may want to come down here anyway."

"For the love of— Put whoever it is on the phone." He looked at the clock again.

"Yes, sir."

A woman's voice floated from the receiver. "I'm sorry to wake you, Sheriff Powell, but this is important. My name is Shannon Reed. I'm an attorney representing—"

"Okay, okay. What has Deputy Gordon done now?"

"Done? Nothing I know of. As I was saying, I represent R. C. Cooper, and he owns the jet that crashed."

"Look, Ms.—"

"Reed—Shannon Reed."

"Okay, Ms. Shannon Reed, I am tired, been going hard all day, and spent half the night at the crash site. See me tomorrow, will ya?"

"Sheriff, there was an impact-proof briefcase on that plane. I need to find it."

"It was a jet crash, Ms. Reed. We can't find much of anything or anyone."

"Has anyone seen a leather-covered metal case in the wreckage?"

"Nope. We poked around that site pretty good. If we can't find the three bodies that were on the plane, how're we going to find a briefcase?"

"It would have survived the crash."

"Ms. Reed, I helped search the scene, and all I saw was a big divot in the ground with a whole lot of burnt plane."

"An old Bible was inside the briefcase."

"A Bible? So what? If you want another Bible, most churches will give you one for free."

"You don't understand: this Bible is worth several millions of dollars, and there is a handsome reward."

"For Pete's sake, if word of this gets out, we'll have every nut within a thousand miles digging up the countryside looking for that thing. Hang on a sec. Let me think." Powell pushed back the covers and swung his legs over the edge of the mattress. The bedroom felt cold. "Okay, I'll call Tanya. If anyone can find your missing Bible, she can, or find what's left of it."

"Tanya? Who is she?"

"It's a long story and one you probably wouldn't believe. We can't search at this hour: too cold, too dark, and I'm too tired. Where did you say you're from?"

"Phoenix."

"The only livable motel around here is the Falcon's Nest just north of town. Check in and rest for a bit. Freshen up. My deputy will make sure you get there. Just sit tight and let me see if I can get Tanya to help out. If so, then we'll start once the sun is high enough for us to see."

6:52 A.M.
SANDY CREEK ROAD

The sheriff closed the car door with a loud thud. Deputy Doug Gordon was sleeping in his parked patrol car . . . again. The sun's glow hued the snow pink as the sheriff rapped his black glove-covered knuckles on the deputy's window. He tapped again and could hear the guttered snore and see his deputy sleeping behind the breath-frosted glass, his head leaning to the right.

The sheriff, a tall man who always wore a side-curled cowboy hat, clenched his jaw in anger as he rapped harder on the window. The glass shook in the door. Doug's eyes fluttered open.

The deputy stepped from the car and donned his black, fur-flapped hat. Doug was the oldest deputy in the small department; his gut hung almost beyond the loops of his Sam Browne gun belt. He often joked that when his belly got bigger than the gun belt he would retire. Sheriff Powell knew the man had grown sick of being a deputy and was just putting in time.

Deputy Gordon turned toward the sheriff's car. Tanya stood by the vehicle wearing a red flannel jacket, her olive complexion framed by coal black hair.

"Why is Tanya here?" The deputy rubbed the morning stubble on his flat chin. "I don't think there are any wounded deer to be found."

"I brought her and Ms. Reed here," Powell said. He offered nothing more. Powell watched Shannon Reed exit the car.

Doug shrugged and looked at the black carcass of the plane wreckage. "Last night I shot at three coyotes snooping around here smelling the scattered whatever."

The sheriff looked at his deputy, embarrassed by his disheveled appearance. He turned to Shannon. "Ms. Reed, this is one of our county's finest, Deputy Doug Gordon." He made no attempt to hide his sarcasm.

"Hello," Shannon said, and held out her hand.

"Hey," Doug answered. He smiled at Tanya. "Hey, Tanya. How ya doin'?"

"Fine." The teenager didn't make eye contact. She seldom did.

Powell did his best not to stare at Doug's shirttail hanging out of his pants. The shirt had yellow stains on the front—what he took to be mustard drippings. Doug's eyes traced Shannon's form. Powell could tell it made her uncomfortable.

"Now that you've had a good night's sleep, Deputy, maybe you could tuck in your shirt and help us find something."

Doug's big belly blocked his view of the shirttail but he reached down, felt his way to the shirt's edge, and quickly stuffed the loose flap of tan cloth into his uniform pants.

Powell rolled his eyes and hitched his thumb in his gun belt. "I didn't want to broadcast it with all the police scanners in this town, but we need to find a briefcase from the crash. It is worth a lot of money to Ms. Reed."

"How much?"

Shannon looked at the deputy. "There is a sizable reward."

"How sizable?" Doug asked.

Shannon said, "Substantial."

"Forget about it," Powell snapped at Doug. "This is part of our official work. Satisfaction is all the reward you're going to get."

Doug started to say something, then thought better of it. Instead he said, "Well, if anyone can find something that's lost, it's Tanya here. She can track a duck across water."

Powell explained. "During hunting season, she tracks in the high country for all the Texans who come here to shoot deer. They know how to wound a deer but can't track one. Tanya can see a tiny drop of blood and a bent blade of grass from fifty feet away. Never once has she failed to find a wounded or dropped deer, even if it took her tracking through a blizzard. She seems to have a special eyesight all right; never seen anything like it."

"She's something of a freak of nature," Doug said.

Tanya walked away, uninterested in anything Doug had to say.

Tanya walked to the edge of the field before the sheriff and the fat deputy had finished talking. She did not like or want anyone prying into anything she did.

She scanned the wide field of wreckage, then turned back to the sheriff. "Everyone will need to stay back. I need to go slowly."

Shannon cried out, "It's a camel-skin-covered briefcase, with an emblem on the front that says Golden Well Drilling Company."

Tanya said nothing and advanced across the field of snow toward the impact site, stepping slowly and stopping at every small clue. She eased her way forward, then stopped and leaned over a crimson smear in the snow. She stepped slowly around it, her eyes drinking in everything. She hesitated when she saw footprints leading from the road across the field and stopping at a pile of churned-up snow. Tanya approached the clump and saw where something had made an indentation in the snow. The detailed impression was the right size for a briefcase. She could even see where the two latches and handle marks had nosed into the snow.

Tanya scanned the area from the wreckage to where she stood. Several indentations spaced a dozen feet apart marred the white field. She nodded. The briefcase had bounced several times before coming to rest at this spot.

She bent and noticed that a person had used a boot to nudge the case. Since a corresponding left boot print had left a deeper impression, she deduced the person had rocked on his left foot and lifted the briefcase with his right. She thought that whoever it was had put their full weight on their left leg. She could see the striation marks left in the snow as the case was pulled free.

Next, she followed the impression that trailed back to the road. She could see they belonged to a man who staggered. The strides were short, but the boot steps were wide and uneven, as if the person had difficulty walking. A right-handed man, she guessed, from the wear on the inner right heel. She could see that the person took slow, awkward strides going into the field and had stopped often, probably watching all that was going on. Moving away from the briefcase, the steps were directional and much faster, all the way to the road, almost running. Tanya followed the tracks to the road a dozen yards ahead of where the sheriff had parked. She found a place where a vehicle had spun its worn tires, making the snow black and sending ice and mud flying behind it.

Tanya, in her faint Slavic accent, called the group over.

"What did you find?" Shannon asked.

Tanya pointed across the field. "A man found the case at that small mound of snow. He pulled it from there and walked in a hurry back to the road—more like he staggered fast. He is the one who found your briefcase. You are lucky there were no other tracks with him. Much of the field has been trampled by emergency personnel."

"You're sure it was a man?" Shannon asked.

Tanya nodded. "His feet are big, about a size twelve, I would say, and he is right-footed."

Sheriff Powell grinned. "Anything else?"

"Yes, Sheriff. The man does not work on a farm. The wear marks are those of someone who does not walk in dirt or rock, but on carpet or smooth surfaces. The inside front of the heel is worn like a man who rests his boots on a bar rail."

Shannon said, "You got all that from a few marks in the snow? How do you know all this for certain?"

"The snow does not lie. Only people lie."

Sheriff Powell spoke up. "Anything on the skid marks here?"

Tanya knelt. "The truck that was here left an impression in the snow that shows the front end slammed into the snowbank. The bumper height tell us that it was a truck—a pickup. Judging from the impression, it hit hard." She ran her fingers on the smooth icy ground. "You can see he spun his tires, trying to free his truck."

"Is that all?" Shannon asked. The words were sarcastic.

"No, the truck owner has a dog."

"How do you know that?" Shannon placed her hands on her hips.

Tanya bent and lifted some dried pellets scatted in the snow. "These are from the feed store in town. It's dry dog food." She rose and grinned. "I buy the same food for my dog, Jane. It was probably loose in the bed of the truck, or maybe fell from the cab when he got out; anyway, it came from the truck that was here."

Tanya stepped to the snow embankment where the truck had slammed to a stop the day before. "Do you want the license plate number of the truck?"

"You can find that?" Sheriff Powell asked slowly.

Tanya moved to the charred piece of metal wing tip and squatted next to it. She scraped the edge of her right hand across the burned, black residue and swept the black granules into her cupped left hand. She walked back to the place where the vehicle had gone nose first into the snowbank and blew the blackened ash on the snow. A rectangle indentation of the truck's license plate appeared like magic. The reversed image of numbers and letters of the plate were also shaded from the sooty pigment.

"That's your man; just find someone who has a truck with those plate numbers and letters," she said with calm certainty. Doug wrote down the numbers and letters and ran his waddling frame back to his car to radio in the plate.

"Is it all as simple as that?" Shannon asked the sheriff.

"It is with Tanya. She never ceases to amaze me."

In a few minutes' time, Doug ran back. The short jog left him out of breath. "The plate and records came back to a Ford pickup registered to a James Ian Orr, who resides at Ute Trailer Park, Slip Twenty-three."

"Jimmy," the sheriff grunted, with a frown. "I'm not surprised." He paused. "Come to think of it, I saw his truck parked near here when I arrived on scene yesterday."

"Wait a minute," Shannon said. "You saw the man here but didn't do anything?"

"Do anything? What was there to do? People were stopping by the dozens until I had the road closed. Besides, I had a burning jet in that field. I was a little distracted."

"I'm sorry," Shannon said. "Of course you had more pressing things on your mind."

Doug laughed. "Yup, a business jet falling out of the sky and killing all onboard does take over a man's attention."

"Doug?" Powell said.

"Yeah?"

"Shut up."

chapter 6

TWO WORDS

7:25 A.M.
UTE TRAILER PARK, SLIP 23

JIMMY SPOKE FROM behind his battered aluminum front door of his mobile home, his words slurred and garbled. "Now why would I, of all people, take a Bible, Sheriff?"

A dog barked from inside.

"Maybe you got religious on me, Jimmy."

"Not likely."

"Open the door, Jimmy, or I will kick it in."

"Wouldn't be the first time, Sheriff."

Tanya had no patience for this kind of conversation. Silently she slipped away, searching the grounds for clues to what the man had done with the case. He either had it inside or had hidden it outside. In the first case, Sheriff Powell would find it; in the latter, she would.

She walked around the side of the mobile home and found a fresh trail of boot tracks. A few moments later, Tanya noticed Shannon following at a distance. She chose not to acknowledge her. A few minutes later, something caught Tanya's eye.

"May I come along with you?" Shannon called from thirty feet back.

Tanya turned and nodded. When Shannon closed the distance between them, Tanya pointed to a briefcase that had slid down the embankment and was now in the clutches of a tuft of sagebrush at the edge of a frozen creek. She trudged through a drift of snow and lifted the briefcase. "Is this yours?"

Shannon ran awkwardly in the snow and snatched the case. "Yes. Yes, it is." She studied it for a moment. "The crash must have broken the clasps."

Tanya shook her head. "Hammer marks and gouges. The clasps were broken on purpose."

"Oh, no."

Tanya heard the woman inhale deeply, then watched as she slowly opened the case as if it were made of glass. Tanya stepped closer to see. Inside rested a Bible.

"Hold the case," Shannon said. "I need to see if the Bible has been damaged."

Tanya held it steady as Shannon removed the book. "It looks as it did the last time I saw it, but I only saw it for a few moments."

"Are you sure it's not damaged?" Tanya asked. "It looks beat up to me."

"As I understand it, this Bible is very old, dating back to the Civil War, maybe older than that. It's seen a lot of history." Shannon slowly fanned the frail, thin pages.

"Wait!" Tanya said.

"What? What's wrong?"

"I saw something. Turn back a few pages."

Shannon did, gently moving each of the yellowed pages.

"There." Tanya, still holding the open case, nodded at the page. "I know those words."

"They look Russian."

"They are." Tanya's eyes were fixed on the two handwritten words. "I saw these words before I came to the United States."

They were the same two words she had seen upon the stone lid of a grave in Leningrad; two words that were now on a page in a very old Bible; two words written in flowing letters from a quill pen; two words in fading brown ink. *Feodor Kuzmich*.

A ghost from her past had found her.

Tanya's heart galloped like a horse, her breathing quickened. Her hands shook as she stepped into the dark hallway of a frightening memory.

"What's wrong, Tanya? You look pale."

"Feodor Kuzmich." She exhaled slowly, trying to keep her voice even. "The gold snuff box of the czar." She realized that she had verbalized her thoughts, thoughts that should have remained tucked away in her mind. She began to sob softly.

Shannon took the briefcase from Tanya and set it on the ground. Tanya felt Shannon's arm drape her shoulders. "What is so frightening about this Feodor Kuzmich, and what in the world is this about a gold snuff box of the czar?"

Tanya pulled away and ran up the embankment. Shannon raised the Bible again and looked at the page with the Cyrillic letters she could not read.

7:46 A.M.
UTE TRAILER PARK, SLIP 24

Shannon spoke softly into the phone, her back turned to the large woman in blue bibs overalls, as she said, "Please get R. C. Cooper on the line."

The woman who lived in the trailer next to Jimmy's bore a face webbed with red capillaries. The neighbor had been friendly enough when Shannon asked to use her phone—but when Shannon said she needed to call England the woman huffed, "Are you crazy, calling all the way to England on my phone?"

"I am beginning to think so," Shannon answered, as she snapped open her purse and laid out five crisp twenty-dollar bills into the woman's open palm. "I will be only five minutes. This should more than cover a quick call."

The woman closed her fist around the bills and looked out her window at a handcuffed Jimmy being led to the sheriff's car. "Boy ain't right in the head. He is nuthin' but trouble since I known him."

Shannon nodded in agreement as her voice traveled to the ear of R. C. Cooper on the other side of the Atlantic. "The sheriff's office has the Bible."

"Excellent; now bring it to me."

"I can't at present. The Bible is part of an investigation."

"I don't care about their investigation; just get it and bring it to me."

"I will do my best."

"I didn't tell you to try and do your best. I told you to get it. Am I clear on that?"

"Yes, sir. Very clear."

"Good-bye, Ms. Reed."

"Wait a minute, sir," Shannon said. "The girl who found the Bible says she knows the name Feodor Kuzmich. The name is written in the Bible."

There was a pause. "Tell me about the girl. I want to know all she knows." His once-tired voice seemed more alive.

"Her name is Tanya Novak, and she's originally from Russia. She is about fifteen years old. She seems to have an eerie ability to see and sense things that others can't. An extraordinary girl, to say the least. Acts older than her age."

"I am not interested in her talents. Tell me what she said. Tell me all of it."

"I really have no idea what the girl's words mean."

"Can you hear me, woman? I am not soliciting your opinion. Just tell me what the girl said. I want it word for word."

"She said something about a man named Feodor Kuzmich and a gold snuff box of the czar."

The phone went nearly silent. All she could hear was Cooper wheezing and the static of water-soaked lines. A moment later he coughed several times.

"Are you all right, Sir Richard?"

She heard him inhale slowly. "The girl may hold the key to wonderful things."

"What kind of things?"

"Get the girl to tell you more about the gold snuff box. I need to know what she knows, and I am willing to pay a great deal for that information."

Shannon explained, "I don't know much about her, but I'm afraid she won't want to talk about this anymore. She was pretty shook."

"She will talk to you. I'll see to it."

SHERIFF'S OFFICE

When they arrived at the station, a news crew from a local television station waited for them. Deputy Gordon saw the reporter and cameraman, and made a scene of removing Jimmy from the back of his patrol car. Shannon had ridden with Sheriff Powell.

"What are they doing here?" Powell said, as he parked in his designated spot.

"You did call them?"

"Of course not. I went out of my way to keep this under wraps, yet here they are. I know nothing went out over the radio. I would have heard it." The sheriff thought a moment. "I think Doug must of made a call from Jimmy's mobile home while I was putting Jimmy in the patrol car." He took off his hat and raked his hair. "It figures. Doug sure does like all the attention."

Shannon could see that. Once Deputy Gordon helped Jimmy out of the patrol car, he walked him around to the front passenger seat, opened the door and retrieved the battered briefcase, then made straight for the reporter. The cameraman rolled video. The deputy stopped for a few more poses.

Shannon and Powell stepped close enough to hear.

"That's the case you called about?" the reporter asked. He looked to be in his mid-forties. His thick, graying hair sat atop a narrow head.

"Yes, sir, it sure is," Doug said. "But the case isn't what's important or the fact that it survived the airplane crash." He opened the case. "This Bible is what's important—"

"Okay, hang on," the reporter said. He turned to the cameraman. "Let's just shoot this now. You good with that?"

"Sure." The cameraman and Doug spoke in unison.

"Rolling," the cameraman said.

The reporter faced the camera. Shannon watched Doug move closer to him, making certain he was in the camera's line of sight. "This is Hector Velázquez on site of the Barnes Crossing sheriff's station, and I'm speaking with Deputy Doug Gordon. As we reported yesterday, a private business jet crashed in an empty field a few miles from town." Velázquez turned to Doug. "Deputy Gordon, I understand you've made an important find."

"Yes, sir. This case survived the horrible crash. Inside, we found this." He opened the case and turned it so the camera could see inside.

"It looks like an old Bible," Velázquez said.

"This book is worth a lot of money—maybe millions. It took a good deal of detective work, but I found it."

Jimmy liked the attention as much as the deputy; he elbowed into the camera's view and smiled. Doug shoved him back and looked at the camera again.

"Millions of dollars?" Velázquez pressed. "What makes it worth so much?"

"Um . . . It's part of an ongoing investigation so I can't reveal everything, you know."

"Does your prisoner have anything to do with the Bible?"

"He stole it from the crash site. Like I said, I found it."

"That does it," Powell snapped, and walked to Doug and the reporter. Before Doug could go on, Powell said, "We thank the media for its interest, but that's all we can say for now."

"But what makes the Bible so important?"

"Thank you for coming out," Powell said. He made it clear the conversation was over. The technician lowered the video camera.

"Come on, Sheriff, we don't get much big news here. If the Bible is connected to the plane crash, then we have a right to know."

"No. The NTSB and FAA are in charge of the investigation. You'll have to direct your questions to them from now on."

Powell and Doug turned and led Jimmy into the sheriff's side office. Shannon followed. In the car she asked if she could sit in on the interrogation. "I know it's out of the ordinary, but I need to report to my employer—and I am an attorney."

"Yeah? Well, you're not his attorney."

"No, but I would still like to listen in. It would be a big help to me and my employer."

Powell groused, but agreed. "You sit where I tell you, and you don't say a word. Can you do that?"

Shannon said, "Maybe."

In the interrogation room, everyone except Doug took seats around a large, abused, green Formica table. Doug stood by the door as if guarding it. Jimmy rattled his handcuffs on the table, enjoying the irritated look on the sheriff's face. Occasionally, he swished back his long hair with a snap of his neck. A tattoo under his chin read "Only God Can Judge."

"Give me a cigarette, will ya?" Jimmy spoke the words as if he were sitting in a bar with his buddies.

"They're bad for your health." Powell leaned over the table.

"Lots of things are bad for your health, like a false arrest lawsuit."

"Stop with the big-man talk, Jimmy. I want to get to the bottom of this."

Jimmy slouched in his chair and grinned. "There's no way you can pin this on me. No one saw me take anything from the crash site, especially a Bible."

"Briefcase with a Bible," Shannon corrected.

Powell frowned at her.

"Okay, *briefcase* and Bible. I know how the game's played, and if there ain't no witness, then there ain't no way to convict me of anything."

"You seem to know your way around the law," Shannon said.

"Practice makes perfect."

Shannon looked at the Bible and case resting on the table. She needed a way to get possession of the case and deliver it to Cooper in England. Ideas flew through her mind, but she'd have to be careful.

"Let me set you straight about a few things, Jimmy." Powell leaned back and spoke in a conversational tone. "We know you were at the site. I saw you there, and if I hadn't been preoccupied with a burning jet, I might have run you through the mill right then. Besides that, your license plate left a pretty detailed impression in the snowbank."

"Snowbank?"

Powell grinned. "Just so happens we found the impression of your plates in a snowbank at the crash site."

Jimmy paled. "So what? Lots of people went to see the crash site. So what if my truck slid into the snowbank? Ain't no crime in that."

"You left bootprints in the snow and we have lots of photos for a jury."

Jimmy said, "This is so bogus."

Powell pushed the case closer to Jimmy. "See those marks on the latches. Those were made by a hammer and probably a large screwdriver. Just so happens we found a hammer and screwdriver in your kitchen. What do you wanna bet a good crime lab can match your tool to those marks?"

Jimmy said nothing.

"I see it this way, Jimmy. You stopped to watch the jet burn; you found the briefcase and took it. What you didn't know was that it held a valuable object—an object worth more than you can imagine. By the way, the value of that book makes this much more than a misdemeanor. So far your criminal career has been nothing but drunk driving, disorderly conduct and other minor stuff. This could get you sent to the big prison. You won't like the big prison, Jimmy. Trust me on that. One day there and you'll be wishing you had cooperated with me."

"I want my lawyer."

"That won't be necessary." Shannon spoke up. "The Bible's owner no longer wishes to press charges."

Powell snapped his head around. "What?"

"I represent the legal owner of the case and the Bible. I'm formally informing you that he doesn't wish to press charges."

Powell shot to his feet. "Come with me, Counselor." He put his hand on her elbow, removing any doubt she may have had about his intent. "Come with me now."

Doug stepped away from the door quickly. Apparently he had seen this look on the sheriff's face before. Powell led her into his office next to the interrogation room and closed the door.

"Sit down," he ordered hard.

"I prefer to stand." Shannon tried to sound confident. She failed miserably.

"I prefer you sit."

She sat slowly onto a chair on the visitor side of the desk.

Powell rounded his cheap metal desk and dropped into a chair that looked older than he was. The office was simple. A college diploma attesting to Powell's degree in criminal science, a marksmanship award on a walnut plaque and a photo of him and someone who looked like a politician were all that hung on the walls.

"Let me get this straight. You're telling me you don't want to press charges for theft."

"That's correct. All I want is the Bible."

"Well, just maybe we will keep the Bible as evidence till we know how this will all play out."

"As I said, Sheriff, my client wants the Bible. He doesn't want it tied up in a case that can't be won."

"Not that easy." Powell glared at her. For a moment she thought she felt heat radiate from his face.

"Why is that?"

"We have a district attorney to deal with. We may not be a big city, but we do have procedures to follow. The Bible will need to stay here as evidence for awhile."

"Look, Sheriff, we both know that it's difficult to get a jury to hand down a conviction on a victimless crime."

"This is unbelievable."

Shannon straightened in her chair. "As I said, the owner wants the Bible now, and doesn't want it tied up in a court trial. So if you want to waste the taxpayers' money and your own time, then go ahead." She smiled. "I like you, Sheriff. If I lived in this town, I'd vote for you. But I'm sure the press outside would love to paint you as a Don Quixote sheriff chasing windmills and old Bibles with his dutiful deputy at his side. And remember, you just slammed the door in the media's face. I've got a feeling the reporter can hold a grudge."

Powell rubbed his eyes, then rose. "Let's go."

"Where?"

"Just come with me."

Shannon followed the lawman back to the interrogation room. He didn't bother returning to his seat. Instead, he picked up the case and handed it to Shannon. "There. Take it and go."

Doug came to life. "Not so fast. It seems we found the Bible as a team, and we should get the reward."

Jimmy jumped up. "Yeah, where's my share of the reward money?"

Powell scowled at Doug. "There's no reward for law enforcement officers. We did our job. We did what we're supposed to do. At least one of us did."

"I'm not a cop," Jimmy said. "There's no problem with me taking it."

Shannon shook her head. "The owner offered a reward to the person who actually found and *returned* the Bible. You found it, but you certainly didn't return it. If anyone deserves the reward, it's Tanya." She looked at the sheriff. "So I am free to leave?"

He nodded and said in icy tones, "Take your Bible. It may be the Word of God, but it's been nothing but a pain . . ."

Jimmy stood. "Nice doing business with you all, but I got to be going as well." He held his hands toward Powell.

"Not so fast. You just sit down, Jimmy," Powell said. "We have some outstanding warrants here on some traffic tickets." He paused. "I got the press here, and I need to arrest someone."

chapter **7**

MURK

FIVE MINUTES LATER, Shannon sat on the edge of an over-stuffed vinyl chair in the Sheriff's Department waiting room; it reeked of urine and was marked with cigarette burns. She held a phone that had a peeling blue sticker that read "Lightning Larry's Bail Bonds." The phone's loose mouthpiece smelled of sour beer. Shannon waited a long minute until she heard someone pick up on the other end. The butler spoke in a monotone British accent honed to aristocratic perfection. "I am sorry, Ms. Reed, but I regret to inform you that Sir Richard C. Cooper has expired."

"Expired? Do you mean he's dead?"

"Precisely. He died about half an hour ago. I would suspect that the strain involved with the acquisition of the Bible proved too great for his frail heart."

It took a moment for her to put words in the right order. "Please give the family my condolences." Shannon's mind was a whirl of colliding thoughts.

"Sir Richard's son, Jason, is here at present; he has explicit instructions for you pertaining to the Bible. Will you please wait on the line?"

"Okay."

A moment later she heard, "This is Jason Cooper, son of Sir Richard Cooper; with whom am I speaking?"

"This is Shannon Reed. I am an attorney on retainer for your father. I helped him in the purchase of the Bible."

Jason Cooper's voice was cold. "I am the only son of R. C. Cooper, so I represent all the surviving family members. We are aware of that insufferable Bible. May I speak frankly?"

"Please do."

"The family is not at all interested in wasting more money on that old Bible. We offer no reward, and don't care if we ever see it. I refuse to even pay the post to have it mailed here. This quest of my father's is the fruit of a senile mind. I want nothing to do with it. Have I made myself clear?"

"Very clear, sir."

"I do not wish to be bothered by you or David Murk again about this matter. I have many more important matters to attend to."

"David who?"

"Are you not working with Mr. David Murk?"

"No, sir. I've never heard of him."

"I see. Very interesting."

"I don't understand. Who is Murk?"

Shannon heard Jason Cooper sigh. "I'll make this brief, Ms. Reed. He is an antiquities dealer, which means he meets men in dark alleys and buys black-market artifacts and relics looted from restricted archeological sites—or maybe pilfered by the nimble fingers of a night watchman in one of thousands of museums around the world."

Shannon was growing weary of the man's snooty attitude. "I assume you know this because he sold your father some of these objects."

"Yes, he sold my father a small fragment of wood he said came from the cross of Jesus. It had been set in a gold frame. It was said to come from a monastery in Romania. My father spent ten thousand dollars for that bit of nonsense. Murk also sold my father a frayed white cloth stained with a brown, blotchy image that when looked upon a certain way appears to be a vague image of a man's blood-smeared face. Supposedly it was scrap from the linen cloth that covered the face of Jesus in the burial tomb. The sellers purported that Charlemagne himself brought the cloth piece to a monastery in the mountains of Spain, claiming it was a holy prize. But legend was the artifact's only pedigree and its provenance will never be proved. Still, my father had to have it, and Mr. Murk was more than willing to make the purchase for my father."

"For a sizeable fee, I imagine."

"Yes, Ms. Reed, for an unbelievable fee."

"So Murk is a crook?"

"Not exactly. My father asked him to get these things and the man did. He is a genius at smuggling. My father told me no one is better than David Murk at finding lost or rare artifacts. His real talent, however, is smuggling these items right under the nose of customs officials." Jason paused. "I am afraid I have no more time to talk. My family is arriving and we have a funeral to arrange. Send your bill for all you have done, and we will compensate you for your efforts."

"Wait," Shannon cut in. "What do you want me to do with the Bible?"

"Clifford—my father's butler—tells me a young girl helped you find it. You may give it to her in lieu of my father's assurances of a reward. I hope she accepts it. Now I am afraid I must be going. I have my father to bury and a company to take control over."

The line went dead.

Shannon set the phone down, her mind a jumble of thoughts. She opened the case on her lap and rubbed the worn cover of the Bible, and thought of its long journey. When she and Carolyn Dawson purchased the Bible in Phoenix less than a day ago, she learned that it once belonged to a boy in the Civil War named Elijah Bell. Too young to fight in battle, he carried the Bible as he traveled with Confederate troops, preaching them fiery sermons before they entered a hail of bullets. In a wet fog on the last day of the Civil War, a Union soldier named Tate shot the boy. Later, as Tate stood over the dying lad, the boy handed his killer the bloodstained Bible.

That set in motion a journey that took the book weaving through history, passing through the hands of a Chinese immigrant working on the Central Pacific Railroad; a woman named Ruth sailing up the Nile; and then to R. C. Cooper, who carried the Bible into battle in World War I. The Bible seemed to be a thread that wove a tapestry of life-changing events. Now she wondered if she herself were somehow being woven into the mysterious saga.

A door opened, and a shadow fell across the lobby floor. A tall man with brown hair and a thin goatee studied her for a moment.

"Would you be Shannon Reed?" The man's voice sounded deep and certain.

Shannon stood. "Yes, and you are . . ."

"David Murk." He smiled and extended his hand. "I've been asked to take the Bible back to England."

Shannon's mouth went dry. "I am sorry, but I can't give it to you."

He furrowed his brow. "May I ask why?"

"Sir Richard Cooper is dead."

"Dead?" Murk said, surprised. "I spoke to him yesterday."

"Well, he won't need the Bible now—" She stopped abruptly, embarrassed by how cold and uncaring her comment must have seemed.

"I suppose not." Murk motioned to a frayed sofa. "Perhaps we should sit for a moment."

Shannon agreed, but sat in the marred chair she had been in moments before.

Murk was a handsome man with a chiseled face, better-looking than she expected an antiques dealer with a checkered past to be. His dark eyes seemed kind. His eyebrows narrowed as he thought. His face seemed scrubbed by desert wind and tanned by tropical sun.

"I just called Cooper's home and spoke to his son, Jason," Shannon said. "He said now that his father is deceased, he and the family want nothing to do with the Bible. He thinks it's a nuisance. When I asked what he wanted me to do with it, he said I should give it to the girl who found it. I was just about to go and see her."

"Girl?"

"Her name is Tanya. She worked with the sheriff to locate the missing case at the crash site. You know about the crash, right?"

"Yes. Sir Richard called me not long after it happened. It's why I'm here. He told me about you, and I offered my assistance with the search."

"Thank you, but your help is no longer needed—considering Cooper's death."

Murk shifted on the sofa. "Why the girl? Tanya, is it? Why give her the Bible? She certainly can't appreciate its importance."

"Because she was the one who found it, and as executor of the estate, Jason Cooper can determine, and has determined, the disposition of the Bible. He wants Tanya to have it."

"Do you know much about her?" Murk leaned forward and rested his elbows on his knees. The ease at which he could pull information from her made her nervous.

"I know she is a Russian immigrant and lives on a goat farm."

"When you say girl—"

"She's maybe fourteen or fifteen."

"Do you think she would be willing to sell the Bible? The Bible is kinda special."

"Every Bible is special, Mr. Murk."

She watched him study her.

"Ah, you're one of those."

"'Those'? A Christian? If that's what you mean, then I'm guilty as charged."

"I wasn't saying anything bad. Look—do you think the girl would be willing to sell the Bible?"

Shannon twirled her hair, trying to think up an answer. "I really couldn't say."

David said, "I assume that if you just talked to Jason Cooper, you got an earful about me."

"I did. He doesn't like you. He said you were an unscrupulous antiques smuggler who took advantage of gullible buyers; that you peddle looted treasures, treasures that should be in museums."

Murk smiled. "Did he really say all that, Ms. Reed?"

"Not in so many words, but it's a fair interpretation."

"Let me explain something. As long as wealthy buyers want to purchase these objects, there will be those who will supply them. I am only a—facilitator. I do not loot, pillage or plunder anything. I am just a middleman who uses creative ways to safely transport these items from seller to buyer."

"You mean smuggle these items to wealthy connoisseurs."

"I have been in this line of work for a long time, and have always been forthright with both seller and buyer. It is governments that I trick. I distrust governments; they take from the paupers so they can eat like kings."

"You have some real issues, don't you?" Shannon said.

David took in a deep breath. "I have worked my trade from Cambodia to the Valley of the Kings in Egypt; from Petra to Machu Picchu. And in every case I performed my duties with fairness to both buyer and seller."

"Mr. Murk, honesty and fairness are not subjective terms. Claiming to be honest doesn't make you honest."

"Okay, Ms. Reed, I see who you are. I can read you like an open book. You are a blueblood whose daddy sent you to an expensive Ivy League law school, and you probably live off a family old-money trust account. You don't drink beer, wouldn't be caught consuming anything someone living in a trailer park might drink. No, you buy wine—not by the bottle but by the case from some vineyard you visited while touring the wine country. You never have dessert after a meal in a restaurant but dig into a quart of trendy-labeled chocolate ice cream when you're at home and no one is looking."

"Really? Is that all?"

"No, there is more. When you travel, you pack your own pillow because you can't stand the thought of putting your face where others have drooled. You go to church every Sunday, probably to be seen by others. You quote Bible verses when it suits you."

Shannon frowned.

David crossed his arms. "Tell me I'm wrong."

She stared at him, mouth open.

"Be careful, or your silver spoon will fall out."

Shannon clamped her jaw shut. "I don't go to church to be seen. I go because I want to worship. Church and faith are important to me. So see, you're not as insightful as you think."

"Am I wrong about the rest of it? Admit it, you're everything I described."

She wanted to deny it all, but she'd have to lie to do so, and she had never grown accustomed to lying.

Murk uncrossed his arms and stared at the floor for a minute. "I'm sorry. I went too far."

"I agree."

"Again, I apologize."

Shannon said, "Okay, what about tricking an old wealthy man into buying pieces of Christ's cross or the face cloth from Jesus' tomb?"

Murk looked as if he'd just bitten a lemon. "I didn't trick him. He heard about these objects and ordered me to buy them. If you've had any dealings with ol' R. C. Cooper, then you know once he decides he wants something, all discussion is over. I gave him what he wanted, nothing more."

Something in the parking lot caught David's eye. "Uh-oh."

Shannon turned her gaze to match his and saw two news trucks pulling through the parking lot. "More media."

Murk nodded. "*National* media. It seems the story is spreading. Did you call them?"

"Of course not. There were a cameraman and reporter here when we arrived."

Shannon continued to watch the trucks. A man donned a suit coat, and another in jeans and a work shirt hoisted a camera on his shoulder. A woman exited the other van.

"We all have a little greed at times, Mr. Murk."

"I am a man who enjoys seeing both parties satisfied with a fair deal. That's not greed; it's facilitating a mutually beneficial transaction. The paying of money for goods has been the basis of free enterprise for thousands of years, and is the cornerstone of capitalism."

Shannon said, "Wow, you sure can put shine on the apple."

"Give me a break. As an attorney, I'm sure you've shined a few apples in your day."

She stood. "I need to take the Bible to its new owner, and I prefer to go alone."

"Fine. Just tell Tanya that I know a great deal about the Bible she has, about its history—and the name Feodor Kuzmich."

Shannon snapped her head around. "You know about the name?"

"The name is well known to people in my trade. You can't be a great antiquities dealer and not know history." He looked at her with a growing grin. "Maybe she would be willing to sell the Bible. After all, I am the best at what I do, and can get her the highest price."

"I don't know whether you are vain or just conceited."

"I am conceited, of course. You see, vanity is a failed attempt to impress others, while a conceited man is sure to impress himself."

Shannon rolled her eyes and stood to leave.

chapter 8

IRENA'S
GOAT FARM

THROUGH HER MUD-STREAKED rental car's windshield, the goat farm looked to Shannon like nothing more than a dated, weathered house trailer perched on ten acres of snow-covered hardpan dirt, dotted with piñon pines and stubble sage. An old woman sat on a wooden stool by a stone wall. The dry, stacked-stone corral had a one-foot-wide gap that allowed only a single goat at a time to squeeze through. The enclosure held a tightly packed flock covered in winter coat.

The woman yanked a flailing goat through the narrow opening and grabbed its sagging udder, squirting a thin stream of hissing milk into a metal pail between the creature's feet.

Shannon had met Irena earlier that day, when Sheriff Powell returned Tanya home after she found the briefcase near Jimmy's place. Jimmy rode in the back of Deputy Doug's patrol car. Tanya and Shannon had stayed with Powell. The simple farm wasn't far off the road to the sheriff's station.

Irena's face was lined and aged from long exposure to the sun. Stress and the ever-present cigarette dangling from her lip didn't help. Shannon knew the air must chill the woman, but despite the seventeen-degree temperature, she showed no sign of being cold, even though she wore only a thin, threadbare coat.

Irena didn't bother to look up at the sound of Shannon's rental car crunching gravel in the driveway; she remained on her three-legged stool milking the bleating goats.

"Hello there," Shannon called as she shut the car door. She slapped her coat and stomped the snow under designer shoes in a futile attempt to get warm. The morning air was still, and a platinum, flat sky hung overhead. A pencil-straight trail of smoke rose from a bent stovepipe crudely affixed, with strands of bailing wire, to the dark tarpaper roof. Opaque sheets of plastic were stapled over the windows to keep the icy winter winds from seeping into the decaying house. Stacked cinder blocks served as the front steps leading to a leaning wooden porch.

Chickens milled about the trailer, pecking in the snow as they foraged for dry corn kernels. Three rusted wire rabbit cages sat by the weathered porch, their white-furred and pink-eyed occupants squirming about.

A movement near her feet caused Shannon to look down. A drooling dog with hair standing up on his thick neck stood a few feet away and was inching closer; its black lips curled, exposing long teeth. It let out a deep, menacing growl. It was a big dog with a head that looked as large as an engine block. Its growl gave it an even more frightening presence. It took another step closer.

"Um . . . Irena?"

The old woman stopped milking, picked up a stone and threw it at the dog. The rock hit it on the right hindquarter. It yelped and turned toward Irena.

"Go from here, dog," Irena commanded, her words cloaked in a thick Slavic accent. She removed the dangling unlit cigarette from her mouth. She yelled something in a language Shannon didn't understand. The dog lowered its ears, eased its hackles and slunk off.

Shannon realized she had been holding her breath. She let it out. "Excuse me for bothering you, but I want to give Tanya something. Is she here?"

The woman turned her face to the house. "Taanyaaaa." She spit a scrap of tobacco on the snow, stuck the cigarette back in her mouth and returned to milking.

The front door to the small farmhouse flung open, and Tanya came bounding down the cinder-block steps. The girl smiled at seeing Shannon again.

"Hello, Ms. Reed," Tanya said, moving up a rutted trail in the snow made by goats. It was stained green from dung.

"Hello again."

"I didn't expect to see you again. Is there something you want, Ms. Reed?"

Shannon held out the case with the Bible. "This book is very old and valuable, and because you are the one who found it, it is now yours."

"What about the man who owns the Bible? He went to a great deal of trouble to get it, just to give it away."

It took a second for Shannon to respond. "He no longer wants it."

Tanya tilted her head to the side. "That isn't true. Your words tell me you are hiding something."

The girl's accusation stung. "The owner died. He was an elderly man. I spoke to his son, and he doesn't want the Bible. He told me I could give it to you."

Tanya looked at the case. "Your words are true now. I'm not sure I want the book, Ms. Reed. There is a name inside that reminds me of a very bad memory."

"What?" Shannon asked. "Why does a name in a Bible frighten you so much?"

"I don't like talking about it."

"Fair enough. I guess I have a few memories that I prefer to keep private." Shannon lowered the case. "Tanya, maybe the Bible found you instead of you finding it. For some reason, I feel this is part of a bigger plan."

Tanya looked at Irena. "May I keep the Bible?"

Irena stood from her milking stool, put her hands in the small of her back and stretched. "*Da*. If you wish."

The black goat she was milking sprinted into a side corral area.

"Your daughter is a special girl," Shannon said as she handed Tanya the Bible.

Tanya exchanged glances with Irena. "We're not related, Ms. Reed. Irena is my guardian. My family . . . is not here."

Shannon didn't press.

"I owe her my life. I am grateful for all that she has done for me."

Irena said nothing.

Tanya looked into Shannon's eyes, and for a moment Shannon thought the girl was reading her mind.

"Sheriff Powell told me you are an attorney."

"That's right. I practice law in Arizona."

"Are you a good lawyer?"

Shannon sensed no disrespect in the question. "I'm very good at what I do."

Shannon shook her head. "I mean, are you an attorney who does good?"

"Yes. I try to be honest in everything I do."

This time, Tanya's head moved up and down. "I hear the truth."

"I don't understand," Shannon said. "What do you mean, you hear the truth?"

Tanya ignored the question. "We need help from an attorney."

Irena gasped. "Say no more, girl!"

Shannon felt confused. "Is there something I can help with?"

"We have no money to pay attorney," Irena cut in.

"That's not a problem. There would be no charge. It's called pro-bono work. Most attorneys do some kind of free work every year."

Irena frowned. "You are kind, but girl says too much."

"We need help with immigration problems." Tanya lowered her voice, as if unseen people might be listening.

"I can help," Shannon said softly. "I would like to help if I can."

Tanya looked at Irena. "Her words are truthful. I spent time with her yesterday, and she spoke nothing but the truth then."

Irena worked her lips for a moment as if searching for a word, but said nothing.

Tanya returned her attention to Shannon. "We escaped from Russia seven years ago, and came to the United States with some financial help from my family living in Toronto. They paid our passage on a ship. They then brought us across the Canadian border to live here in Colorado. Colorado is in the middle of such a big country, we thought we could live our lives unnoticed."

"Go on," Shannon said.

Irena spoke up. "Ms. Reed, you are only lawyer we have ever met. I trust you only because Tanya says your words have truth. What I say about the girl was hard for me to believe when I heard it seven long years ago."

"Heard what?"

"Girl has rare gift known as the Pravda."

"The Pravda?"

"Yes, it is a gift that allows the girl to hear lies in voice of others."

"She hears lies? Like a human lie detector?"

"Yes. Every few generations, in far north of Russia, a special girl is born, a girl from a special bloodline. That girl has the Pravda gift."

Shannon rubbed her forehead. "Ever since I got involved with this old Bible, my life has gotten weird. Why do I think it's about to get a whole lot weirder?"

Irena said, "There is no one else like her. It is why we fled Russia. There are those who want to make use of her gift."

"Wait a second," Shannon said. "How is it possible that you can tell when someone lies? A polygraph measures changes in blood pressure, pulse and respiration. Are you saying you do that?"

"No, Ms. Reed, it is a physical ability. I can tell when someone lies just by hearing his voice. I hear it and know. I have read books from our school library and they say when people lie, their voice creates a sound that scientists call a microburst. It is like a very faint, faraway FM signal on a radio. I can hear that very faint sound."

Shannon shook her head. "I'm sorry, but I find this all very hard to accept, Tanya."

"The Pravda comes only in my family and appears in a girl every fourth or fifth generation—always a girl. My great-great-grandmother Olga had it, but we know little of her life."

Shannon brushed back her hair. "And I'm supposed to believe you have this ability?"

Tanya nodded. "Truth should always be known, because truth can always be tested."

Shannon cocked her head and stared at Tanya. "What do you hear when someone lies?"

"It is hard to describe. It's like the whir of a hummingbird's wings, or a teapot a moment before it starts hissing. But it's not just a sound that I hear; it is a kind of irritation in my inner ear, like a knife scraping across a plate. It is very faint, but I can't ignore it. It's unmistakable to me."

Shannon sighed. "I knew this was going to get weird."

"When you told me the owner of the Bible no longer wanted it, I knew you weren't telling the whole truth. Only after I said so did you tell me he had died."

"I wasn't lying, just trying to keep an unpleasant fact from you. Maybe you noticed my discomfort and assumed I was keeping something from you."

"Test me," Tanya said.

"That would be silly."

"It's not silly. It's the only way for you to believe me. Test me."

Shannon shrugged. "Okay. I was born in July."

"That is untrue," Tanya said quickly.

"I was homecoming queen in high school."

Tanya smiled. "You are beautiful, but you weren't homecoming queen."

"All right then, I have a brother who is a doctor in Phoenix."

Tanya narrowed her eyes. "That is true and false. You have a doctor in the family, but not from Phoenix and this person is not your brother."

Shannon began to feel uncomfortable. "My sister is a doctor in Seattle."

"That statement is true."

Shannon was stunned. "I had chicken pox in the fifth grade."

"Again, true and untrue: you got chicken pox but not in the fifth grade."

"You're right, it was the sixth grade."

Irena said, "The girl is never wrong, I know. I have lived with her for seven years." She looked at Tanya. "It is most hard not to lie a little."

"Maybe Tanya's just a good at guessing."

Tanya shook her head. "You know I'm not guessing. You believe now. You believe I have the Pravda. Your words tell me you believe."

Shannon closed her eyes and tried to clear her colliding thoughts. "I need to know the whole story here. Is there someplace we can discuss this?" She flapped her arms. "I'm freezing."

"In our house," Irena said. "It's not much for Americans, but for me it is a good place. Please come and I can make some tea."

"I could use something hot," Shannon said, and followed Irena and Tanya to the rundown home.

Five minutes later, Shannon sat in an unsteady fiberglass folding chair at one end of a rickety card table that served as the kitchen table. She set the case with the Bible on the floor next to her chair. The inside of the home smelled musty, and looked only slightly better than the outside. A woodstove in the living room poured out heat. The plastic sheets over the windows meant to keep out drafts, but the aged and dust-filmed coverings also kept out most of the daylight. On the table rested several dark biscuits—breakfast, Shannon assumed. Unwashed dishes sat in a suds-filled metal sink, a washcloth and towel resting to one side. Tanya must have been cleaning dishes when Irena called her outside. In short order, Irena placed a cup of steaming tea in front of Shannon. The woman then served up two more cups.

Once the others had joined her at the table, Shannon said, "Maybe you should start at the beginning."

Tanya sipped her tea before speaking. She stared into the cup as if seeing images from her past swirling in the steamy fluid. A moment later, she told of the trip to a Russian monastery, of the stone coffin and the gold snuff box.

"How do you know it was Feodor Kuzmich's coffin?" Though Shannon warmed her hands on the cup, still something inside her felt very cold.

"I remember seeing the Romanov imperial double-headed eagle on the top of the box. The lid of the snuff box had been sealed with red wax. The priest gave it to my father. I never saw the gold box again after that night; I don't know what my father did with it. I've always believed he hid it somewhere. There is a note inside that I was to read."

"What is your father's name?" Shannon asked.

"Yuri Novak."

"Where is your father now?"

Tanya seemed to melt in the chair. She started to speak, but nothing came from her open mouth.

Irena clutched a cube of sugar between her teeth and sipped her tea. She swallowed a sip, then said what the girl could not. "We do not know. We have heard rumors that he is in a prison camp in the far north of Russia. We cannot say if he is alive or dead."

"That's a horrible burden to bear," Shannon said.

"We live in hope," Irena said. "And when hope is all we have, it is enough."

"What happened next?"

Shannon listened as Tanya told of being pursued by a KGB man, about her wounded father, and how a one-armed man saved them by striking the pursuer with a shovel.

"Did you ever find out who the one-armed man was? Do you remember much of him?"

"He is my brother," Irena said. She brought a match to the unlit cigarette she had been hanging onto since Shannon arrived. Blue smoke rose to the tarnished ceiling. She coughed as she took a drag and released the smoke in a long exhalation. "My brother Sergey worked at the monastery. In America he would be called janitor. He was war hero, wounded several times in battle of Stalingrad and received many medals, which he always wore pinned to his coat. He killed many Germans in battle, but one day he killed a young man, no more than sixteen, who was captured and then lined up against wall with other prisoners. Sergey was told to shoot boy by his commander. Sergey refused. He believed shooting prisoners was murder. His commander told him to shoot or be shot for disobeying order.

"He raised his rifle, aimed at boy and said, 'God forgive me.' Sergey said the boy tried to cross himself with his tied hands. He could hear the prisoner mumble a prayer in German. Sergey . . . pulled the trigger. The boy slumped to his knees, then toppled over. Before Sergey could lower his rifle barrel, a bomb went off close to him and . . . next thing he remembered was being placed on a stretcher. He saw an arm covered with rubble on the ground. He recognized the battalion markings on his coat sleeve. It was his arm. Next to his severed limb lay body of commander who had ordered Sergey to shoot the prisoner."

Irena inhaled more smoke. Shannon saw her hand shake.

The woman continued. "Sergey believed he was being punished by God—punished for killing boy. He dedicated the rest of his life to the service of God. After the war my brother worked at monastery, scrubbing floors and repairing place the best he could with only one arm."

"What happened to Sergey, your father and you after that night?" Shannon asked.

Tanya said, "Sergey took my father to a nearby abbey where he could be cared for. He was too injured to travel far. My father pleaded with the monk to get me across the border to Finland, to safety. Leningrad is close to the border, you know."

Tears pooled in Tanya's eyes. "I haven't seen him since that night. He promised that he would find me—that no matter what, he would find me. That night Sergey and Irena drove me to the village of Viborg, near the border of Finland. We waited by the road in a clump of trees a long time. Sergey said good-bye to Irena. She cried and said she could not leave him, but he insisted that it was better to save a life and live apart than to be together and see a life ended. They took several cases of vodka from the trunk of the car and motioned for me to crawl in. Irena gave me a sedative to keep me calm. I became very dizzy. Sergey scooped snow from the ground and sprinkled it on me so heat sensors at the border would not detect me. He wrapped a blanket around me and covered me with the bottles of vodka. He told me to stay quiet, then closed the trunk. The bottles were heavy, and it was so dark. I remember shivering. A moment later I felt the car moving. We were soon stopped at the border crossing."

Irena smiled sadly, showing nicotine-stained teeth. "I will tell rest of story," she said, then fought back a tear. "When we reached the border crossing, I told the guards I was taking a load of vodka to Finland so I could bring back bottles of whisky for some high-ranking Communist Party officials. They asked for my papers. I told the guards that the party officials were all very drunk and ordered me to tell border guards to let me pass. They weren't interested in what I had to say. I told them I would be in big trouble if I could not get men their whisky from Finland. They laughed at me. I offered them six bottles of whisky on my return trip. That wasn't good enough. They wanted to see vodka in trunk. I got out of car and walked to the back. The guards looked in trunk with flashlights. They said, 'Six bottles for us now and six later.' I gave them the vodka and said, 'Na zdorovye,' which means, 'To your health.' They waved me through. When we passed into Finland, I heard on the radio the song of Sibelius's *Finlandia* and turned it up loud to let Tanya know we were free."

"That's amazing," Shannon said.

Irena laughed weakly. "I bet those stupid guards are still waiting for me to return with whisky."

"Where is Sergey now?" Shannon asked Irena.

"I think that if he is alive, he still works at the monastery. I doubt the KGB ever found out that an old one-armed man knock unconscious that big oaf of a KGB agent. I am sure Yuri alone was accused of all that happened that night." She paused. "May I see the Bible that Tanya found?"

Shannon retrieved the book from the case and set it on the table. Irena pulled it close. "I think God brought this Bible as an answer to our prayers." She ran her fingers over the worn leather cover. "Perhaps this Bible is a holy messenger, a thread that sews us together for a reason only God can explain."

"We need your help, Ms. Reed," Tanya said. "Irena is a good woman. She has been good to me even though I'm not her blood relative, but it's a lonely existence for us both. We're afraid someone will discover we're illegal immigrants and send us back to Russia."

"I won't let that happen," Shannon said, defiant. "How is it you got in school, Tanya? Didn't they ask for a birth certificate or other documents proving you're a U.S. citizen?"

"Occasionally, we encounter a kind person. The school administrator looked the other way."

"After hearing that story, I can't decide if your life is cursed or charmed."

"We are poor, but alive," Irena said. "That counts for something in this world."

"I suppose it does," Shannon said, then added, "The Bible is legally yours to do with as you please and it could be worth a lot of money."

Tanya stared back in surprise.

"There is a man in town who wants to buy it, and I know he is willing to pay a large amount of money. His name is David Murk, and he told me he knows about Feodor Kuzmich."

Tanya stiffened at the mention of the name.

"Do you want to meet him?" Shannon asked.

Tanya hesitated before saying, "Yes."

"I'll arrange it. Is there some place in town—some public place—where we can meet?"

"There's Michelle's Diner," Tanya said.

"Great. I'll pick you up in the morning . . . say, eight o'clock?"

"Do you trust this man?" Tanya asked.

Shannon grinned. "I guess it wouldn't do to lie to you, would it? I don't know, Tanya. I honestly don't know."

Tanya nodded. "You're being truthful."

"One more thing," Shannon said. "I suggest we don't tell Mr. Murk anything about this special gift of yours."

chapter 9

C-23

A HUSKY GUARD CRUNCHED snow under his thick, felt-lined boots as he made his way through the dark morning to Prison Ward 8. He pulled a brass key free from the big metal ring tethered to his uniform belt. It took two tries before his gloved hand managed the task. This far north, a man never removed his rabbit-fur gloves to take hold of something made of metal.

He stooped in front of a thick planked door that was pitted from blowing snow and ice crystals. His shivering right hand prodded the stem of the key into the rusty, worn lock. The metallic clink of key striking lock echoed inside the dank corridor of the prison cell.

The big door swung open followed by an invading bitter blast of air that slapped Yuri Novak awake. Sixty-six men lived in Ward 8. Sixty-six battered, worn, weary shells of humanity were yanked from the painless hours of sleep by the guard's bellowing. Yuri lay in Bunk 14, a raw board bed supported by wood poles, which he shared with four other men. He had been in the gulag seven mind-numbing years.

Every day he felt his heart atrophy a little more, slowly dissolving in his chest. He knew his muscles were being consumed by his own body to compensate for the lack of nutritious food. The skimpy diet his captors served was not enough to sustain his weight. He had lost thirty kilos since coming to this place.

Work Camp C-23 had been restored from one of the many infamous Stalin gulags. It had been specifically modified to punish men for subversive acts against the Soviet state. It lay somewhere in the endless taiga of the north, planted in the dark pine and conifers, far off from the prying eyes of human rights activists, and far from any hope of any freedom.

Only one long and lonely road led in and out. In winter the snow piled up to the rafters. When the short Arctic summer came, snow melted fast, creating muddy, boot-sucking bogs.

Coils of razor-sharp barbed wire trimmed the tops of concrete pillars and the tall fence that rimmed the perimeter of the compound. Four stilt-timbered watchtowers, manned by bored, machine-gun-bearing guards, occupied each corner of the property. The fence was an unneeded expenditure. If someone made the foolish attempt to flee, they would die in the snow-choked forest. It was an unforgiving patch of ice where lungs could freeze from inhaling the icy air, rubber tires would split open and hardened metal would turn brittle.

All who tried the equally insane attempt at escape in the summer were hampered by endless quagmires of tarry muck, their feet sinking with each step, gaining unwanted weight from the mud that clung to their legs. Then there was the constant assault of female mosquitoes, relentlessly injecting their syringe-shaped beaks into the pale skin of their victims. No one had ever escaped from Work Camp C-23 and lived.

The short days were consumed with raw-bone labor and the nights filled with icy wind lashing against the thin-walled barracks. Despite the risk, such conditions pressed some men to attempt escape no matter how dire the odds. Their frozen bodies were usually found within ten kilometers of the camp. The guards called it "the Zone of Death." The frozen corpses were allowed to be gnawed at for a day or two by hungry creatures that roamed the dark green forest. It served as a stomach-turning warning to the prisoners and made for lighter loads for the guards, who would sling what remained of the frozen blue bodies onto a wooden cart, then push the cart to the cemetery just beyond the coils of barbed wire rimming the prison's perimeter. The corpses would be dumped onto a stack of other dead, contorted, chewed-over prisoners awaiting burial when the rock-hard soil thawed in the late spring. They were then dropped unceremoniously in a common unmarked grave for eternity.

"Up! Get up, you lazy dogs!" the guard roared in the darkness of the ward. Several prisoners moaned from their beds. Nighttime dreams were their temporary escape from the sea of white death that awaited them beyond the barbed wire.

Yuri joined in the groaning. The thought of blowing shards of ice chewing at his unprotected face ate away at his resolve to live another day. His stomach ached from hunger. It always ached from hunger.

Yuri heard a sulfur match hiss to life as the guard walked to the middle of the room and lowered the tiny flame to the nub of a candle resting on a small wood table. The candlewick slowly ripened into a faint orange glow. Sullen faces with sunken eyes void of hope peered at the light from the rows of plank bunk beds. No electric lights were allowed in the ward; too many prisoners would use the wire to end their misery.

The men said nothing, and offered the guard only frowns from blue lips bunched tightly behind unruly beards. Their dry lips hid a sparse array of teeth. Many of the men's teeth had fallen out due to malnutrition. Some, like Yuri, countered the lack of vitamins by drinking tea made from pine branches boiled in water. Most men found the taste so offensive they refused to consume it, but those that did kept their teeth and lived a little longer.

A few of the men could not stir for the first minute or so and lay in a fetal position. Their muscles had been punished hour after hour in the coal mines, only to be tortured even more at night from the unforgiving wooden slats and sparse straw bedding of their bunks. The straw was little comfort. Some had to urge their cold limbs to move by massaging them with coal-stained fingers. Then, if possible, they forced themselves to stand. If they didn't, the guard would drag them outside into the snow, where they would be left to shiver away their last breaths.

A month ago, Yuri had seen a prisoner who refused to get out of his bunk pulled outside and left to the elements. The next time Yuri saw him, the prisoner lay on his side like a marble statue. His last gesture of defiance: a raised fist. He froze in that position.

One by one the prisoners swung their legs over the bunk's edge, revealing bone-thin limbs covered with a dark patina of coal dust or soiled with gummy tree sap. They picked their shaved heads with dirty fingernails and flicked off new scabs of dried blood left from lice that had nibbled on their salty flesh. Those who had not been at the prison that long stood quickly, almost defiantly, but they would all be broken soon enough by the menacing, soulless guards.

Yuri exercised a different kind of defiance.

MICHELLE'S DINER

Shannon sat in the back booth with Tanya and Irena. She raised a hand when David Murk entered the diner. The café smelled of disinfectant and grease. David smiled and gave a short wave.

As Murk approached, Shannon smoothed her blue wool suit and crisp white blouse. When she had entered and followed the waitress to their booth, she felt the stares of ranchers and a trucker who, apparently, weren't used to seeing a well-dressed woman in high heels gracing the dingy diner. With every step she took, her heels clicked on the hard surface of the floor, making her more self-conscious.

Murk greeted them and slid into the booth.

"I think this should prove to be an interesting morning," Shannon said. "Mr. Murk—"

"Hold on." Murk raised a hand. "First names, please."

"All right. David, this is Irena and Tanya. Irena is Tanya's guardian." After a moment she added, "And I'm their attorney."

Murk grew a slow grin. "I see. Picked up a new client after our little talk, eh?"

"That wasn't my intent, but another matter came up and they asked for my help."

"Attorneys make their living on 'another matter.' I hope it's not something too taxing."

"Sorry, but it's confidential; attorney-client privilege and all that. I'm sure you understand. I can tell you it has nothing to do with the Bible—but I still represent them."

A fiftyish waitress with a tight bun of gray hair pinned to the top of her head came to the table and took orders. Shannon's appetite had been stolen by the sight of a bug scurrying along a windowsill. She ordered coffee, but drank it only after examining the inside of the cup. Murk said he never ate breakfast, but encouraged the others to order whatever they wanted; he was paying. Tanya requested eggs and pancakes; Irena ordered the same.

Murk turned to Tanya, but shifted his gaze to Irena from time to time. Shannon didn't know if he was being polite or trying to read the old woman's expression. "I'm an antiques dealer. I work with old objects such as your Bible. I would be willing to buy it for a good price if you would be willing to sell it."

Tanya turned to Shannon. "What is an antiques dealer?"

Shannon answered with sarcasm. "They're smugglers."

Murk frowned. "Antiques dealers find people with rare, ancient objects of great value, and then they find buyers who want to purchase those objects. The seller gets paid for the object, the new owner gets something he wants and the dealer makes a commission on the sale."

Shannon glared at Murk. "And once they find a buyer, they smuggle the object to its new home."

Murk said, "I prefer 'creative transportation of rare and valuable goods.'"

"It still sounds like smuggling to me," Shannon smirked.

David narrowed his eyes, then spoke to Tanya. "The Bible is worth much more money than you might think."

"Why?" Tanya asked, her demeanor belying her young age.

"I am told the book has the name Feodor Kuzmich written in it. That name alone makes it valuable."

"Just because of that name?" Irena asked.

"Yes, ma'am," David said. "Of course a handwriting expert would need to analyze the writing. If verified, that Bible would be worth big bucks."

"He's telling the truth," Tanya said to Shannon. She turned back to Murk, who gave her a puzzled look.

Tanya asked, "What do you know about the name Feodor Kuzmich?"

Murk explained, "Well, my client, Sir R. C. Cooper . . . I suppose I should say 'ex-client' . . . owned your Bible during the First World War and for a short time afterwards. He remembered seeing the name of a Feodor Kuzmich written in Cyrillic."

Tanya spoke up, "Does R. C. Cooper read Russian?"

"No. However, while he was a soldier fighting for Great Britain on the Western front, he made friends with a Russian soldier. It seems that in February 1917 the Russians agreed to send two brigades of twenty thousand men to fight in France and Belgium. In the spring of that year, they took a beating in what is known as the Nivelle Offensive. Some Russians mutinied after that campaign, but some volunteered to keep fighting. They called themselves the Russian Expeditionary Force. One of the Russian soldiers befriended Cooper and translated the note in his Bible."

"Who is Feodor Kuzmich?" Shannon asked.

"He was a wandering monk who lived in Siberia in the mid-1800s."

"Why would that make the Bible so valuable?"

"It wouldn't if that were the end of the story, but many historians and scholars believe that Feodor Kuzmich might be more than he seems."

"Such as?" Shannon prompted.

"None other than Czar Alexander I of Russia, the duke of Finland, the king of Poland, the great conqueror of Napoleon Bonaparte."

"Say that again," Shannon said.

"I know it sounds crazy, but your Feodor Kuzmich may have been the emperor of Russia who allegedly died in 1825."

"Allegedly?" Shannon said.

"Some notable historians believe Czar Alexander faked his death, then traveled by private yacht to Palestine. That's where the trail goes cold. About eleven years later, around 1836, a man who looked and spoke like Czar Alexander I turned up in Siberia as an itinerant monk. Those who had known the czar well, and even several members of the royal family who met the monk, were convinced he was the czar."

"Why would a man do that?" Shannon asked. "Shrugging off

such power, wealth and prestige to become an impoverished monk seems too much to believe."

"I suppose," Murk said, "but surprisingly there are many experts on the subject who believe just what I told you. The czar staged his own death, thereby avoiding an assassination attempt. It's said that a woman warned Alexander I that an assassination plot was brewing against him. If the faked death and secret abdication of the czar is true, and if he penned the signature of Feodor Kuzmich in your Bible, and that signature can be matched with the czar's known handwriting, then you have a very valuable historical document. Many collectors of czarist artifacts would salivate at the thought of owning a Bible with Alexander's autography on one of the pages."

"What does . . . *autography* . . . mean?" Irena asked.

"It's like the word *autograph*. It refers to something written in one's own hand."

"Would the snuff box also be valuable?" Tanya asked.

"Incredibly valuable," Murk said. "Not to mention that it's a huge piece in the historical puzzle about the missing czar."

Tanya's eyes drifted to a distant spot in the café. Shannon noticed the teenager was breathing faster and deeper.

The waitress brought two plates of eggs and steaming pancakes dripping with butter, set them in front of Tanya and Irena, then moved to the next table.

Shannon said, "I would think that if this is such a big mystery, someone in Russia would exhume the czar's body and the controversy would be solved with a little DNA testing."

Murk flashed a Cheshire grin. "This is the good part. Count I. Vorontsov-Dashkov, the former viceroy of the Caucasus in the 1880s, went to the Cathedral at the Fortress of St. Peter and St. Paul, and, under orders of Czar Alexander III, opened the tomb of Alexander I. The count was the only minister of the court who had keys to the cathedral doors. At his direction, stoneworkers and laborers pried open the tomb. Want to guess what they found?"

"I'm not good at guessing."

"They found nothing. The tomb was empty. Then much later, in the 1920s, the Bolsheviks, wanting money for military needs, opened the tomb searching for imperial jewels rumored buried with the czar. They also found an empty crypt."

"There's one big fly in the ointment of this wild theory," Shannon said. "How does Czar Alexander, the same man who defeated Napoleon and his powerful army, a few years later run away from all his wealth and power to become a poor monk in Siberia?"

"Czar Alexander fled the throne the same way he defeated Napoleon. History teaches that in 1812 Napoleon invaded Russia with a massive army. As Napoleon pushed deeper into the heart of Russia, the farmers burned down their homes, their barns and their crops. It's called 'a scorched-earth tactic.' The French soldiers were left with nothing to gather from the land, and by the time they reached Moscow in September they found the city shrouded in smoke and almost completely empty of anyone."

He took a sip of his coffee, scowled and pushed the cup away. "Most buildings burned to the ground; only a few sections of blackened walls or columns here and there remained standing. In the poor quarters of the city, a smattering of stunned people wandered in the choking smoke with their clothing almost burned from their bodies. Multitudes had abandoned the city, carrying what few belongings they had, and Napoleon found himself uncharacteristically baffled by it all. He retreated back to France not long after—defeated."

"As amazing as that story is, I don't see how it relates to Alexander's departure."

Murk said, "A man who would order a large part of Russia burned to ashes to save his country would be the same sort of man who would leave his own throne in ashes in order to preserve his life."

"I suppose in a strange way that makes sense," Shannon said.

"Look, I don't claim to be an expert on the subject, but I know someone who is. There's a man at the Institute for Soviet Studies in Washington, D.C. He has spent years researching the legend. If you want all the facts, then you need to visit him."

Tanya asked, "Will he know why Feodor Kuzmich might be buried with a gold snuff box?"

"Maybe. The best way to know is to go and see him."

"What do you think, Tanya?" Shannon asked. "If you want to go to Washington, then I think we should go. I have some contacts there and we can better deal with that other matter as well. Maybe David's friend can help with the mystery name in the Bible. You shouldn't sell it until you know what you have."

"We cannot afford such a trip," Irena said.

"I will take care of that," Shannon offered.

Tanya and Irena stared at each other for a long moment. Shannon imagined that a great deal of conversation was wordlessly exchanged between them. Shannon could see the eagerness on Tanya's face and the concern on Irena's.

Shannon touched the older woman's arm. "I'll take good care of her, Irena."

Irena shifted her gaze to the table.

Tanya spoke softly but firmly. "This may solve our problems. I want to go."

"I have done my best to protect you and teach you strength," Irena said. "I've also taught you to be suspicious of others." She paused. "I will not stop you, Tanya. I suppose I can manage the goats for a while without you."

Tanya hugged Irena.

"If the Bible is as valuable as I think it is," Murk said, "then you will never have to take care of goats again."

Irena said, "I like the goats, but a young girl today needs more in life. Go, my dear."

"Fine, then. I'll arrange for the tickets right away," Shannon said. "This is becoming an adventure of sorts. I haven't had this much excitement in my life since I was in the wilds of Africa."

Tanya looked surprised. So did Murk. "You were in Africa?"

"I'll tell you the story on the flight to D.C."

Tanya reached up to Shannon's neck and pulled her close. She whispered in her ear, "He is telling the truth."

"I think he's a pirate." Shannon winked.

Tanya shrugged. "Then he is a truthful pirate."

chapter 10

LABOR

THE FREEZING BITE of morning was like all the others. Yuri stretched, then pounded his stiff, cold legs until his circulation returned. He would soon have an axe in his dry, skin-split hands and would spend the day swinging it. He felt as if his blood had chilled to sludge. From his bunk, he put on his rancid, padded winter bib pants, and then his padded jacket. Next came the unpleasant task of pulling his damp, felt-lined boots over already cold feet. His boots were better than those the other prisoners wore. Most prisoners were given high-topped boots called *valenki*—a boot made from a mixture of mud bound together with hair. They wore out quickly, but were relatively waterproof and somewhat warm.

Yuri, however, had well-made boots. A year earlier, a kindly guard had become so sick he had had to be sent from the camp to Moscow to receive medical care. He was a rare, caring guard in a system filled with brutality. He gave his boots to Yuri before being helped aboard the big rig coal truck that carried him from the camp. To prevent such coveted boots from being stolen by another prisoner, Yuri painted a Jewish star of David on them with leftover yellow paint he found outside the camp supply shed. When he'd checked out his ax for his daily excursion into the dark forest, he'd slipped the can under his coat. Afterward, he used the tip of his finger to paint the bright yellow symbol on his boots. No one touched them after that.

Yuri trudged from the prison ward. Above the prisoners, clusters of brilliant stars lit their way to the camp kitchen, each man taking a place directly behind another, forming a long, snaking line.

There was no hurry; the morning meal that awaited him would be the same as it had been for the past seven years—a single slice of bread and a ladle of slightly warmed herring-head soup. But by the time the soup in their tin cans made it to their mouths, it had a glaze of ice on top.

The guards considered the prisoners nothing more than animals. The prisoners came from all over the Soviet Union: Latvians, Lithuanians, Poles, Ukrainians, men from the Balkans, even a few Chinese. All had been condemned for being spies or dissidents. The general citizenry hated them; so did the guards. They were enemies of the state who had disgraced the motherland. Most, however, had done little more than be in the wrong place at the wrong time, or knew someone less than supportive of the cause of communism. Each man had been tried and faced a judge—not that it mattered. They were guilty before any words were spoken in their defense.

Now they were nothing more than forgotten men with numbers tattooed on their arms. They were forbidden to use their birth names. When they were called on they answered with their assigned numbers. The goal was to completely strip the men of their identity. They made it so that the men would have nothing to live for, nothing to pray for and nothing to hope for.

Yuri stood patiently in the long line, waiting for his single ladle of the diluted fish soup and piece of bread. The man in front of him shivered and ran a hand over his shaved head. He looked the same as the other men: weary, forlorn expressions, holding their small tin cup waiting for a pitiful meal that would stave off hunger for only a short time. They were a haggard lot with their shaved heads and unshaved faces set atop stooped shoulders; living corpses adorned with torn and filthy jackets that were dusted with a skim of fresh Arctic frost. The only thing that made Yuri different was the boots with the yellow star.

The bedraggled line would move a single short step at a time, like a slow-moving machine. The shuffling cadence was the norm and Yuri had no reason to expect any change. Almost everything done in the camp was done in mindless repetition. In time, he would come to the serving area where the cooks stood.

As he neared the serving window, Yuri saw a haggard-looking Polish prisoner raise his cup a little too late to receive his morning meal. The cook, who worked with the same sense of forced automation as the prisoners, missed the container with his ladle. The broth splashed on the ground at the prisoner's feet. Only a small amount of the soup made it into his small tin cup. The man's hand began to shake. To not get anything meant his muscles would fail to work in the cold.

"You fool," the prisoner shouted. "That was my food for the whole day, and now it is on the ground!"

The cook gazed dispassionately at the man. He then dipped the ladle back into the soup and flung some of the broth into the man's face. The surprised prisoner stood motionless for a few seconds, then lifted his hand and pulled at his beard as if milking a cow, squeezing any remnant soup drippings into his cup.

As the unfortunate man moved away, Yuri stepped forward and lifted his tin cup, steadying it the best he could. His eyes followed the ladle's path until all the liquid hit its intended mark. He was handed a slice of bread. He consumed the meal before the soup had a chance to freeze.

While others went to the coal mine, Yuri and his team of nine other cutters—all dressed in their padded outer-ear fur hats, padded pants, jackets and gloves—started the two-mile hike with a surly guard. Aluminum snowshoes crunched on the snow with every stride. Slung over their shoulders they each carried an ax that had been checked out of a tool shed tended by an old Ukrainian guard.

Yuri was not even sure exactly where his prison was located. He knew it had to be near the Arctic Circle and northeast of Leningrad.

The daylight was brief, the only light being a teasing sun that skirted the frozen horizon for a few short hours, only to drop back into the winter abyss. He knew the name of the prison was C-23; he could see the name painted on the front gate every day as he returned to the camp. But knowing distance or direction really didn't matter. He would not escape; certain death would find anyone trying to flee across this vast wasteland without a good map, provisions and clothing that would allow travel across such an unforgiving environment.

This time of year, most prisoners would go months without seeing the light of day because they would march under the stars and blue moonlight to the grimacing stone face of the coal mine. They would enter the mine's maw, load themselves into coal carts and ride deep into the darkness, their only light coming from flickering lamps attached to the tops of their dented helmets. The crammed carts rattled over steel rails to the end of the mine, where they would swing picks into wet black rocks that stubbornly clung to the slick walls. The fallen coal would be scooped by wide shovels and then dropped into the coal carts that, when full, would be sent wobbling along on the narrow rails outside the mine, their contents to be stored in high, conical piles. When enough coal had been extracted and brought to the surface, a front loader would fill a BelAZ 27-ton quarry dump truck for delivery to places only the commandant of the mine and the drivers knew.

Yuri had it worse than those poor souls in the mines. In the mines, the temperatures were better than the harsh elements outside.

He was a lumber cutter assigned to a gang of ten men who waded daily through the thick mantle of snow and into the nearby forest. There he and his gang cut logs with long oak-handled axes. Each log would then be moved by the men who pulled it sled style, harnessing themselves with ropes to the fallen tree.

Each log was dragged down the sloping hill to lumber trucks that waited on the road plowed daily by a military truck with a large front blade. The trucks then drove off to an unknown town. Yuri saw many men crushed by runaway logs.

His gang of cutters had a daily quota enforced by the guard. Ten trees had to be felled; ten dragged to the lumber truck. The quota remained the same, even near the winter solstice when daylight was its briefest. Ten trees. Always ten more trees. It was cold, hard, backbreaking, miserable work. Hacking through frozen trees was like chopping iron.

Yuri was the team leader, elected by the other nine workers.

They had chosen him because he was the smartest. He could find more ways to confound the guards than anyone else. One day last month, his crew did not have to chop a single tree, because Yuri found a pile of logs that had long ago been felled by another gang of lumber cutters. For some reason the logs had been abandoned, probably because of sudden snows that could quickly bury the big trees.

Yuri had spotted the felled logs peeking from under a shroud of snow. He had his crew chip away the dark ends of the abandoned logs so that the weather-stained area would have the appearance of being freshly cut wood. The guard never discovered the trick, because he spent his day drinking vodka to stay warm as he sat on a log, hunched over and half-drunk. Yuri doubted the man cared how the logs were harvested as long as ten trees went to the trucks.

Despite his intelligence and the respect other men held for him, some chose to attempt escape. Yuri would plead with them not to try. Those who turned a deaf ear to him died and returned to camp as frozen corpses.

Yuri wouldn't make that mistake, nor would he surrender his will to the guard beasts of the taiga that tormented him daily. Yuri would wait for opportunity to arrive. If it ever did.

chapter 11

THE FLIGHT

TANYA ADMITTED SHE had never been on an airplane, and Shannon could see that the Boeing 727 intimidated her.

"It's bigger inside than I thought it would be."

"It seems to get smaller with every flight," Shannon said. "Especially the seats."

Tanya fumbled with the seat-belt clasp. Shannon helped her.

"Mr. Murk isn't flying with us?"

Shannon shook her head. "He flew out last night. He said he had to meet with a client in another city and would meet us later." What Shannon didn't mention was the relief she felt at not having Murk seated beside her.

"I'm nervous," Tanya said.

"No need to be. It's safe."

Tanya looked forward. She didn't seem comforted by Shannon's reassurances. The stewardess closed the doors, and a few moments later the plane began to move back. Shannon could see the girl's white knuckles as she squeezed the armrests, her body rigid, her eyes pinched almost closed.

Shannon squeezed her hand. "Really, Tanya, it'll be fine. Flying is the safest way to travel."

"It wasn't safe for the private jet that crashed near Pueblo."

"That's different . . . All right, you got me there, but flying is still very safe." Shannon hadn't considered the impact of flying so soon after Tanya had walked the disaster field looking for the Bible and case.

"You're telling the truth."

"I have an idea. Maybe a story will help. May I tell you a story?"

"Yes, please."

Shannon waited until the stewardess had finished her safety spiel and the jet started to taxi. "It is a story of when I was young, but not as young as you. After I graduated from college, I traveled to Africa."

Tanya's eyes widened. "At Michelle's Diner, you said you went to Africa."

"That's right. After college and before I went to law school, I worked for a year as a Christian missionary."

"Did you live in a mud hut?"

"Well, it wasn't a mud hut. We lived in buildings with windows and doors, but once I lived for two weeks out in the wild, sleeping in a tent in Gonarezhou National Park. That's in the southeastern corner of Zimbabwe." Images from the past flooded her mind. "It was a strange and beautiful land."

"Gonarezhou? What does that word mean?"

"It means 'Place of the Elephants.' I learned some very strange things about wild elephants." She leaned closer to Tanya. "I found out they have strange powers—unusual abilities concerning their voices and ears."

"Like me?"

"Yes, in some ways, like you."

"Do the elephants have the ability to tell the difference between truth and lies?"

"In a way. Once I was walking in the brush just after sunrise. I brought my Nikon camera and was snapping pictures left and right. The sunlight was bright orange against the Chilojo cliffs. The cliffs are so high you can see them from thirty miles away. The muddy Runde River winds through a small valley, and all along its banks are trees and brush, including some large acacia trees."

Tanya sat with her mouth agape as Shannon spun the tale. "That morning I watched a herd of elephants wading in the water. After awhile they came out, with slow, heavy steps that shook the ground. I stepped into a clearing and raised my camera to snap a shot of a big cow."

"Cow?"

"That's what you call a female elephant."

"Oh."

"Anyway, she must have been the leader because the small herd trailed behind her. Maybe the sound of my camera startled her, I don't know. I do know she suddenly spun her gigantic frame so gracefully she looked like a huge ballerina. Then she started to come toward me in a dead run."

Tanya's eyes widened more.

"My heart pounded so hard I could feel it in my temples. I stood frozen by fear. Then in a cloud of dust she stopped—stopped as quickly as she had started. I could see her eyes set on me. They looked sad, and moisture leaked from her facial glands."

"Go on. What happened?"

"Her expression changed. It seemed to soften. Her swaying trunk lowered, her ears relaxed and flattened back against her head. She expelled a grunt from her massive lungs, turned and walked to a large acacia tree. She nudged her broad skull against the limbs, shaking the clustered seed pods loose. The pods are ripe with protein and flavor. The fat seeds dropped all around her until they littered the ground. She rubbed the tree for the benefit of the rest of the herd."

"So they ate the seed pods?"

"They started to, but then something happened. She must have heard something in the distance. With the wave of her trunk, she signaled the rest of the elephants gathering around the tree. Somehow she communicated with her clan. I couldn't hear a sound, but I could see that the herd got the message loud and clear. The animals stood still, like big gray statues. Two big bulls faded deftly into the brush, as the females nudged the smaller elephants behind them. They formed a defensive circle around their young. They stood in a fearless stance with tattered ears flapping and their long trunks probing for a scent on the morning air. It seemed as if the African breeze was sending them an important message.

"It was then that I saw the wisp of dust trailing a Land Rover coming my way. In the back of the truck I saw the dark figures of men. I knew they were poachers when I saw rifles sticking out from under a canvas tarp roof. When they drew close, they began shouting as they approached the herd."

"What did the men want?"

Shannon's stomach turned from the memory. "Ivory. Ivory brings big money. It's worth several hundred dollars for a single kilo."

"They kill the elephants for the ivory?"

"Yes. It's horrible. They cut away the tusks with hatchets, leaving the elephants to rot in the sun."

Tanya looked stunned.

Shannon continued the story. "The elephants had heard the sound of the Land Rover long before I did. They knew from instinct—or maybe from experience—that the sound of rifles followed that of the Land Rover. They seemed aware that some of the herd would soon be dead. The elephants seemed to have an innate instinct about the impending danger and huddled even tighter."

"What did you do?" Tanya chewed at one of her fingernails.

"I climbed on a big rock outcropping and took off my jacket. I waved it wildly so the approaching men in the Land Rover could see me. I hoped it might scare them off, but I didn't hold much hope. To my surprise, the car slid to a stop and made a hasty U-turn. In a matter of minutes the Land Rover disappeared over the ridge. I guess they thought I was a park ranger.

"In any event, they didn't commit their carnage that day. The elephants, seemingly sensing that the danger had passed, relaxed and returned to eating the pods on the ground.

"When the female signaled the others in her herd, it was done in a tone that only the herd could hear." She stared into Tanya's wide eyes. "Tanya, if you ever hear something in the words of others that you recognize as a lie, then give me a signal that only you and I know." Shannon caressed Tanya's hair. "You've decided to trust me. That makes me feel like part of your family. Just like the elephant in that herd, I am here to always protect you."

"I hear truth in your words, and that makes me feel better."
The plane continued to climb.

WORK CAMP C-23, NORTHERN SIBERIA

The morning light bathed the ground in a misty pink hue. The guard and prisoners followed a path made by their daily march into the tall timber of the taiga. At times snow could gather into drifts that reached the roof of the prison ward, but the repeated footfalls of the gang of ten cutters and one guard packed down the trail, making it passable, at least until the next snowstorm.

The relentless wind blew across the wide valley and through stone pine thickets, making visible dry winter brush that bristled in the cutting breeze. Ice particles stung their eyes as they walked. Most had ragged scarves wrapped around their faces and rags tied around their boots. For added protection, the men had packed dry moss next to their skin and dry grass inside their boots. It was an old Yakut technique to stay warm and prevent frostbite that could take toes and fingers.

As the men all trudged forward, Yuri heard a strange sound. He had made this trek many times and had never heard such a noise before. He lifted his ax and tilted it in a defensive angle. Only a month ago a guard had been mauled by a big brown bear. The event left the men wary of any sound that didn't belong. The guards were just as troubled. The men joked among themselves. "Guards are as fat as pigs and prisoners are thin and sinewy. Bears are not dumb creatures and can tell the difference between a sparse meal and a good one."

Yuri heard it again: a disturbing noise—the sound of desperate grunting and frantic thrashing in a thicket of brush. Yuri gripped his ax tightly and slowly moved into a morass of dead limbs. A dozen steps later, he came face-to-face with a large stag. The creature's yellow-rimmed eyes darted about as he struggled to get his wide-beam antlers untangled from a mesh of twisted branches.

The guard appeared behind him and raised his rifle. "We will have fresh meat tonight." His words crackled out in the cold air. The thought of roasting deer flesh dripping droplets of fat over licking flames flashed in Yuri's mind, but he knew the prisoners would never receive a bite. The guards would eat it all, and what remained would be tossed to the guard dogs.

The snared deer sensed Yuri's presence and began flailing its hooves in the snow. The big animal urinated in fear. Yuri raised his ax and hushed the guard's excited movements.

Yuri motioned for the guard to back away. "You may need that bullet for one of us prisoners. There is no need to waste ammunition when an ax will do the job just as quickly."

The guard lowered his rifle. It was clear the stag could go no-where. Yuri closed the distance between himself and the buck, push-ing dry limbs aside, many of which snapped in Yuri's hand. Slowly he made his way to the trapped animal, and stepped onto a log that lay near the creature.

Yuri studied the buck. Its mouth hung open as it coughed up a frothy drool that dripped from its protruding, pink-gray tongue. Yuri's shadow fell across the deer's frantic face. The creature expelled a moan that sounded as if mourning the loss of its life.

Yuri raised the ax high over his head. The frightened deer's eyes rolled up. Yuri waited a second, taking precise aim.

The guard issued an order. "Be sure, prisoner; be steady and sure to kill."

Yuri didn't bother looking at the guard. "I never miss where I swing."

The animal seemed to calm in the next moment, as if sedated by the acceptance of its fate. It stood still, like a figurine in a shaken snowglobe. Yuri tightened his grip, set his jaw and sent the ax slic-ing through the air. His blade lopped off the gnarled branch that snared the deer's antlers. The stag pulled free, hunched his body, splayed his legs and stood frozen in a moment of paralyzed uncer-tainty. It flared back its ears, snorted, then bounded clumsily over the dead brush as it made its escape. The guard fumbled as he set his machine gun to his shoulder and squeezed the trigger. The crackle of the spewing bullets filled the air and rounds sent plumes of soft snow skyward with each impact. The stag scampered out of sight.

"You fool!" the guard shouted, and pounded the butt of his weapon in the snow. "Fresh meat! Lost! All because of you."

Yuri did not change his expression. "It would be meat for the guards, and you have plenty enough already. That animal was trapped, just as we are trapped in this stinking place. I could not let him die a prisoner. Not when it was in my power to do something about it and set him free."

"You are a fool." The guard shouted the phrase over and over. "I should shoot you for such stupidity."

Yuri turned the ax in his hands and looked at the blade, now powdered with snow. "I use this ax to cut trees that I do not sell. You guards tell us to eat and I eat; you say work and I work; now you say kill, but I refuse to kill. It is a good feeling not to kill something when you can, and it is an even better feeling to free something when you are able."

Yuri jumped from the log, his legs disappearing to his knees in a drift of snow. He held up the ax in one hand, like it was a hammer ready to strike another blow. The guard stepped back, raising his gun. His eyes widened in a way that reminded Yuri of the stag he had just released. Yuri sighed and lowered his ax. "You should try letting things go free."

The guard growled. "You are crazy." He spat in the snow.

Yuri smiled. "Sometimes, dear guard, the captive feels freer than his captor."

The guard shouldered the leather sling of his Kalashnikov. "If I report this, you will be in trouble." He paused. "Of course, I would be in trouble as well."

Yuri laid the ax's handle over his shoulder. "They killed a good carpenter two thousand years ago for setting the weak free, and thought him crazy as well, so I am in good company with what I do." He laughed at the guard. "And you are in miserable company for what you do."

The guard raised his voice over the gathering wind sifting through the boughs of the stout pines. "You might be right, but I will be free from all this in due time. I will be able to go home and have a wife serve me endless bowls of hot borscht."

"Perhaps, but you will never be free from yourself and the misery you have brought to so many. On your deathbed, with a stomach full of borscht, you will pass away with a life drained of good. In the end, you will be like that deer, waiting your judgment."

The guard stammered as he pointed down the snow-clogged path. "We—we must get our wood cut and get back, or they will think we both tried to escape."

chapter 12

STOCK'S STORY

INSTITUTE FOR SOVIET STUDIES, WASHINGTON, D.C.

DAVID MURK LED Shannon and Tanya down a dark hallway of the Institute for Soviet Studies, known as the ISS. Murk, who had been waiting for them in the lobby of the multistory building, shared what he knew of the Institute. "Basically, it's a think tank of brilliant minds that have contracts with the United States government for special research projects. It's the mission of the ISS to know every detail of the Soviet Union, with an emphasis on Russian military, government, history, literature and culture."

"So your friend is more than a history buff?" Shannon said.

"He's a student of all things Russian, but his love is history."

An elevator took them to the third floor and opened on a simple lobby with the kind of nondescript furniture found in most government lobbies. The receptionist's desk sat unoccupied. Not that it mattered. Murk moved through the space as if he owned it. He led them to an open door to the right of the lobby, started to knock on the jamb but hesitated.

Murk saw Jeffrey Stock sitting at his desk reading what appeared to be a history book, probably something by a Russian historian. The man seemed unaware that an early spring day was blossoming outside. Murk knew him to be a boring man to most everyone. He seemed to hate life, people and his mundane job. Every time Murk had seen the man he wore the same clothing: a wrinkled white dress shirt, polyester clip-on black tie and cheap brown shoes with thick rubber soles. Perhaps he did so to avoid thinking about something as inconsequential as wardrobe.

He had salt-and-pepper hair—more salt than pepper. His lean face sported a strong jaw that always looked as if it needed shaving even if he had shaved ten minutes before. A pair of black-framed glasses perched on his nose; white tape had given a temporary fix to one of the arms. Stock had a reputation for losing things. Once he admitted to losing his car keys so often he had taken to having ten made at a time. Like other scholars', his was an intellectual world where he lived deep in thought, so much so that his external world often went ignored.

At forty-three, he was an average man with features that would be forgotten once he left a room. He had never married and had never visited Russia, but felt linked to it by heritage. Murk knew these things about Stock because Murk liked to research his topics and acquaintances well. Stock, he came to realize, worked for the pay and retirement, and nothing more. Murk knocked on the door-jamb.

Stock looked up and said, "Oh no."

Shannon stood just behind Murk as he rapped his knuckles on the door. The door face bore an imitation wood-grain nameplate mounted in a cheap brass holder. The white letters read: DR. JEFFREY STOCK, PHD.

Shannon tried to read the man's face. He showed no joy at seeing Murk, nor did he show any other emotion. "I thought you two were old friends?" she whispered. She tightened her grip on the Bible.

Murk replied in a similar hushed tone. "Let's just say Dr. Stock and I have history; we help each other out from time to time."

"I hope you don't mean out of jail."

Murk stepped into the office and approached Stock. "May I introduce Ms. Shannon Reed, a lawyer from Phoenix, and Tanya Novak from Colorado?"

Stock rose. "It's very nice to meet you." He faced Murk. "Did we have an appointment, David?"

"Appointments are for strangers, not friends." Murk motioned for Shannon and Tanya to sit in the guest chairs opposite Stock's desk.

Shannon and Tanya stepped around a stack of books, and then waited a moment for Murk to clear off the two chairs that held rolled-up maps and papers stuffed into a cardboard box. Then he retrieved a similar chair from its place near the side wall and all were seated. "We have a special question to ask. The kind of question only a man of your education and interest can answer."

"Go on, David."

"I'm sorry," Shannon said. "We were under the impression that David had contacted you about this."

"I must have missed his call." He sounded surly.

"You'll brighten up in a moment, Jeffrey." Murk scooted his chair to the side of the desk. "We want to learn everything you know about Feodor Kuzmich."

Stock pulled a cigarette from a pack on his desk and held it with nicotine-stained fingers. He coughed twice. "I see. Feodor Kuzmich." Stock cleared his throat, as if saying the name choked him.

Stock studied Tanya for a moment. "You're a Russian girl, aren't you?"

Tanya's face revealed her surprise. Shannon spoke for her. "How do you know that?"

"It's easy to see. Your eyes dart about my office, taking in the environment, but your head remains still."

"I don't follow," Shannon said.

Jeffrey Stock explained, as if he were a professor lecturing a classroom full of students. "In Russia, newborns are bound in swaddling cloths, strips of cloth or a small blanket, that hold the infant's legs and arms close to the body. It keeps the child immobile. This goes on for about five or six months, but some parents swaddle babies even a little longer."

Shannon said, "That's cruel."

"To Americans it is, but Russian women think it keeps the babies from mischief and out of harm. The babies are kept bound all day, except of course for feeding, changing and bathing. The baby learns the only way to explore their world is by moving their eyes." Stock stared at Tanya. "When you entered my office, your eyes scanned the space, but your head remained still. I'd bet real money you were a swaddled as a baby."

Tanya said. "I was. I do not remember, of course, but my mother told me she swaddled me for six months."

"Wait a minute," Shannon said. "Don't other countries practice the same thing? How can you make a connection to Russia?"

Stock shrugged. "It was a safe conjecture on my part."

He put the cigarette between his lips, then reached into his other coat pocket and removed a metal Zippo lighter. He flipped the lighter open with the snap of his wrist, his thumb running over the knurled striker wheel. He put the flame to the end of the cigarette and took a long drag. A second later he exhaled white smoke. He placed the lighter on the desk. Shannon saw that it had been engraved in small letters:

DR. JEFFREY STOCK
20 YEARS OF SERVICE
ISS

He must have followed Shannon's gaze. "It was a gift; a gift for enduring two decades here. Not much of a gift."

The trail of the smoke drifted into Shannon's face. She coughed. "That is a really bad habit you have." The black marble ashtray on his desk was filled with discarded cigarette butts.

"I suppose it is. I excel at bad habits. Will you be staying in Washington?"

"No. I don't like all the crowds and traffic and the sirens blaring all night long. I found a beautiful bed-and-breakfast in Petersburg. It's a drive, but it's where I grew up. Tanya and I'll be staying there for the next few days, then I have to get back to my practice in Phoenix, and Tanya has to get back to school." Her eyes followed Stock's hand as he flicked ash into the stuffed ashtray before him; some of the ashes missed and landed on his desk.

He leaned back in his chair. "So you want to hear about Feodor Kuzmich."

"David has told us some of the legend." Shannon decided she didn't like Stock.

Stock tilted his head down and looked up over his glasses at Tanya. "I'm impressed that you are so interested in Russian history. It's sad that most Russians have little interest in their past. They have few heroes because of this."

He set his cigarette down. "I am too busy now and have no time to go into great detail about all this."

Shannon forced a warm smile at the man. "It is very important for us to hear what you have to say on the matter."

Stock smiled back and puffed out his lower lip. "I've researched the legend extensively; it has been a fascination of mine since I was a young boy. Even Leo Tolstoy, the famed author of *War and Peace*, studied the imperial legend for many years before he died. It was to be the subject of his next novel. Unfortunately, he died before he could start. Tolstoy believed the legend to be true." His chair creaked as he shifted his weight. "In a nutshell, the legend states that the czar faked his own death to take a new identity as Feodor Kuzmich, a *starets*."

"Starets?" Shannon said.

"It's a Russian word referring to monks, or holy men, that roamed the countryside doing good."

Shannon asked, "Do you have any proof he faked his death and took on a new identity?"

"I know it sounds crazy, but when you consider all the facts it makes a lot of sense."

"What facts?" Shannon pressed.

"Just like a lawyer to go after the facts. Czar Alexander I was without a doubt a great man of history; after all, he defeated Napoleon. Many consider him the savior of Europe. After Napoleon's defeat, Alexander I entered Paris as a hero, riding high on a dark Arab mare. I think he must have cut a dashing figure with his blue sash draped across his dark blue uniform. On his shoulders were large gold epaulets, and upon his chest a row of ribbons and medals. He spurred his dark horse with his polished knee-length black boots, and the people went crazy as he passed by. They shouted, *'Vive Alexandre! Vive les russes! Vive les allies!'* Which meant, 'Long live Alexander; long live the Russians; long live the allies.'"

Shannon said, "I thought the Russians were France's enemy."

"They had been for a long time, but the French were weary after two decades of Napoleon killing off their sons in bloody war after bloody war, so they hailed Alexander as their hero, as a national savior of sorts. On that March day back in 1814, thirty-thousand parading Russian troops made their way through throngs of cheering people that lined the Champs-Élysées. It took six hours for the Russian soldiers to complete the parade route. It was as if a conquering god had come to visit.

"But despite the accolades for his military accomplishments, Alexander I was also a deeply troubled man. Early in his life, he was smothered by a domineering grandmother, Catherine the Great. Then, as a young man, he loosely participated with the conspirators who assassinated his own father, Paul I. That was in March of 1801. That guilt ate at him until it almost made him go mad. He became irrational, eccentric, consumed by paranoia. And ultimately he became a fanatical religious mystic."

"Fanatical?" Shannon asked.

"He prayed incessantly and immersed himself in Bible study. He read the Book day and night. It is said his knees were worn raw and bloody from daily prayers spent on hard wooden floors. His servants often heard him ramble incoherently, and on many occasions he remarked that he would someday escape the throne to seek a life of solitude serving God.

"A plot was discovered by one of the czar's close confidants. Liberal young nobles, enlightened by the French revolution and filled with romantic zeal for release from an archaic czarist system, were planning on taking the czar's life. The plot was uncovered, and all the conspirators were discovered. A woman known only as 'the Yakut' was instrumental in foiling the plot and identifying the would-be assassins. The legend says she had a strange ability to detect when a person was lying."

Tanya looked at Shannon and drew her hands into nervous fists. Shannon glanced at Stock, who seemed too lost in his lecture to notice the teenager's reaction. One look at Murk, however, told Shannon it didn't get past him.

Stock continued, "It might surprise you that many historians believe in the imperial legend. Even the Grand Duchess Olga, sister of Czar Nicholas II, said, and I quote, 'We have no doubt that Alexander I and Feodor Kuzmich were the same person.'"

"So you seem to believe the legend as well."

"I do. Without reservation, I might add."

"Sounds more like a fairy tale," Shannon said.

"I admit it sounds contrived at best, but I have researched this story thoroughly for many years, and I believe it has merit. Shall I finish the story?"

"Go ahead," Shannon urged, with another warm smile.

"Well, as the legend goes, in 1825 the czar took his very sick wife on a fourteen-hundred-mile journey south from Saint Petersburg to the remote port city of Taganrog on the Sea of Azov. To most, this seems odd from the beginning. Why would he take a sick wife on such an arduous journey to a dirty, forsaken, distant place like Taganrog? The place was a putrid-smelling town with few if any medical facilities, poorly suited for any sort of recuperation. Such an odd choice, when you consider all the warm-weather cities he had to choose from—cities of flowering villas and good doctors—yet he chose a smelly, filthy, backwater town.

"Anyway, when the entourage arrived in Taganrog, the czar became ill. Mind you, he was a man of robust health who suddenly fell sick. No one knows what afflicted him. But here is where the story gets interesting.

"The czar mysteriously died from an illness that no one could diagnose. Some have suggested malaria, some typhoid, some think some other maladies did him in. But in any event, no autopsy was performed until thirty-two hours after his supposed death, and when the autopsy *was* performed, the body was described as having deteriorated so badly that flesh was falling off his neck. Now this was in winter, mind you, and skin would not decompose that fast even in a sweltering jungle."

Tanya grimaced and raised a hand to her mouth. Shannon put a hand on her shoulder.

Stock brought his smoldering cigarette to his lips. "Reports say the face on the czar's corpse was disfigured so much that even his closest confidants found him unrecognizable. The face was described as being black, and the nose was nothing more than a rotted-away nub, almost no nose at all. Two French doctors who had seen the czar only a few days prior wrote in their memoirs that there was no way a corpse could decay so much in such a short period of time. It was impossible that the dead man they saw could have been dead any less than two weeks—not two days. All this to say that a body in the cold of winter does not do that for several weeks or more. Nor would they keep the body in a heated room for long; it would stink up things pretty fast." Stock paused and rolled the cigarette between his yellow-tinted fingers. "It is also odd to me that no official record exists of Alexander's death, a virtual impossibility with an imperial leader—unless the death was fabricated by those close to the czar. It seems possible that a soldier who died weeks prior was substituted for the supposedly dead czar."

"How could such a thing be pulled off in the first place?" Shannon asked.

"The only way the czar could possibly execute such a ruse was if he had the aid of his trusted Chief of Staff, General Diebich. It was said that he was the one who brought the recently deceased soldier from the Semeonovsky regiment and put him in the czar's coffin. The soldier had died at a military hospital in the Taganrog region two weeks prior. It is most interesting that there are no records of the soldier's burial—an odd thing for a military establishment that was known for keeping impeccable records."

Stock's thin lips curled into a grin. "But if he were a substitute corpse, he would not have had his own burial, would he? The soldier that had died was reported to be the same size as the czar, and had died of a disease that made his face black and deformed. No one would be able to recognize him.

"Some say the substitute corpse was put in a wooden bathing tub, covered with a blanket and taken to the czar. The body was placed in the coffin and the czar climbed into the wooden tub that was again covered with a blanket. The czar was taken to a waiting yacht in the harbor, and that night escaped to Palestine. From there, the trail goes cold until eleven years later, when a strange monk riding a white horse rode into the Siberian outpost of Krasnoufimsk. He had no papers, nothing to show who he was. The monk spoke

French, English, Latin and Slavic. Those that had seen or served the czar recognized his speech and his features, and many soon believed the man was none other than Czar Alexander I.

"But because he didn't carry the required papers, he was arrested and sentenced to twenty lashes for vagrancy. Alexander's younger brother, Grand Duke Michael, heard of the punishment and sent a military attaché to stop it. He ordered the judge to be lashed if the sentence was carried out. Of course, the judge relented. Over the years, others in the Romanov family made the long journey to visit the monk Feodor Kuzmich, and all said they had no doubt he was the missing czar. Some even bowed, tearfully kissed his hand and said, 'Blessed Emperor.'"

"There must be death records of some kind," Shannon said.

"You'd think so, but in the case of Czar Alexander, the records are a minefield of contradictions. You see, when a sovereign dies, there is a very strict protocol of reporting that needs to be done. Meticulous records for time of death, those in attendance and thorough medical reports need to be completed. Then the records are sealed, but in this instance the documents are incomplete, contradictory, unsealed and, at best, contrived. Memoirs of those in attendance at the supposed death are so conflicted as to be useless. The czar's own doctor, Dr. Tarasov, was absent during the autopsy, and the czar's wife didn't bother to travel back to Saint Petersburg with the casket."

"So," Shannon said, "there was no one who bothered to look closely at the body in the coffin. I would think that many would stop to pay respects."

"It's true that in those days the open coffin would be placed on display, but in this case the casket was kept closed. On the rare occasion when it was opened for dignitaries, a black cloth covered the deceased's face. Oh, and another thing: this czar was an over-the-top religious zealot. While he was alive, priests surrounded him at all times; yet during the last four days of his illness, not one clergyman was called to his bedside. It is hard to believe that a deeply religious man would not have prayers read over him if he knew he was dying."

Shannon tried to take in every detail of the story. "So they had a funeral with a substitute body?"

Stock grinned. "Yes, March 13, 1826. The funeral was a grand affair, complete with slow, muffled drumbeats and equestrian Cossacks who escorted the casket. It must have been quite impressive as the Cossacks rode in the cortège, sitting ramrod-straight on magnificent high-stepping horses. Cartridge belts crossed their red tunics, and at their sides hung long, glinting sabers. Their heads were covered with tall black Persian-lamb caps studded with the golden insignia of the two-headed imperial eagle.

"After the Cossacks came, the Prussian royal guards of cuirassiers marched by and then the Russian imperial guard of dragoons and hussars. All the while, weeping citizens lined the cobblestoned streets as the cortège passed by. They had no way of knowing it was all a sham."

Shannon's mind raced with questions. "If the czar was not in that casket, and instead very much alive, then how could he possibly escape his own country? Wouldn't everyone recognize him?"

Stock raised a finger. "Ah, remember the yacht I mentioned earlier. That's how he escaped undetected. You need to remember that they were in a small port city on the Black Sea, but ships from all over the world anchored there. That late in the season, all the ships would be gone, all but one: a yacht under a British flag named the *Britannia Seas*."

"How could you possibly know that?" Shannon asked.

"Lloyd's of London insured just about every British ship in the nineteenth century, Ms. Reed, and they kept impeccable records. They were very helpful when I researched this part of the legend. They confirmed the craft had indeed visited Taganrog and that it sailed under a British flag. The sailing ship was either owned or leased by the British ambassador to Russia, the first earl of Cathcart."

"I find it very coincidental that the yacht was anchored in the Taganrog harbor the very day the czar died and that it sailed off for Palestine later that very same night. Oh, and this earl of Cathcart and the czar were close friends. Seems a bit much . . . Wait a second. What did you say the name of the ship was?"

"*Britannia Seas*. Why?"

Something she had seen in the Bible came to mind. On the

same page as the Cyrillic name Feodor Kuzmich was another note, this one in English: *Captain W.P.,* Britannia Seas, *1825.* As fascinating as Stock's story was, she had been inclined to dismiss it as fable. Now she wasn't so sure.

"Shannon?" Murk said. "Are you all right?"

Shannon set the Bible on Stock's desk and pointed at the faded signature.

Stock pulled the Bible closer and studied the signature. Shannon could see him read it and read it again. His face paled. He blinked several times.

"It is there, all right; it is certainly right there."

Murk stood and bent over the desk. "Is that the signature of the ship's captain, right below the name of Feodor Kuzmich?"

"It seems to be." Stock smiled like a child on Christmas.

"What do you make of it?" Murk asked. He had sat in silence while Stock told the long story. Shannon assumed he had heard the details before, but now they were down to the business they had come for.

Stock studied the inscription for a moment.

"Well?" Murk said.

"Sit down, David. I need a minute." Stock pulled a magnifying glass from his desk and held it over the page. "The ink is browned, as one would expect from an old signature." He rubbed his chin. "It is from a right-handed man who has a flamboyant and confident writing style—certainly not the kind of signature I'd expect from a *staret.* They were usually uneducated, itinerant and monks."

He shifted his position so that more light from the window behind him fell on the old pages. "This is absolutely amazing. Beyond amazing. Do you know what you have here?"

"An old Bible," Shannon said.

"It's much more than that. There are thousands of old Bibles, Ms. Reed. This one is unique." Stock took in a deep breath. "I think I know how this Bible may fit in all this."

"I'd love to hear it," Shannon said. She shifted in her seat.

"In the archives at Lloyd's of London is a ship's logbook that is inscribed by a captain named Wilber Purdue. He could be the Captain W.P. in this Bible. It is interesting that the ship's log was missing ten pages of entries, starting on December 1, 1825. Captain Purdue retired with an unexplained fortune shortly after a voyage to Palestine. He retired early and beyond the means of a small yacht captain."

Stock returned his attention to the Bible as if speaking to the pages instead of the people in the room. "A private collector in England claims he has the missing pages. He's not willing to sell them for any sum of money."

Murk said, "I have heard that line before."

Stock ignored him. "The Purdue family found the log pages hidden in the lining of the captain's steamer trunk. Presumably he had torn the pages from the log as soon as they arrived in Palestine."

"Is there any way we can see those missing log entries?" Shannon asked.

He shook his head. "The family agreed to remain silent as to the content of those entries. At the time of the sale it was a condition of purchase that no one would ever know anything about them."

"I think I can get those logbooks," Murk said smugly, as he laced his fingers behind his head and grinned.

"That will be most difficult." Stock sniffed.

Murk stood. "Stock, you know that if it's difficult I can do it, and if it is impossible, then it will take me just a little bit longer."

Shannon rolled her eyes. "Are you thinking of stealing them?"

"'Creatively procure' is the best description."

Stock's eyes glazed over as he stared forward and mumbled, "I have been impressed with Murk on other occasions."

"Thank you, Stock."

"If you can get the logbook pages, then just maybe we can unlock a mystery for the ages. I have not had much of any life and maybe this is something that will be part of history."

"Do you know where Old Ebbitt Grill is?" Murk asked.

"Of course. It's a famous haunt for congressmen and lobbyists. It's on Fifteenth Street, not far from the White House."

"Good. Meet us there tomorrow and be prepared to be impressed again." He then looked at Shannon and Tanya. "How about a tour of D.C.? You know, the Lincoln Memorial, the Washington Monument and all that."

Tanya stood, but did not turn to leave. Instead, she looked straight at Stock. "Can you tell me anything about a gold snuff box and how it relates to Czar Alexander I?"

"I suppose I can do a little research on that. Why is the gold box important in all this, anyway?"

Tanya said nothing as she turned and left.

chapter 13

THE CARPENTER

As HE DID every day, the guard flung the prison ward door open, chanting his daily mantra, "Get out of bed, you lazy dogs!"

As he did every day, Yuri donned his heavy padded pants, gummed with tree sap and years of grime. He slipped on a jacket still frosted from the day before and then pulled on his felt-lined boots, with the yellow painted star of David on them.

But this day was different: The guard walked to him and said, "It is your lucky day, prisoner. The camp carpenter died last night from a knife fight with the Ottoman. He insulted the Turk and paid dearly for it. You will come with me to the commandant's home and make shelves and a door for his pantry."

Yuri stood and stared at the man as if he were speaking a foreign language.

"You are a carpenter, aren't you? Your records show you were one before your offense."

Yuri cinched his jacket. "I once was a good carpenter, but that was long ago. Now all I know how to do is cut down trees with an ax."

"Well, you better remember how to be a good carpenter again, or we will both be in trouble."

"Will I work in a warm place?"

"The commandant's home is heated. If you do a good job it will reflect favorably on me, and as a reward you will be given an extra ration of soup."

Yuri nodded. "I will do as you ask. What happened to the Ottoman? He is a friend of mine."

"He was put in the 'intestine' last night and was found as frozen as a carp this morning."

The intestine—as the prisoners called it—was made from a cement drainage pipe a meter in diameter. Men who were to be punished were put there, but it wasn't punishment—it was execution.

After his meager breakfast, Yuri and the guard walked side by side past the guard's mess, past the big coils of wire, past the machine gunners who followed their every move, past the barking guard dogs.

The commandant's house faced south to shield it from the harsh winds. The snow-covered roof trailed a gray wisp of smoke that rose toward a still starry sky. When the guard knocked on the cabin door, a yellow candle floated past the windows that were covered with dried, stretched fish skins.

The door creaked open and a woman stood before them. She bowed but did not speak, then motioned for them to enter.

Yuri stomped the snow from his boots and entered behind the guard, who slipped off his sheepskin gloves and gray rabbit-fur hat. The home was built from stout logs, with smooth, varnished pine planks on the interior wall. It smelled good; smelled of a woman's presence—a smell that flooded Yuri's mind with memories of his home in Leningrad and his wife. A cast-iron stove sat in the corner, its round belly rumbling with flame. On top was a blue pot wobbling nervously as steam poured from its spout.

Yuri was instantly warm—too warm with his padded pants, heavy jacket and woolen gloves. He began to sweat. He had not perspired in months and had almost forgotten what it felt like. He stood, uncertain what to do, awkward in the presence of a woman. He could not take his eyes off her: her form; her pink, clean skin; her light blue eyes.

The woman lifted her hand and pointed at Yuri's thick coat, which seemed to steam as warm air melted a thin membrane of frost.

He removed his coat and handed it to her. She took it from him and carefully hung it on a wooden peg by the front door. Her movements seemed effortless and as graceful as a cat's.

Yuri had not seen a woman in seven years. She was so small that even the emaciated men in the prison seemed larger. She had a lean, handsome face, with high cheek bones, a delicate nose and smooth complexion. She wore a thick-clothed skirt that reached the wood-planked floor. A wool cardigan covered a white embroidered blouse, and from her neck hung an apron. Her hair was coiled in Russian fashion about her head. Yuri marveled at the washed sheen of her locks. He was finding it hard to breathe.

The woman never let on that she had noticed his gaze. He fought hard not to be obvious, but was losing the battle. Yuri felt a flood of shame at his foul smell, disheveled appearance and matted beard. He removed his hat suddenly, realizing it was the proper thing to do. His manners in the presence of a woman were almost forgotten. He knew that he looked more like a creature that emerged from the wilds of the thick forest around them than a human being. The woman smiled, and for a brief moment Yuri felt like a welcome guest instead of an animal just released from his cage.

The guard looked at Yuri. "She's deaf as a rock and seems every bit as stupid; can't speak a word. So it might be difficult to under-stand what she wants." The guard turned his attention to the woman. "She's a fine-looking woman, I will give her that. It is too bad she is the commandant's sister and also that she is considered mentally deficient."

Yuri furrowed his brows.

"Don't worry, she can't hear us."

Yuri stared deep into the woman's warm eyes, slowly lifted his hands and made a series of gestures.

"What are you doing?" the guard asked.

"My wife was a deaf mute. I learned sign language long ago when we were courting." Yuri thought of Tanya at that moment.

A wide smile crossed the woman's face as Yuri communicated with signs.

"What are you saying?" The guard seemed nervous.

"I told her my name."

The woman signed back.

"She says her name is Anna."

Tears trickled down her face. She wiped at them with the back of her hand and moved to a straight-backed chair by the iron stove.

"Why is she upset? Did you say something to hurt her? If you did—"

"No, I only told her my name." He signed to her again, then translated her response. "She says she has not communicated in sign language to anyone in over five years. Seeing someone use sign language has made her happy."

There was more that Yuri didn't translate. Anna felt like a prisoner in her brother's house. At times she felt the prisoners were better off than she. At least the inmates had others to talk to. She had no one to communicate with.

Yuri understood. Early in his relationship with his wife she had shared how lonely a deaf person could be, always surrounded by empty silence.

Anna's heart was a churning cauldron of emotion. When she opened the door, she had expected to see a guard and a prisoner. Her brother had made it clear that someone would be coming to the house to work. What she did not expect was to have her first conversation in five years. The sight of someone using sign language made her heart dance, but also made her stomach sour. The man was a prisoner. He was allowed in the house only because her brother needed work done, and once the job was done, she might never have a chance to talk to him again.

She was a prisoner as well. She might live in a warm home, eat decent food and sleep in a bed with warm blankets, but she had no freedoms. Her days were occupied with cooking and cleaning for her commandant brother, who demanded his home be impeccably clean and orderly. If there was a single boot mark on the wood-planked floor, then the whole floor had to be mopped. Tea glasses needed to be wiped of dust twice a day, and the commandant's uniforms were washed and ironed daily. At night, after she fed her brother, she would shine his boots while he sipped vodka and inspected her progress. Books were not allowed in the house. Books were considered a distraction that would keep Anna from her domestic responsibilities. Prisoners in the camp worked in the coal mine or in the forest harvesting trees. Anna was also a prisoner, who worked in the house she was confined to.

With Yuri she could communicate her thoughts, her lost feelings. She had known him only moments, but they shared the knowledge of sign language and that made him welcome in her world. How could a prisoner know how to communicate in sign language? Her brother had never taken the time to learn a single word; he simply pointed and gestured.

It was clear he felt ashamed to have a physically defective sister. Even as children, he treated her as an embarrassment. She knew if it had been up to him, he would have put her in an institution for the mentally ill long ago. Their sickly mother made him swear on a Bible that he would care for her. He was callous and cold, but feared an unseen God. He was not a worshipper, but her mother told her that her brother knew the same God who took the girl's hearing could do worse to him.

The door swung open, and the commandant entered and stopped short. He sniffed the foul air that was foreign to his home. Yuri lowered his eyes, knowing better than to make eye contact. The commandant snarled as he looked at the pathetic prisoner, his unwashed skin pocked with grime, his clothes soiled and reeking with body oils that had fermented into a pungent stench. He turned to the guard. "He stinks. Bring me a carpenter that does not smell so horrid."

The guard stammered, "Sir, the men cannot bathe until spring. All the water in the washtubs is frozen. I am afraid any man I bring will smell the same, maybe worse. He is a lumber cutter; the coal workers smell far worse. Besides, this man was a carpenter before coming here. He has the most experience."

The commandant sat in a gaudy, red-upholstered chair. He waved his sister to remove his leather boots. She quickly obeyed, and pulled off the scuffed boots. She placed them neatly beside the stove. A second later, one of the boots toppled against the side of the red-hot cast iron. The smell of singed leather wafted from the boot.

Anna grabbed the fallen boot in her trembling hand and hurriedly rubbed the leather, trying to remove the burn mark. The commandant stood, stepped to the woman and snatched the boot from her hand. His eyes widened when he saw the blemish. He flung the boot against her head. The heel struck the left side of her face, knocking her to the floor. Blood oozed from a split in her eyebrow. She didn't scream, but her face made clear the pain she felt.

Yuri made a move to help her, but the guard grabbed his collar. "You stay where you are."

For an instant, Yuri felt the urge to knock the man's hand away, but it died as quickly as it came. The woman pushed herself to her knees, then took the hem of her dress and wiped her blood from the floor.

The commandant looked at the guard and shouted, "See to it that this disgustingly filthy beast is bathed before you bring him back here to start work." He plucked a speck of dirt from his uniform shirt and flicked it to the floor. "Is that clear?"

"Yes, Commandant. Very clear."

"I do not want his putrid smell contaminating the air in my home ever again."

"I will see to it, Comrade Commandant. I will do as you instruct." He grabbed Yuri's coat off the wood peg and shoved the soiled jacket into the prisoner's arms.

"He can start tomorrow."

"Yes, Commandant."

As Yuri slipped into the heavy coat, he caught a glimpse of Anna's face. She looked more disappointed than hurt. Yuri felt himself pulled to the door. The guard flung it open and shoved Yuri back into the dark cold of morning.

Yuri was led back into the compound and across the parade ground to the kitchen building. The guard, with Yuri in tow, shouted to the prison cooks to heat pans of water; that the commandant wanted the prisoner cleaned of his stench and made presentable.

The cooks complained that they would not use their cooking pots for bathing the tick-infested clothes of a prisoner.

The guard's words were menacing. "You cooks get your fill of bread and work in warmth every day. If you want to keep those benefits, then I suggest you do as the commandant orders. I'm sure the commandant will not hesitate to find coal miners who will trade places with you."

The cooks grabbed large pans and refueled the stove fires from a pile of coal in the corner of the room. Another cook took a pot outside to scoop up snow to bring it back inside for melting.

In an hour, the cooks were pouring hot tubs of water on Yuri's cold, shaking, naked body. Yuri rubbed a black bar of soap on his wet skin, sloughing off months of dirt and grime. The hot water soon warmed him. He had forgotten the feel of skin free of filth-clogged pores.

He was even given a straight razor to shave his coarse beard, but the guard wanted it back as soon as he made the last slow swipe.

One of the cooks saw the gunshot scar on Yuri's exposed leg and asked how Yuri got the wound.

"I was shot by the KGB."

One of the cooks chortled. "Shot by the KGB. You must not be such a bad fellow, after all."

chapter 14

THE CRAFTSMEN

YURI KNOCKED ON the door, and a second later it swung open. Anna stood at the threshold, smoothing her blue cotton dress and adjusting her knitted shawl. She would have looked lovely if her left eye hadn't been swollen shut and rimmed with blue and purple.

She signed "Hello" before Yuri and the guard entered. As soon as she closed the door behind him, she handed him an ornate egg, decorated in the traditional Ukrainian way. The guard snatched it from him and put it in the pocket of his gray coat.

Anna signed, "It is Easter Sunday tomorrow and a priest will come here so we can celebrate communion. I found a communiqué on my brother's desk that said the priest comes all the way from Leningrad." She wrinkled her nose, then let her fingers make the words, "I suppose only the priest and God know why he would come to this horrible place."

Yuri had not taken the Eucharist in years, so long it no longer mattered to him, but if Anna would be there, he would go.

Yuri carried his toolbox and walked to the food pantry. The toolbox contained a hammer, plane, handsaw, cloth measuring tape, wood rasp, pencil, sandpaper and a brown paper sack of nails. Every nail would have to be accounted for by the guard. He had checked out the tools and nails from the tool shed attendant. The guard stood behind Yuri, holding several rough-cut flat boards, which he propped next to a wall.

The guard shoved Yuri in the back with the butt of his AK-47. "You are a prisoner and need not be concerned with socializing, especially with the commandant's sister."

Anna turned and moved to the kitchen. Her steps were quick; her expression told Yuri she had lip-read enough of the guard's words to be embarrassed.

As Yuri inspected the pantry, the guard warned, "Do a good job with the shelves, prisoner, or the commandant will be angry with you, which means he will be angry with me. It will add to your misery."

Yuri smirked. "You can offer little misery that I have not already received." Then he took the measuring tape and pencil and started planning out the job.

He was more than a typical carpenter: he could inlay wood floors, making intricate patterns with expensive and exotic woods. He was a true craftsman. He had helped install the parquet walnut and oak entry floor of the famed Hermitage Museum. He had worked mostly in government buildings and was known for his skilled hands and clever mind. That was a lifetime ago.

Yuri looked into a side room. A small wooden desk supported a pink-plastic-shelled phone and a teletype machine that ticked out a narrow slip of paper that rolled into a curled pile below.

Above the desk was a map that had no names, only numbers with the words *prison camp* painted in red before them. He saw Work Camp C-23 in the north country, about four hundred kilometers or so northwest of Leningrad. In a nearby open closet hung cold weather gear, heavy rubber felt boots, a long parka with fur collar and padded insulated pants. The clothes were designed for the brutal cold of the place. It was cruel that the commandant had such well-made clothes hanging unused in his closet while just a short distance away, men under his charge were clothed in decaying rags and dying of hypothermia.

"Get to work, prisoner," the guard snapped. "You are not here to look but to make shelves."

Yuri returned his attention to the pantry. It was a simple job that could be finished in an hour or two, but he wanted to spend as much time in the warmth of the small house as he could. He also enjoyed the kind smile of the woman. The cut of each board would be made slow and sure with lingering stokes of the sawblade's dull metal teeth.

The smell of baked bread filled the house. Yuri inhaled deeply, even though the tantalizing aroma made his stomach hurt with hunger. Except for his aching belly, he felt as if he were in Heaven. For a brief moment, he forgot he was a captured animal and that soon he would be taken back to his filthy, lice-infested prison ward, to sleep in misery on bunk number fourteen.

Yuri pushed the small hand plane over the rough-cut boards, shaving them down, curling slices of wood peeling from the top of the plane. Soon the rough boards were smooth. He then cut the boards to length with the handsaw and sanded them.

After two hours, Anna brought out a silver tray with two clear glass cups and a porcelain tea pot. In order to avoid cracking the cups, she put a silver spoon in each to absorb the heat from the boiling tea as it was poured. She sweetened the brew with two lumps of sugar and handed a glass to Yuri.

"Prisoners are forbidden such pleasures," the guard snapped.

"She can't hear you."

Anna smiled and nodded to the commandant's large, over-stuffed chair. The guard returned a slack smile and sat. She gave him a hot cup of tea and a crisp, ironed napkin holding a slice of bread with wild raspberry jam smeared on its surface.

The guard took it and immediately bit into the bread.

Anna handed Yuri a jam-covered slice of bread and a cup of tea.

The guard growled through his stuffed mouth, "No food for you, prisoner."

Yuri ignored him and drank the tea. It was hot and flavorful. The warmth spread in his gut, the sugar delighted his tongue. Despite another warning, he took the bread and jam and devoured it in seconds.

"You better not get me in trouble, prisoner." The guard drained his tea cup and asked for more by raising his cup.

Anna dipped the spout of the pot into his cup, and then set it next to the man. She turned to Yuri and signed. "She says you should finish the rest of the tea."

The guard grunted, then said, "*Spasibo.*"

Yuri signed, "Thank you."

Anna hurriedly stepped behind the guard and signed to Yuri,

"Will you be at Easter Mass tomorrow? I pray you will be there." Since the guard watched his every move, Yuri said nothing but indicated his answer with a slow nod.

Anna signed back. "I have put some canned meat in your jacket. Be careful that the guard doesn't see."

When Anna looked at her feet, Yuri knew she could feel the vibrations in the floor even though she couldn't hear the commandant on the porch stamping snow and mud from his boots. The guard shot from the chair so fast he almost dropped his cup.

The front door swung open and the commandant plunged in, followed by a swirl of blowing snow. The guard promptly stood erect and put the cup of tea behind him. Yuri saw Anna discreetly take the cup from the guard without her brother noticing. The guard seemed relieved.

The commandant moved to the pantry and inspected Yuri's work carefully. The guard walked to a spot just behind the camp leader and rose on his toes to see over the tall commandant's shoulders.

"Excellent. This is most excellent work." The commandant looked at the prisoner. "Are you finished?" He sounded almost cordial.

"I just tapped in the last nail."

The commandant nodded. "You have done a competent job— no, an exceptional job." He scanned the shelves once more. "I need a cabinet for my guns. I want it made of white birch and sanded to a fine finish. I want the varnish to be like window glass. You will make this for me."

Yuri lowered his head in submission.

"Good." The commandant sniffed. "Very good."

The camp leader then looked behind him at the surprised guard, who came to attention, tucking in his double chin. "You will go into the forest with him and find the wood he needs. Start tomorrow. I am taking him off lumber detail. A skilled man like him should be used more efficiently."

"Yes, sir. I agree."

"I assumed you would."

Anna stepped forward and held up a wooden bowl filled with

colored Easter eggs. She shifted her eyes to the prisoner. The commandant read her intent. "Yes, such a good job deserves a reward, even if he is an enemy of the state." He faced Yuri. "Take an egg for your reward, prisoner; you will need food for the task tomorrow."

The woman held the bowl with one hand, touched a crucifix around her neck with the other, and stared at her brother.

"What are you trying to say?"

She motioned to Yuri.

"Commandant, my wife was deaf," Yuri said. "I can read her hand signs if you wish."

"If you can understand this gibberish, then tell me what she wants."

"Yes, sir. She wants to know if I can be rewarded by going to mass tomorrow, since tomorrow is Easter."

The commandant shrugged. "Well, I suppose you may go to communion in the morning, but right after you will go into the forest and find a fine birch tree for my gun cabinet. Is that understood? I have little to look forward to in this place, and I want my gun cabinet as soon as I can."

"It is understood, sir."

The guard saluted and snapped his boot heels. "As you wish," he stammered.

The commandant walked to his chair. "Take your egg and leave me." He sat and pointed to his boots. Anna set the bowl of eggs down and moved quickly to the chair to help remove her brother's boots.

Yuri turned, took his jacket from the peg by the door, and slipped on his coat. He felt the weight of the cans Anna had put in his pocket. He did not look at them and was careful to ease his coat on so the cans made no noise. The last thing he needed was for the commandant to think he was stealing food.

chapter 15

OLD EBBITT GRILL

SNARLED TRAFFIC MEANT Stock arrived at the Old Ebbitt Grill thirty minutes late. Murk, Shannon and Tanya were already seated and had chatted about their visit to the Lincoln Memorial and the Washington Monument. Shannon had enjoyed herself and Tanya seemed captivated by the sights. The afternoon had been perfect, with only one incident that gave her pause: a sedan had driven by and Shannon saw a camera with telephoto lens appear out the driver's side window. For a moment, she thought the camera was pointed at them. She dismissed the idea. This was Washington, D.C.—tourists with cameras were everywhere.

A crisp linen cloth and silverware adorned the table. Mahogany siding and brass fixtures lent a warmth and charm to the restaurant that only age can create. Stock walked by the old ornate mahogany bar where many a congressman had struck informal deals over a cocktail, or two, or three. He plopped a file folder on the white table.

"What's this?" Murk asked.

"It's a file full of information about Czar Alexander I." Stock took a seat at the table. "I've been poring over every small detail of his life and came up with some very interesting things." His eyes looked Shannon up and down. She felt a shiver of disgust. His smile showed yellow teeth.

Shannon forced herself to return the smile.

A waiter came by and handed out menus. A young woman followed, filling glasses with water from a metal pitcher.

"We need a little while before we order," Murk said. The waiter nodded and left to attend another table.

Stock turned to Tanya. "All right, young lady, you wanted to know about the gold snuff box, right?"

Tanya sat up. "Yes."

"Before I begin, I want to know how a young girl like you knows about the snuff box in the first place. Before I get any deeper, I need to know why you are asking me all this. What's going on?"

Tanya turned to Shannon. Shannon nodded. "It's okay, Tanya. If we are going to get to the bottom of all this, he has to know." She leaned over and whispered in her ear, "There's no need to talk about the . . . other matters."

"Okay," Tanya said.

"What's that all about?" Murk asked.

"Nothing. Just consulting with my client." Shannon winked at Tanya.

Tanya looked at Stock. "When I was a child, my father took me to a monastery in Leningrad. That was about seven years ago. A monk led us down some steps to a tomb. It was the stone crypt of Feodor Kuzmich. Some monks took off the lid and the priest removed a gold box with the Romanov seal on its face—you know, the double-headed eagle. The monk said a message, along with the bread from Heaven, a glass vial of the manna from God, was in the gold snuff box. Before we could open it, a KGB man came and we ran. My father was shot in the leg and was taken to an abbey, while I fled the country with the help of the woman I now live with."

Stock was clearly taken aback. "Where is the gold box now?"

"My father took it. I haven't seen him since."

"You haven't seen him? Where is he?"

"Some family members wrote and told us he was taken to a prison somewhere in the far north country."

Stock rubbed his chin. "That's a very remote and rough area."

"Please tell me what you found out about the box. I need to know."

"Okay," Stock said, as he opened his file folder and leafed through his notes. "Here it is. According to statements and memoirs of those who were there that night in 1801, it happened like this: Several conspirators, mostly men from the highest ranks in the palace, wanted Czar Paul dead. Remember, he was the father of Alexander. The murderers thought Czar Paul was mentally unbalanced and growing worse. They feared he would soon ruin the whole country."

"Why would they think that?" Shannon asked.

"Paul had made many erratic decisions. He sided with the French and broke an alliance with the British, which meant a complete stop of trade through the Baltic. Nobles lived in fear that the crazy czar would invent charges against them and they would be exiled or killed. A plot was hastily hatched to get the czar to abdicate the throne and let his son Alexander be crowned the new leader. Paul, however, disliked his son, and grew paranoid about him. He believed his own son was trying to steal the throne.

"At about eleven that night, the conspirators left their homes to meet at the quarters of General Talyzin, commanding officer of the Semeonovsky Regiment. After downing many snifters of cognac to bolster their courage and recounting why the czar had to go, they decided to act.

"The drunken mob marched into the night and down the deserted city streets. As the conspirators entered the garden of the Mikhailovsky Castle, a thousand crows were startled from their perches in the old linden trees and took to flight, screeching in a cacophony of wild sounds. The conspirators froze like stone statues in the dark, hoping the bird noises had not awakened the emperor. No light appeared in the czar's window above, so the men slowly advanced to the castle entrance as the birds swirled off into the night.

"The lead conspirator was a crafty man named Count Peter Pahlen, who was the czar's closest and most trusted aide. He had convinced young Alexander that his father was a threat to him. He warned that he, his mother and his brother Konstantin were about to be placed under house arrest for being a part of a plot to overthrow the government. It was just another manipulation, but it let Count Pahlen convince Alexander that he needed to sign an agreement that he would take control of the throne, after his father was forced to abdicate and then taken away to his peaceful retirement. Pahlen knew that Alexander could be easily influenced; that he was, by nature, a lazy young man who was content to live an idle life of privilege and ease.

"To cement the young man's cooperation in the plot, Count Pahlen told Alexander that Catherine, his youngest sister and favorite daughter to the czar, was to marry a German prince by the name of Eugene von Württemberg and that Czar Paul was to bypass Alexander as the true successor to the throne and name his new son-in-law to be emperor of Russia. To avoid such an unspeakable act, Alexander signed the document. Of course, this made Alexander part of the plot to murder his own father. Later in life, his involvement in his father's death would drive him mad."

"He turned on his own father?" Shannon said.

Murk answered. "Remember, Alexander thought he and the rest of his family were in imminent danger from Czar Paul. That's why he agreed to the plot."

"I've already mentioned that." Stock continued. "The conspirators slipped into the castle, aided by guards who were in on the plot. They made their way to the czar's bedchamber. A man named Platon Zubov found the czar's bed empty. He said to the others, 'He has escaped.' As the group of killers entered the room, someone saw bare feet under the fireplace screen. It was the startled czar, dressed in his night clothes.

"A large man with a barrel chest, named Nikolai Zobov, picked up a gold snuff box from a table. He staggered toward the czar and smashed the box into the left side of the emperor's head. The force was so great the emperor's eye was knocked out. The czar fell to the floor. Someone grabbed a sash from the bed and placed it around the unconscious czar's neck and strangled him. They kicked his lifeless body until Czar Paul I was unrecognizable."

Shannon cringed. "I can't believe you're telling us this right before dinner."

"You asked me to tell the story. Shall I go on?"

"Yes," Tanya said. She looked pale but resolute.

"The family was allowed a private viewing of the body. Alexander was there with his mother. Special surgeons and artists were brought in to mold the czar's deformed face back into place. He was whitewashed and then painted with a grotesque pink blush. His hat was cocked to cover his left temple and eye.

"The reports say Alexander fell to his knees in horror at seeing his father's mutilated body. This was not what the conspirators promised. Czar Paul was to be exiled, not killed. He must have felt that he was one of the murderers. In a sense, he was—he had affixed his name to the document. For the rest of his life, he considered himself guilty of patricide."

"Patricide?" Tanya asked.

"Someone who kills his father," Shannon said.

"Oh."

"The assassination was the beginning of the end for our Czar Alexander. After that night—after March 11, 1801—guilt would haunt Alexander day and night. He would spend the rest of his life trying to find peace, which he never did. In desperation, he turned to mysticism, the occult and finally the Bible, to escape the demons that chased him."

Shannon's lips felt dry. She took a drink of water. "Who told Alexander that his father had been murdered? I mean, who delivered the news?"

"Nikolai Zubov."

"The man who hit his father? The man who crushed his temple with the snuff box?"

"The very same. In a bit of irony, Alexander had given the box to his father as a birthday present."

Murk asked Tanya, "Why would the priest at the monastery take the gold snuff box out of the grave and give it to you?"

She shrugged. "I don't know. He said it held a message for me."

Stock leaned back and addressed Murk. "What about the logbooks of Captain Wilber Purdue? In my office you implied you could lay your hands on some copies. I assume you have people working on that."

"Perhaps."

"Can you get those?" Shannon asked.

Murk blinked twice. "Maybe."

"You already have them, don't you?" Tanya said.

"Excuse me," Murk said. "How would you know if I did or didn't have them?"

"You have the logbook, don't you, Mr. Murk?" Tanya's gaze was intense.

Before Shannon could speak, Murk slid a leather valise onto the table. "Yes."

Shannon had seen the case when they arrived at the restaurant, but didn't inquire about it. She had a feeling it wouldn't do any good to ask.

"How did you get copies of them?" Stock stammered.

"What makes you think they're copies?"

Stock's eyes widened. "No, you're not telling me you have the actual logbook. How?"

"I made a few calls. I know a guy who knows a guy. I brought them with me." He turned to Shannon and Tanya. "It's the reason I didn't fly out with you. I know enough of the story to guess that that logbook might have some bearing."

Shannon glanced at Tanya, who gave a slight nod. Murk was telling the truth.

"Why did you lie about having them when you were in my office?" Stock said.

"I'm a cautious man, you know that. I wanted to see if you'd come through with the information we needed."

"Read them," Shannon insisted.

"Let's order our food now. I'll tell you after we have our meal. Besides, I don't want food and drink around when I open this case."

"Read them now." The story had seized Shannon's attention. "We can eat later."

chapter 16

LOGBOOK

SHANNON WATCHED MURK slide out a set of old, brittle pages and said to Stock, "Before I read these pages, do you have any more information about our captain?"

"I want to hear what's in the logbook," Stock replied. "The rest can wait."

Murk refused to budge. "Tell us first about the captain, then I'll read the logbook to you all."

Shannon saw Stock's jaw clench, then relax. "If you insist."

"I insist." Murk grinned.

"The captain was raised in Douglas, on the Irish Sea, an impoverished place where poor deckhands were spawned, not captains who plied the seas under a British flag. Captains usually came from prominent families. They were groomed early on to be gentlemen, tutored in Latin, history and the Bible, attended the finest private schools—schools for the privileged upper crust. The town of Douglas was poverty-ridden, nothing more than an isolated spit of land with wind-scrubbed hills that met the sea. All that was in Douglas was a few herring sheds and one small shipyard. But somehow our captain found his way to Portsmouth and worked from ship's helper at ten years of age to being a master's mate in the Royal Navy. Subsequently he became the captain of the frigate *Gossamer,* owned by the East India Company. He had an honorable career, but lost his ship during a trading run. He ran the ship aground on some unseen rocks. Apparently too much rum precipitated a navigational error. After he lost his ship, he went bankrupt. Facing debtor's prison, he signed on as captain of a yacht leased by the first earl of Cathcart.

"As I said before, the name of the schooner was the *Britannia Seas*. It was a large pleasure yacht made in Holland in 1817. She was a two-master with a sleek, copper-sheathed hull. The yacht had a cockpit, deckhouse and helm. Belowdeck were four cabins, a dining room and a galley.

"It seems the captain returned from that assignment a wealthy man, but he never revealed how he earned such a fortune, or anything about that mysterious journey." He sipped his water. "That's about it."

"Okay," Murk said, "now it's my turn."

The waiter appeared and offered to take their orders.

"Not now," Shannon snapped. A moment later, she apologized. "We'll order a little later."

The waiter glanced at a line of people waiting for a table and frowned. Shannon opened her purse and handed the man a twenty. He took the bill. "I'll be back later. There's no hurry."

Shannon motioned to Murk. "Come on, David, read the blasted log before I explode."

"Here goes." He took a breath and began to read, speaking just loud enough to be heard around the table.

Log Entry, December 1, 1825

Gray morning, sky filled with gulls and the sound of death bells tolling from the small town of Taganrog. The news came from a passing skiff that Czar Alexander died today. It is a strange feeling to think that his demise occurred while our vessel lay under anchor at the very port where the emperor was visiting. I have been given orders to await a passenger this night. No more description of passenger given, only that I should await them and be off to Palestine in the most expeditious manner. It is well that we go; the sea here smells putrid and being anchored here for five interminable days has made the crew restless to depart. In the meantime I keep them busy scrubbing the deck with vinegar, mending sails and storing stocks of provisions for our anticipated journey. No rum allowed the crew this night.

LOG ENTRY, DECEMBER 2, 1825

Last evening, in the dark of night, our passenger was rowed by escorts to the ship's side. A man of about fifty years of age dressed in the garb of an Orthodox monk was the first to be taken aboard. The man's hands were smooth, like a child's; it was as if they never had so much as plucked a potato from the earth or touched a plow. This is not what I would expect from a servant of God who had to endure a harsh monastic life. His mannerisms were odd for a man who had agreed to forfeit worldly pleasures in the pursuit of servitude and piety. He moved not as clergy but as a man of position accustomed to the ease of life. The monk kept his head raised; chin up with a regal cock of the head. His stare was penetrating, yet at the same time dismissing of those around him. Two uniformed men followed the monk aboard and bowed at his every move. It was most strange to see soldiers with gold-embroidered collars and breast coats covered with shiny imperial emblems treat a simple monk with such respect and honor.

The uniformed men offered a fond farewell. Several wept. Their lingering bows and flowing tears were, in my estimation, quite strange.

I had my crew show the monk to his cabin. His only belonging was a small canvas sack. The uniformed men paid the fare for the passenger by handing me a sack of gold coins. They said that if I delivered the monk safely to a home in Jerusalem, I would be paid ten times more.

I have never seen such a fortune and agreed to the terms readily. The military men asked if the ship had a

Bible and I informed them that it did and I retrieved same from my cabin. I was asked to place my hand upon the Bible and swear an oath to God Almighty that I would never reveal any of what I had just seen or where the passenger was being transported, and that if I did they would see to it that my life would be expeditiously ended. I believed them, and fear writing this entry in the ship's journal. Perhaps in doing so, I have blasphemed God and breached my agreement with the soldiers. But a captain has a solemn duty to make accurate log entries on any voyage, so I will continue to make a daily account of our journey to satisfy my responsibility as captain, and then rip these pages from the logbook and leave them with my family to be posthumously read. In this way I will fulfill my duties to both the Lord and the time-honored rules of the sea.

Log Entry, December 3, 1825

Set sail for Palestine last evening under full sails with a lively wind backing to the north. Heading out in the Sea of Azov; met with a frothing chop. Passenger not seen on deck, perhaps due to cold winds and rolling swells that would render a disagreeable stomach to any land dweller. Chamber pots delivered to his cabin. Ship's mate said the man did not respond to his knocking.

Log Entry, December 6, 1825

Today we passed through the Bosporus. Our passengers still remain sequestered, except for meals. They all seem fit for the journey. Seas calming, a favorable wind bloats our sails. We are making better distance than expected.

Log Entry, December 7, 1825

The Aegean Sea greeted us with robust winds. The monk stays in solitude, confining himself to his cabin. I passed by his closed door this morning and heard what sounded like a man mumbling Russian words, which I took to be prayers. Sea calmed with the setting of the sun.

Log Entry, December 8, 1825

Weather turned wet and raw; battened down all hatches as seas became confused and contrary. Waves broke over the gunwales. Crew pumped water from belowdeck all night. Rain and lightning increased with each hour.

Log Entry, December 9, 1825

Troublesome waves concealed the sight of land. Our monk appeared in the main cabin; it was a Sunday and I was reading my Bible to the crew. We held communion with bread and wine. It was very difficult as the hull rode high atop each oncoming swell and then dropped into the trough. The monk wept as he saw us in holy remembrance. To my surprise, he spoke English and asked to participate in communion even though we celebrated in the Anglican manner.

Log Entry, December 11, 1825

Weather quieting, the Mediterranean seas abating before morning light. I ordered sails trimmed at dawn's full glow. The monk asked if he could read my Bible this morning. I was surprised at his proficiency with English. He said there was not a whole and complete printed Bible in all of Russia. I afforded him my Bible to read, which he did all that day and into the night and also the next night.

LOG ENTRY, DECEMBER 13, 1825

Long night, could not sleep thinking of the strange passenger Feodor Kuzmich. His mannerism of placing his hand on one hip and assuming the stately posture of wealthy gentlemen belies the stature one expects of a poor, pious monk. He returned the Bible to me this afternoon and said he enjoyed reading it. I asked him to note his favorite verse, along with an accompanying signature for a remembrance of his passage. He told me that man will pass away like grass withering in the summer sun, but the Word of God will remain forever. I had the first mate retrieve a gull-feathered quill and a small glass well of India ink from my quarters. The monk made the most graceful movement while placing his signature.

Strong wind eddying, black night, no stars, only the dark abyss of infinity above me and the ship's rhythmic thrust and heave under my legs. The creaking blocks, cordage and canvas slapping in the wind was a soothing sound in the dark of night. It was unusually black, an intense gloom past anything I have ever witnessed.

LOG ENTRY, DECEMBER 14, 1825

Feodor Kuzmich came on deck today. He seemed to offer me the affection that one affords a close friend. He complained, however, that his knees were sore, so I had the ship's cook look and he found them both rubbed bloody. I asked the good monk how his knees came to be so injured, and he said he had spent most all of the previous several nights and mornings in

prayer. A salve was administered and the man's afflic-
tion seemed to relent.

LOG ENTRY, DECEMBER 16, 1825

Arrived at port in Palestine, time was late in the evening, weather was fair and sea was quieting beneath a
warm westerly wind. It had been a voyage spared of
calamity by the grace of our Lord. We will stay on ship
and be quarantined for two days before being allowed
to disembark.

LOG ENTRY. DECEMBER 18, 1825

Quarantine complete. Set to shore. Feodor Kuzmich
donned a white-lined skull cap and led us down the
gangplank to a string of camels that awaited our group.
A young man also waited. He was dressed in a frayed
robe and had bare feet blackened by dust and sun.
He spoke in the Arab tongue. I learned his name was
Eliezer. I was not privy to what was being said; however, I was solicited not to understand but to deliver
my passengers to a home in Jerusalem.

Our small caravan commenced and proceeded
across barren, stony hills toward the city of Jerusalem.
We lodged the night at a stone-walled inn. An Arab
girl tending to the service of food looked with fascination at my seafarer's blue coat with its white piping
and tasseled epaulets. The fare was quite good, with a
fire-roasted lamb served cubed and on metal skewers,
accompanied with yellow rice with raisins and a most
aromatic spice.

LOG ENTRY, DECEMBER 20, 1825

We were blessed with the sight of the holy city. It was
the first time my eyes fell upon the holy ground, the

very dust that was trod upon by our Lord and Savior. The Muslim minarets and Christian church cupolas, some gold, some silver, some in tiled mosaic, glittered in the clear, dry air.

The monk ordered his camel to kneel with the light touch of a stick to its rump and a clicking noise created in his mouth.

The fly-swarmed beast folded its legs underneath and lowered to the ground. The Russian monk slid from his saddle and dropped to his worn knees. He made no indication of having pained knees but began to weep prodigiously. The man was moved to a state of emotion I had never seen from either man or woman. He prayed unceasingly for two hours; then, as abruptly as he began, the monk ceased his pious display and gathered himself to his camel once again.

When we entered the Damascus Gate, we found crowds of men screeching in an ever-present cloud of foot-stirred dust. In the city the stench was most profound. Garbage was piled everywhere, and women from second-floor windows tossed the contents of chamber pots onto the passing pedestrian without aim or concern. Blind beggars cried out for alms with outstretched arms. At the Wailing Wall we saw Jews beat their chests repeatedly and bob forward, then back, in a steady dance of prayer. This they did at a temple that was long ago destroyed. Destroyed, the Jews say, but never forgotten.

Eliezer led us all through the throngs of camels, donkeys and men. We arrived at a wood door set in a mud brick building with a weathered Star of David carved on its surface.

Inside, under candlelight, sat a very old man in a robe. He was hunched over a tarnished roll of sheepskin. Surrounded by a cloud of incense, he read from the document with yellow-rimmed eyes and seemed unaware of our presence. We stood in silence, waiting a long while till the old man finished his reading. He then bowed our way and Eliezer took Feodor Kuzmich into a side room. I was told to stay out.

The door was left ajar and I positioned myself close by. What I heard next chilled my soul.

The old man spoke in a strange language that my ears had never heard. Eliezer had a moderate understanding of English, so he translated the old man's words. "I am Rabbi Solomon from the land of Ethiopia. Many years ago, long before your Jesus was born, a small band of Jews migrated to the highlands of Ethiopia. They were escaping the brutal reign of the Israelite King Manasseh. They settled in the area of the Agaw tribe and over time intermarried and took the native tongue of the Agaw.

"My forefathers carried with them a great object of God, the lost golden jar of manna that was stolen by the Philistines when they captured the Ark of the Covenant as it made its long journey to the Holy of Holies on the Temple Mount."

It shames me to confess, but hearing was not enough to satisfy my curiosity. I peeked through the small space between door and jamb and saw the man open a wood box with black iron hinges and carefully remove a gold jar. It had two angels for handles, their faces pressed into the golden urn with their stretched-forward wings appearing as if they were embracing the object. Their wing tips touched. The golden object was exquisite.

Feodor Kuzmich wept as he stared at the object and handed the man a small glass vial. The old man scooped, with the utmost of care, a few granules from the golden jar with the glass vial, and said, "Now that you have some manna from God, I want my Siberian diamonds."

Feodor Kuzmich handed the man a full leather sack the size of a large hen's egg. The man loosened the drawstrings and poured out a glittering spectacle of ice-clear stones. The man said with glee that the diamonds would feed many who were starving in Ethiopia.

It was then that I pushed the door open, pretending to summon the monk, but what I really wanted was to have a closer inspection of the treasures being traded back and forth. In the angriest of tones, I was ordered to leave.

David Murk stopped reading. He looked up. "This is how it ends. Nothing more is written."

Stock stammered, "There . . . there must be more."

Murk slowly shook his head. "I'm sorry, but that's it."

"Amazing," Shannon said. "Amazing and unbelievable."

"I don't follow," Stock admitted. "Can someone explain this manna thing?"

Shannon leaned forward. "Okay, here's the *Reader's Digest* version. The Bible tells us that about thirty-five hundred years ago the Hebrews fled Pharaoh. Later in the journey, artisans, at God's direction, made several key objects. The Ark of the Covenant was one of those creations. The Ark was a box covered in gold, inside and out. It held certain precious objects, including Aaron's rod that budded, the stone tablets of Moses and a golden jar of manna. Manna was what the Hebrews ate in the wilderness."

"What kind of food is 'manna'?" Stock asked.

"The word 'manna' is Hebrew for 'what is it.' They had never seen that kind of food before. The only description of manna comes from the Bible. It was a kind of small wafer that the Bible describes as being like a coriander seed. It was sweet like honey, and it fed the wandering Hebrews for forty years. Anyway, some manna was put in a golden jar by Moses for future generations to see, and placed in the Ark of the Covenant along with the other items I mentioned. Many years later it disappeared, lost to the ages."

"Until now." Stock's gaze shifted to images only he could see. "You mean hundreds of people lived off this manna for forty years?"

"More than hundreds. Some scholars think that as many as two million people made the Exodus."

Stock stroked his chin. "Imagine if the story is true. I mean the part about the manna feeding all those people for so long. Who knows? It just might hold the nutritional secret of the ages. Maybe this secret could feed the starving people of the world." He grinned. "Maybe this kind of discovery would be worth millions or even billions. If the glass vial with the manna still exists and if our sea captain is telling us the truth of what happened back in 1825, then we could all be rich."

"Rich? How?" Shannon leaned back, uncomfortable at what she was hearing. "God provided the manna from Heaven. It's not a human product."

"I don't know," Stock said. "But where there's a will, there's a way. Maybe a chemical analysis could give us a clue, but even if it didn't, the stuff would be the most valuable historical artifact ever. You're the antiquities dealer, Murk. What would a vial of manna be worth?"

"I couldn't begin to guess. I know some artifacts have gone for tens of millions of dollars. This would be worth much more."

"More . . ." Stock whispered.

Murk looked at Shannon. "I guess that's why a few monks and a priest would die to make sure the right person had the manna, but why would it be passed down to a girl? Why did they choose Tanya to have the gold box with the manna inside?"

Murk and Stock gazed at Tanya.

"How should we know?" Shannon said. "We're here to get information, remember. We don't have answers—"

Tanya cut Shannon off. "If my father knows where the gold box is, would you know someone who can get him out of prison?"

Stock wasted no time answering. "Yes. Good thinking. I know people who can get your father free. When we get the gold snuff box, we can all share in the riches it will bring."

"What do you mean 'we'?" Murk said.

Stock's face hardened. "Do you have a way to get the girl's dad out of a Siberian prison?"

Murk didn't speak. Stock kept his eyes on him. "You're a pirate, my friend. Let's say we somehow manage to get Tanya's father out of prison. I will be more than happy to share any profits. What do you say?"

"I learned to say very little at times like this."

Tanya turned to Shannon. "Remember the elephants."

Shannon nodded. "I believe it's time to go now."

"What? Why?" Stock said. "And what is with you and elephants?"

Murk rose. "What about dinner?"

"I've lost my appetite." Shannon stood, took the girl by the hand and headed for the restaurant door.

As they reached the restaurant door, Tanya said, "Mr. Stock lies. He has bad intentions."

chapter 17

THE COMMUNION

IN THE PRISON, there was nothing to look forward to. Each day melded into the next with little to distinguish one day from the previous. There was nothing to break the laborious madness that made for a somnolent mind, with one exception: each year the commandant allowed the Orthodox Church to conduct a formal communion celebration at Easter. The camp leader was less religious than practical, knowing a few hours spent worshipping God might discourage future disobedience by the prisoners.

Anna was seated in the front row of the log room, wearing a fine white linen scarf covering her kind face—a face that looked angelic in the yellow glow of candles on the makeshift altar in front of her.

Seeing her made Yuri remember his wife and daughter and the past Easters they had shared. It was the only time he would go to church. The Communists allowed the ancient Orthodox practice, but frowned on people using religion as a way to seek out truth. Truth to Communists was not to be found on the pages of an archaic book. Truth, they believed, was acquired only by the organic evolution of the mind.

Yuri thought back in his evergreen memory to the time when he and his wife attended the long Easter vigil. The next day, when the Easter fast was over, was his favorite day of all. It was a day when his wife would set a table with traditional dishes of kulich, a thick, tasty bread, and white, sweet paskha cheese. He remembered his family bringing eggs of red, blue, yellow, green and even some in the ornately painted Ukrainian style. As each guest arrived they would say, "Christ is risen," and the guests would reply, "He has risen indeed."

But this cold day in Work Camp C-23 he would worship in a room full of sour-smelling men and one angelic-looking woman. He could not escape the thought of how she looked so much like his long-ago departed wife.

Yuri stood next to a brass stand topped with a cluster of sputtering candles. A priest in a draped habit stood next to the stand and slowly swung an ornate silver incense burner filled with small, smoldering coals. Aromatic smoke hung in the air.

To be allowed to receive communion, prisoners were required to first go to confession. The confessional was nothing more than a small storage room with a sheet hung between the priest and prisoner. None of the prisoners confessed a word to the priest, fearing the guards had placed a microphone in the confessional. Since no one would say confession, the priest told them to confess in silence; God would hear them, and then they would be allowed to take communion.

The candles were made of beeswax and brought by the priest. The wax of the bee was a symbol of purity and sincerity. On a table at the end of the room was a cloth sheet: on the sheet were several polished brass icons and a large painted wooden cross with the image of Christ, bleeding from His hands, crossed feet, side and from the crown of thorns on His head.

Everyone stood during the liturgy. Yuri's eyes grew moist as he recalled memories of his wife and young daughter, Tanya. He thought of the times they had picnicked along the grassy banks of the Neva, eating herrings, pickled mushrooms or cabbage soup made thick with sour cream. He could see his wife's beautiful face, her dainty nose reddened from the summer sun. Her soft blue eyes appeared in his mind, as well as her blond hair curling over narrow shoulders. He could remember every line of her lean form as she lay on a blanket in her thin cotton summer dress. He smiled as he remembered Tanya playing at the river's edge, poking a stick into the reeds trying to prod out green frogs.

Recollections of his wife's illness flashed in his mind. The illness had come quickly, but it took her six tortuous months mired in the socialist medical system to see a doctor. The waiting list was so long it seemed as if it would take forever to see the physician. After the long wait, there was only a ten-minute medical exam, followed by the doctor saying that death was imminent. The stoic doctor refused to go into details, because he had another twenty patients waiting for him. He said he was sorry and that it was an unfortunate illness. He patted her shoulder and left the exam room.

Natalia died three months later, her stomach wracked with pain. The last words Yuri signed to her were, "I wish you could hear the words when I say I love you."

She signed back, "Your lips could never speak love as much as your heart has said in silence."

Her last request was that he take Tanya to the monks at the monastery. The story of the Pravda had been passed down in their family from babushka to babushka: when a girl is born in the family with the special gift in her ears, she was to visit the monastery and be given a message hidden in the grave of an old monk.

After his wife's final request, her body slackened and she died in Yuri's arms.

Yuri fulfilled his promise and took his daughter to the monastery. What had been a simple act of obedience to his wife resulted in his being shot in the leg and his sweet Tanya being spirited across the border and into Finland. He considered her escape a miracle; it was his only consolation.

Soon after, he was arrested at an abbey while recuperating from the gunshot wound. He was charged under Soviet penal code number 58:6—espionage.

Two men in black coats handcuffed him and delivered him to a dark building somewhere in downtown Leningrad, where he was dragged downstairs deep into the bowels of the cement structure. He was then put in a concrete room with one chair. A lone light bulb hung from a wire in the ceiling. He could see black scuff marks on the floor right below his chair . . . the results of flailing heel marks made by tortured prisoners. On the bare walls he saw the brown splatters of dried blood that painted an eerie testimony of what had happened many times in that place.

A woman entered the room. She held a cup of tea resting on a porcelain saucer in her right hand. "Drink," she said, as she plopped two sugar cubes into the hot amber liquid and handed it to Yuri.

Yuri took the saucer and cup, then looked around. "I am not thirsty." He had sounded meeker than he intended. Two men entered and stood in a dark corner of the room.

"Drink," one of the men said.

Yuri sipped the brew. It tasted like tea, but within a few minutes he began to feel hazy. His jaw slackened and his hands slipped to his lap, sending the cup and saucer to the floor where they broke into uncountable shards.

He awoke as the woman pushed a pill into his mouth, tilted his head back and poured a fluid into his throat. Things darkened. When he became cognizant again, a piece of paper lay on his lap and a pen had been pressed into his hand. The paper bore a signature—his signature. It was crude, rough, nothing like the way he signed his name. He tried to lift his head, but a sharp, burning pain threatened to split his head like a meat cleaver. He was force-fed another pill, and the next day he awoke with the same intense throbbing in his head. It took several minutes for him to take in his surroundings. He was on a train, reclining on a tuft of straw. He could hear the steel rails clatter and the shrill blasts of the train's whistle as they passed through a tunnel.

He forced himself into a sitting position and rubbed the back of his neck. As he looked around, he saw thirty or so men sitting or lying on planked bunk beds supported by cross beams. There were no mattresses, only a stack of straw piled in the corner that each man took from to make his own place to lie down.

In the middle of the train car was a small bucket of coal. Next to it rested a cast-iron stove on bricks. The stove's stack rose through the roof. The coal was to last several days, so the fire was sparse, just enough to keep the bucket of water from freezing and the men inside barely alive.

Next to the stove sat a metal-covered barrel partially filled with waste. The waste would normally be kept in the corner, but it too needed to be kept from freezing, or else they would be unable to toss the waste through the small window set along the upper edge of the rail car.

The men took turns looking out this small opening, craning their necks and calling out a description of the passing countryside.

One would cry out, "I see a farmhouse." Later another at the same window would say, "There is a bridge coming." Or "I see a woman in the field." Several men would drag the man away from the tiny window so they could catch a rare glimpse of the female walking in the distance. All knew they might never see such a thing again.

Yuri could see the weak light of the winter sun pressing through gaps in the planked sliding side door. He asked a man lying next to him what time he thought it was. The man said, "Does it matter what time it is?"

After a minute or so, Yuri asked the man, "Where are we going?"

The man's vacant expression looked up, and his red, worried eyes peered out of a black coal-coated face. "Nothing matters, my friend—not time, not place, not death—for you are now an orphan of God."

The train stopped once a day so meals could be brought to the prisoners. When the train slowed the cars would bang into each other, starting with the forwardmost car; then, one by one, they would slam into each other as the train fought its momentum.

Guards climbed on the top of the railcars and held rifles, watching for someone to run off. It was a useless effort. The men's legs were so cramped from standing or sitting on hard, cold boards that it was difficult for them to walk, let alone run away. Once the meal of cabbage soup was delivered in metal tubs, the doors were closed. The guards on top of the car came down and the train lurched into motion again. The men were left to themselves to divvy up the small ration of soup.

A priest from Latvia was given the job of making sure the soup was dispensed in proper proportions, but he died the first night and the men decided to pass the duties to Yuri. He would ladle each man a small portion, not more than a mouthful. Each man would take his turn. It was a fair system. Yuri knew that starving men would always complain for getting too little, but would kill if they were cheated in the slightest.

After four days and nights, the train made its final stop; the doors slid open and the men were ordered out. Yuri's cramped legs almost folded beneath him as he hopped off the train. He struggled for balance. As he was ordered to move on, Yuri's shoe fell off. He turned to get it, and a rifle butt slammed into his temple.

Yuri staggered to a log building, where his clothes were taken and boiled to kill all lice. They shaved his head and powdered him with disinfectant . . . some of which they threw in his face. As he stepped away covered in powder, he felt a tap on his shoulder. Yuri turned and saw a big man, covered in the same chalky film that covered him. Yuri would later learn the man came from Turkey, a man known only as the Ottoman. He held a shoe in his hand and gave it to Yuri. Yuri was pleased, if only for a moment, that someone had shown him an act of kindness . . .

Yuri was pulled from his past thoughts when the priest wearing the traditional Easter vestments of red and orange stepped in front of him, holding a wide golden spoon that had a wine-soaked piece of bread resting on it. Yuri quickly made the sign of the cross, his thumb and two fingers joined at the tips, his third and fourth fingers curled into his palm. He touched his brow, his chest, his right shoulder and left shoulder. It was an orthodox symbol of committing the mind, heart, soul and strength to the service to God.

The priest said, "I am more for tending the souls of men than digging up the dead."

Yuri had heard these words before. His stare locked on the old priest's eyes. He was the same priest who had taken him and his daughter, Tanya, down to the grave of Feodor Kuzmich, the one who handed him the golden snuff box. The priest's spoon was put in Yuri's mouth as the old cleric said, "This is the blood of our Lord and the body of Christ. Take this in remembrance of Him."

Yuri couldn't form words into a sentence.

The priest leaned forward and whispered, "A Yakut man waits for you in the forest. He will take you far from this place. He watches from the forest as you go out each day and cut down trees. Go with this man; he will take you to freedom and the girl with the Pravda."

Yuri looked at the other men waiting in line. "Hurry it along," one man murmured.

Yuri looked back at the priest and remembered his face from a night seven years ago. The same large silver cross hung around his neck.

"Priest, remember that the last time I trusted you, I was shot."

A guard stepped forward and pushed his rifle barrel into the side of the priest. "No conversations allowed."

The priest bowed slowly and moved on.

Yuri stood in silence. *What does this mean?* His mind whirled as he tried to comprehend the priest's statement. The words were easy to understand; the concept of escape, however, eluded him. Seven years of confinement had made freedom an impossible concept to grasp.

He looked at Anna, who had raised her face from her prayers. She made eye contact with Yuri and raised her hands to form the words, "My heart sings a new song this day, it sings at seeing you again."

Like a small boy awkward at his first encounter with romance, he looked away from Anna. Anna's eyes saddened, but he saw them smile again when he looked back and signed, "There will be a place someday where we will be together and free far from here."

That night, while lying in his bunk, he whispered a prayer, pleading with God to give him an answer as to what the old priest meant. Who was the Yakut man the priest said was waiting for him in the forest? Maybe it was all a dream, or, worse, a trap. Or maybe, just maybe the Divine Hand had come down out of a dark winter sky and touched him. Would he be free soon? Impossible. He dismissed the notion as madness, but the priest was right in front of him when he whispered the words. That was no dream.

As he prayed, he visualized himself running free from the prison one instant . . . and the next he would see himself as a gnawed-over blue body tossed on the pile of corpses outside camp, awaiting burial after the late spring thaw.

chapter 18

THE MEETING

The Rezidentura (KBG operations center)
Soviet Embassy, Sixteenth Street, Washington, D.C.

WITH ITS ORNATE and graceful Parisian lines, the exterior of the building exuded grandeur and a turn-of-the-century charm, but inside it was a dark and soulless environment filled with spartan furniture.

The building was originally built by the famous railroad millionaire George Pullman for his family's home, but it was never occupied: the Pullman family sold it at the start of the century to the Russian czar to be his personal palace. It was now being used as the Soviet Union's embassy.

On the fourth floor, behind a cramped corner desk, sat Victor Pochinko. Victor had the stature and personality of a brick. He had never married; never wanted to. The only passion he felt was for his career; his only craving was for advancement.

He felt there was one problem with his career desires: he had the misfortune of being born the son of a miller who had fought as a White Army officer against the Bolsheviks. Anyone who fought in the civil war following the Russian revolution and sided with the White Army would forever be marked as a counterrevolutionary and considered an enemy of the Soviet state. The career of such a man was considered tainted and doomed from the beginning. That is, unless that son of a White Army soldier showed overwhelming skills beneficial to the U.S.S.R.

Victor had shown such skills and loyalty over and over in his career, yet the U.S.S.R. held too fierce a prejudice against such a family lineage to fully embrace Victor Ivanovich Pochinko. His career had, against all odds, sprouted and grown, but not to the level he felt he deserved. His favor was won largely on his talent for being ruthless for the cause of Communism. He had a special fondness for inflicting pain on others, of seeing a prisoner bent as far as possible and then breaking the man's will. Victor savored such things. He especially liked to see men die.

When he worked at the infamous Moscow prison Lubyanka, he was reported to have a perfect record for getting confessions from every prisoner he interrogated, even if the poor soul wasn't guilty. Insiders said he was a man who would kill his mother to advance in the ranks of power.

Now his job was counterintelligence operations in Washington, D.C., but he worked undercover as the cultural attaché for the embassy.

When Victor looked in a mirror, he saw a bulky man with a neck as thick as a birch tree. His wide Slavic face seldom allowed a smile; his sullenness was legendary. When he curled his lips, it was not to grin; it was to grimace. When his lips parted, they revealed an upper band of silver teeth set in a tight row like metal bullets in a bandolier.

He was about to interview a walk-in informant whom he guessed was at that moment riding the elevator past the ambassador's office to the fourth floor. A thick metal door would be opened by a uniformed Soviet soldier, who would then key in a code to a digital lock. The whole floor was lined with metal sheathing to foil eavesdropping equipment used by the FBI.

Victor liked interviewing Americans. He liked to frighten them. They were all so weak, with their love of money and their addiction to a decadent lifestyle, that they could be bought off so easily. He welcomed the distraction this day—anything to spare him from the mountain of mundane paperwork strewn in piles across his desk. Such paperwork was compulsory for all who worked in the Rezidentura. It was a trait of all good Communists to spend much time on reports, a meaningless effort that usually resulted in nothing more than unread paperwork filling space in long rows of file cabinets.

The American was escorted into the cramped, low-ceilinged office crammed under the mansard roof. The nervous man shook hands with Victor. The visitor's hand felt clammy. The man seated himself in front of Victor, inhaled deeply, fidgeted in his chair and repeatedly pushed up his silver wire-rimmed glasses that refused to stay perched on the ridge of his aquiline nose.

The American's voice cracked. "I . . . I am not a traitor; I am just a man who wants what is fair. I have given my life to my job and to America and have never been appreciated—not once. I work like a dog and get treated like one as well. This is only an attempt to obtain fairness; to get what I deserve."

Victor could see he was a timid man, trying feebly to be brave. It probably took all the courage he had just to arrive and sit down.

"What do you have for me?" Victor asked.

The visitor sat up as if he were at a job interview. "I am skilled in many areas, but currently work in accounting for the Department of Defense."

A nobody. Just a low-rung employee in a government office who spends his days entering numbers into ledgers, then checking them over only to add more numbers.

Victor sighed. "What is it you have for me?" He tried not to scowl.

"I have information."

"What kind of information?"

"I have a file that was left at a copy machine near my work area. I put it in my briefcase without anyone seeing and I have those papers with me now."

"The information will not be important to me. Americans are not that irresponsible with information."

"You'd be amazed by how careless people are in my division. I can get as much information as you want. Of course, I want to be paid, and paid well, for what I provide."

Victor couldn't know for certain, but he had done enough of these interviews to guess the man had a bad habit of betting on horses and greyhounds that always seemed to lose. Perhaps he owed a bookie more money than he had, or had taken an advance from a loan shark. Perhaps he spent money designated for the birth of a new baby and his wife was about to find out. The reasons didn't matter; the need was the same. He wanted money. Now he hoped his newly acquired information would be easy cash. He hoped his misfortunes would be rectified in the next few moments.

The accountant sat in silence, waiting for Victor to speak. Like a boy slowly burning an ant with a magnifying glass, Victor made him wait another minute. "What is it again that you have for me to see?"

"I have secret information from the U.S. government and it's for sale—for the right price, of course." The man licked his lips.

Victor snapped his fingers over his desk. "Show me."

The man opened his briefcase and carefully removed a manila envelope and set it on the desk. He removed some photocopies marked DEPARTMENT OF DEFENSE. On the first page were the bold letters KH-11 SATELLITE OPERATIONS MANUAL.

Victor thumbed through the thick stack. When he had finished, he tossed the documents on his desk. "This is of no value to me."

The man straightened, and a frown crossed his face. "What do you mean? This is top-secret stuff."

Victor lifted a hand. "We had an American defense worker walk into our Athens office with the same material. They purchased the documents. Your government is either unconcerned or foolish to let such documents be so easily procured. The material we bought was of little value then; it is worth no more now."

Victor pushed his chair back from the desk. "Agents from your government arrested the man within hours after he passed the information. They find security leaks very fast and they plug those leaks with efficiency. Do you understand what I am saying?"

The man squirmed in his chair, and beads of sweat dotted his brow. Once again he pushed his glasses up his slippery nose. "How did the Americans find out about the man? I mean, he was in Athens, right?"

Victor leaned forward. "Snakes that make a habit of slithering across roads will eventually be crushed under a tire. Major governments have agents everywhere. It is no surprise he was caught. Most men who do what you're attempting get caught. Tell me, don't you fear rotting in jail as a traitor?"

The man swallowed hard and stood. He reached over Victor's desk and gathered the papers. He gulped for air and looked as if he were about to buckle at the knees. Victor loved seeing men tremble at his words. The man started for the door. A high-cheekboned Ukrainian man appeared and took the visitor by the arm. Victor listened to the footsteps of the men as they walked down the corridor. Victor shook his head. Americans were so stupid.

He stood and walked to a small dormered window, gazed to the street four stories below, watching the would-be traitor walking briskly across Sixteenth Street. Victor had to bend slightly to accommodate his six-foot, three-inch frame. Some of the plaster around the window was black from a roof that leaked like a colander. Rusted, poorly painted water pipes clung to the wall.

An FBI agent was talking to the man before he made it to the other side of the street. The agent took the man's briefcase and pointed to a waiting car. "Such a stupid man; such a snake." Washington was rife with spies, double spies and even triple agents. Victor's job was to find information and pass it to his superiors—supervisors who took any or all the credit. Both sides spent so much money securing secret Cold War information that it created a climate ripe for betrayals. Money could make someone change allegiances. It was as true for the Soviets as for the Americans.

Informants who could be bought off made his job much easier. Mercenaries would walk to the Soviet Embassy and simply ring the doorbell, saying they had secrets to sell. They expected a big payday. Their secrets were usually nothing more than valueless government statistics. Often the seller would be some disgruntled government worker angry with a "jerk boss." But usually the traitor was someone who would sell out because he needed quick money to fix a messed-up life.

Once, however, an informant had come to Victor with material of great value. A double agent in the CIA handed over information on a bit of espionage called Red Ears, a clever project in which the Americans tapped into a secret Soviet underwater communications cable running between the Kamchatka Peninsula and the Russian mainland. The Americans were able to intercept all communications between the submarine base at Petropavlovsk and the Pacific Fleet headquarters in Vladivostok. Most of the communications from the Soviet Union's military were coded because those communications traveled by satellite. Since this cable was under the sea, the Soviets had not been concerned with coding their transmissions. The Americans managed to send divers from a submarine and tap into the lines with battery-operated listening devices. It was an intelligence goldmine. The Americans had retrieved unbelievable amounts of information . . . until, that is, Victor learned of it.

The Soviets had their tricks, too. Once notified about the breach in security, the Soviet military began sending false information over the same cable, tying up the Americans for months as they chased fabricated leads. Victor expected that obtaining such crucial information would earn a promotion, but the head of Soviet counterintelligence in North America took the credit, leaving Victor completely ignored. Victor was a man with a healthy ego, and the lack of respect and credit ate at him. He found himself hating the country that betrayed him, just like the disenchanted people who came bearing secrets harmful to the United States. He despised them. Now he fought not to despise himself.

The FBI and the CIA had the Soviet Embassy watched night and day. Victor could look out his office window at any time and see the shadowed shapes of the American agents behind the blue-shaded window across the street. Their black binoculars were pressed tightly to their eyes, probing, searching, observing—eyes of young, ambitious agents, thinking they were conducting a stealthy surveillance.

The building across the street looked to be empty. A sign hanging above the entry read FOR LEASE in large block letters. A phone number had been painted below.

On a whim, Victor called the number several times but got only the sultry voice of a woman saying, "Thank you for calling Capital Central Preferred Leasing Corp. Please leave your name and number at the beep, and we will get back to you as soon as possible." Victor left his number each time but never received a call.

Victor calculated that the man who had just left his office was already caving under the pressure as the FBI peppered him with questions. No doubt the CIA was there lending a hand. The man was probably sniveling and spilling his guts. He could just hear the

man saying how some big, dumb KGB agent had just tried to re-
cruit him at the Soviet Embassy and that he was only participating
in a patriotic scheme to trap the Commies.

In Washington, D.C., government and defense workers weren't
all that suspicious of others, even though they were the information
nerve center for the entire nation. The place pulsed with the blood
of democracy. In Moscow things were different. Victor knew what it
meant to be constantly watched. A Soviet citizen could be impris-
oned or even shot on the false accusations of a nosy neighbor gossip-
ing about some unusual or suspicious activity. It was because of this
that everyone in the Soviet Union learned to say little or nothing to
strangers. When someone walked down the street, they did so with
eyes down.

In America, Victor had noticed the opposite. People here were
friendly, even jovial. They would walk the streets with eyes lifted and
offer a cheery hello as they passed others. It was a bad habit. Many
American spies in Moscow gave themselves away simply by being
friendly. In Moscow, if you wanted to find an American spy all you
needed to do was listen in a restaurant for a hearty laugh and loud
talk. Only Westerners did such things.

Victor believed that Americans were weak because of the life of
ease they led, a life with too much time for leisure. He nurtured an
attitude of supremacy, believing his genes were superior to those of
the Americans. He came from stock forged in adversity and passed
down from the hearty ancestors who defeated Napoleon, and who
had repelled the powerful German armies.

He moved from the window. It was getting late and his thirst
for whisky was growing stronger. He grabbed his coat from behind
his chair. Within half an hour he would be across town and seated in
a Georgetown bar. If things went well, in two hours he would be
drunk.

chapter 19

THE
SABLE HUNTER

THE NEXT DAY, at 10:00 a.m., Yuri walked with the guard toward the front gates. The late morning light was a soupy pastel pink, muted by a frigid haze that blanketed everything with a crusty frost. They walked past the coils of rusted barbed wire, past the machine-gunners peering down from their tower perches. The tower guards always looked eager to shoot, if for no other reason than to break the monotony of standing with frozen gunmetal in their hands. The barrels followed their every step as they walked atop a blanket of snow that crunched under their insulated boots.

Anna stood on the front porch of the commandant's log cabin. She stood in her long dress but wore no coat, not even a scarf to ward off the icy breeze. She smoothed her hair and dress, and then raised her hands and hurriedly signed, "I read the weather report off my brother's desk. A horrible storm comes this way."

Such storms were not new to Yuri or anyone who lived in the region. The guards called the dreaded storms *burany*—a vicious white tempest with icy fangs that would eat warm flesh.

Yuri, with his ax propped on his shoulder, nodded to Anna.

She returned a forced, nervous smile, then signed, "I worry for you, Yuri."

The sentiment warmed him. He returned her a wide smile.

Yuri returned his gaze to the road as he and his guard walked from the prison. The guard chortled. "Find a good tree, prisoner, find a quality birch. The commandant is very particular about his furniture."

"So it seems," Yuri said, as he thought of Anna. No one had cared for him in such a long time.

As they made their way deeper into the forest, a red sable darted in front of them, its fur pulled tight to its body. A dog bounded from the trees, pursuing the fleeing animal. It was a large dog with long, coarse brown hair and a wide, flat face. Its tongue flapped from one side of its mouth.

The snow in the area was deep and the dog's weight—Yuri guessed fifty kilos—made him sink to his chest with each leaping stride.

A middle-aged man with eyes closed to mere slits slogged through the snow on wooden framed snowshoes following the dog. One glance told Yuri the man was a Yakut, a member of the indigenous people who lived close to the Arctic Circle. Yuri had never seen a Yakut nomad this deep in the woods. They hunted on the lower hills and herded reindeer. The nomad was a short man, but looked hardened by the toil of eking out a living in some of the harshest elements on earth.

He wore a thick, long bear-hide coat that was cinched with a smooth leather belt and brass buckle bearing the Soviet hammer and sickle.

From his feet to his head he was dressed in furs, testaments to the many animals he had killed. Four dead black sables hung over one shoulder. Blood from the creatures dripped down his back and had frozen in the hairs of the coat. Yuri could see that each of the sables had been shot in the head to avoid any loss of meat or fur. The Yakut carried a rifle in his fur-gloved hand. A reindeer skin bundle hung from his other shoulder.

"*Estrayvucha.*"

The guard returned the greeting cautiously. "What brings you this far into the woods?"

"I hunt sable. Their furs are fullest this time of year. They are crafty creatures, burrowing in the snow before I can get a shot off, so my dog digs them out." The man seemed proud.

The guard said, "Well then, what if the sable runs and hides deep in the rocks?"

The Yakut shrugged. "I smoke them out with a fire made of green sticks."

The guard motioned to the dead sable hanging on the man's back. "You seem good at your trade."

"I am. I get one hundred rubles for black sable, half that for red ones." He shrugged again. "It is a good arrangement—if not for the sables."

The guard looked again at the limp, black-furred animals dangling from the man's shoulder. "There are wolves that would not think twice about attacking you with that feast on your back."

"Better still." The Yakut held up his rifle. "I get two hundred rubles for a fine wolf's hide."

The guard grumbled. "You make more money with one hide than I make in a month."

The Yakut laughed. "That is because I am a capitalist and you are a Communist."

"We are all Communists in the Soviet Union."

The Yakut laughed again. "Not all of us. I am a nomad like my father and his father. We live off the land and you Communists live off of people."

The Yakut reached into his coat and pulled out a liquor bottle. "But there is one thing we share, and that is our love of drink." He unscrewed the cap. "This keeps my bones from freezing."

The guard licked his dry lips. "Is that cognac?"

"It is, and fine cognac." The Yakut held the bottle out to the guard. "Take a sip, my Communist friend."

Yuri stood in silence and watched the events play out before him.

The guard took the bottle and chugged down several mouthfuls, then wiped his smiling face with his coat sleeve.

The Yakut lifted his arm and made a slight motion with his wrist, giving the guard the freedom to drink some more. The guard nodded, and lifted the liquor to his cold lips.

The Yakut pointed at Yuri. "What about your comrade? I am sure he would like a taste as well."

The guard looked at Yuri and laughed. "He has no choice in the matter; he is only a prisoner of the state, a traitor to the cause." He took another swallow, and when the Yakut man turned to call his dog in from sniffing around some nearby underbrush, the guard finished off the bottle. "I am sorry, my dear Yakut, but I seem to have drunk all your fine cognac." He slurred his words.

"No matter."

Yuri watched the guard sway, roll his eyes skyward and then drop to his knees; his Kalashnikov slipped from his shoulder, the bottle slipped from his hand. A moment later he fell face first into the snow, unconscious.

The Yakut stepped to the guard and nudged him with his rifle. He didn't move.

"I will be killed because of this." Yuri was angry.

"Not to worry, friend. I will take you far across the taiga. No one will catch us. Now, let me shoot this fool guard and we will be off." The Yakut raised his rifle and pointed the barrel at the guard's back.

"Stop," Yuri shouted. "He is a fool as you say, but like me he has to do what this government tells him to do."

"I am Yakut. My only law is the forest and the snow and the wind."

"Please, don't shoot him."

The Yakut stared at the guard's large form. "A pity to let such vermin live." He lowered his rifle. "I still prefer shooting him."

"Who are you?"

He looked up. "My name is Tengri Boo."

"A strange name."

"It means 'sky shaman' in my language. When I was a boy, a bolt of lightning from a summer storm flashed across the sky and hit me on my shoulder. It knocked me to the ground. I could not stand again until the next day. After that, the elders called me Tengri Boo. They believe I have much power, a gift from the sky god. I became a great hunter, renowned among my people." He puffed out his chest. "My clan has never gone hungry and has always had much fat to roast over their fires."

"Why do you do this for me?"

"The old priest, he told you I would come, did he not?"

"Yes."

"I am to take you far across the mountains to a secret place where those that wish your escape await for you."

"Why?"

"Why is not important."

"Then where?"

"I will not say where, because if we are caught they will torture you and you may tell them where we go. It is best you do not know too much." He paused, then whistled through stubby teeth. His dog bounded toward them.

He looked back at Yuri. "I have another reason to help you, but I cannot say until you are far from here and safe. All I know is that you are a man who carries with him valuable secrets that many seem to want."

Yuri studied the man's weathered face. "Why should I trust you? Maybe you are tricking me into escape, only to kill me."

Tengri grinned. "If I wanted you dead, you would be lying in the snow with this stupid guard." He took off his left glove and twitched a nub where his forefinger used to be. "The KGB did this to me a long time ago. They wanted me to talk after they arrested my father. I said nothing, even as they used the wire cutters on my finger. That is why the people hired me to help you escape; they know I hate the Soviets and that I will never talk if caught. I can be trusted."

Yuri glanced at the guard, who moved slightly and then released a shallow moan.

Tengri Boo said, "The drugs I put in the drink will keep him unconscious for a while. I will take you to a valley, to people who have an automobile." The Yakut propped both his hands on his hips. "Do you trust me now, prisoner?"

Yuri nodded. "I have to."

"Good, then we must go."

"Wait. We cannot go now. There is a woman back at the prison camp. She is the commandant's sister, and she is as much a prisoner as I am. I will not leave without her."

The Yakut sniffed the stirring wind. "I smell snow coming. It will come upon us fast and deep. You must forget this woman. We must go now."

"I will not go without her."

The Yakut moved close to Yuri. "You are like a bird freed from the cage. I suggest you fly fast and not be so foolish as to fly back into the cage again."

"I have an idea—a plan in mind."

"Does your plan explain how you will get out of the prison after the guard tells his superiors what happened to him today?"

Yuri smiled. "He won't speak a word to anyone. If he does, he will be in more trouble than me."

"What is this plan? That is, if you really have one."

"Please be here tomorrow, and I will come with the woman at this same time. Trust me as I trust you, and help me take the woman far from here."

Tengri raised his voice against the rising wind hissing through the tall pines. "Do you love this woman?"

"I do not know what love is anymore," Yuri said.

Tengri shook his head. "Love has killed many a man." He removed his fur scarf from around his neck.

Yuri searched the man's brown face to look for a clue as to his thoughts. He huffed. "This will get us all killed." He handed Yuri his rifle. "If the guard wakes up, hit him in the head real hard with the butt of this gun."

He knelt in the snow and unfurled the bundled reindeer skin. Yuri marveled at the mound of fur clothing that spread out. There was a heavy knee-length fur coat that Tengri called a *doha*. "It has fur on both sides; it will keep out the wind and keep in the warmth that the body makes."

He spread out several items: a headband of fur with ear flaps; a chin band and face shield of sable fur; a blue fox fur cap; undergarments made of thick deer suede; two sets of socks made of finely cured calfskin; leggings made from reindeer hide; and mittens crafted from squirrel.

"These are all to keep you from dying in the cold." There was a neck scarf of red fox that was long enough to wrap three times around the throat and boots made of heavy fur. The soles of the boots had pads from wolves' feet sewn on with deer sinew. He then pointed out a pair of snow shoes made of bent pine boughs and webbed with dried fox guts. "This was meant for one person. If we take a woman who is not hardened to the cold like you and me, she might not make it."

Yuri said, "I do not need these things. I cut timber all day in the clothes that I wear now. I have padded pants and good boots."

"It is not enough. We will be going in a snow that will kill you if that is all you wear." He rose and grabbed Yuri's jacket. "The stuffing comes out of the seams and your miserable boots will not keep your toes from freezing. This might be good for a few hours of cutting timber and then retreating to the protection of the prison ward, but we will be four days in the jaws of a storm—a storm that comes tonight."

Tengri stepped away. "Even as a Yakut man, I fear such a storm. It may help us because they will not search for you during a storm. It will give us time to make distance. The guards will wait for the storm to quiet before they let loose the dogs and follow us. A storm will also erase our tracks."

He looked Yuri up and down and wrinkled his small flat nose. "I could stuff your boots with ugunnya."

"Ugunnya?"

"Dry grass. It lies under the snow. It will help your boots stay a bit warmer." The Yakut rubbed his fur glove under his chin. "I will dig deep in the snow and forage some ugunnya, and I will also gather some tree moss. I will put what I gather over a fire tonight and it will be more insulation than your old coat. Maybe it will be enough to keep in your body heat." He looked at his blood-smeared sable skins that now lay at his feet. "These will be for your hands. I will cut up these four skins and make gloves. There will be enough hide to make a hat maybe."

"What will we eat on the way?"

Tengri Boo looked at his dog. "He will be our food in a day or two, if we do not find anything to shoot. We do not have the strength to carry meat far distances. For water we will melt snow. For sleep we will dig out snow caves and sleep on pine boughs." He looked at Yuri. "I hope the woman is fatter than you, my skinny friend."

"She is thin as well."

Tengri frowned. "I hoped she was a woman with padding. Thin is not good in the taiga." He looked up at the darkening clouds. "We will have no stars to guide us at night for the next night or two. We will have to travel by day when we can see the moss growth on the north side of trees. That will be our guide to direct our way."

"You do not have a compass?"

"I have no use of compasses. Compasses are unreliable this far north. The trees will be all we need, but we must be careful to hide from the planes when the sun is up."

"We will be far away from here by then," Yuri said.

"You have not walked far through deep snow, have you?"

"That is correct."

"The skinny woman will slow us, not to mention that we will waste a full day with your crazy scheme to bring her along. You can be sure that men with planes will come searching for us."

Yuri shook his head. "No one has escaped the camp and lived. They will think us dead and not bother searching for us."

"I am sorry, my friend, but stealing away the commandant's sister will change everything. Believe me, prisoner, the sky will have many planes, I fear. Yes, they will come, and they will find us when we cross the treeless tundra after they see our tracks." He paused. "That is, unless we are like the white rabbit or Arctic fox of winter whose coats are difficult to see against the fresh snow."

"What do you mean?"

"We need a white covering, a kind of camouflage."

Yuri thought for a second. "The camp hospital will have white sheets."

"Can you get three?"

"I will get the sheets and be here tomorrow just as I said."

The guard moaned again. He was coming out from under the influence of the drugged liquor. Tengri reached for his rifle. "I should kill the guard."

"No. He is of more value to me alive. He is part of my plan."

"I will be here as you wish, but I don't expect to see you again. The guards will make sure of that."

"Tomorrow you will see that I am here and a man of my word. Just make sure you are a man of yours."

The Yakut frowned, gathered his things and left.

A short while later, Yuri's guard propped himself on his elbow and rubbed his throbbing head. "What . . . what happened?"

"You drank too much of the cognac, and you drank it too fast."

The guard looked about. "Where is the Yakut?"

"Chasing sable. He left as soon as you passed out."

The guard struggled to his feet, stepped to the nearest tree and leaned against it for support. "My head hurts."

"Such is the way with cognac. We should get back now."

"Not without the wood. We cannot return without the birch or the commandant will have both of our heads."

"I have found the perfect tree while you were passed out." He pointed his ax at a large birch that had fallen in the snow. "It looks as if it fell some time ago, maybe last winter. The wood will be drier than a freshly cut tree. Dry wood makes better furniture. It will make a good gun cabinet." The corners of Yuri's mouth turned up slightly. "And you won't have to listen to so much chopping."

The guard rubbed his head. "Do what you need to do."

Yuri used his ax to cut off limbs that would catch on trees and other foliage. With each swing of the ax, the guard swore and rubbed his temples. An hour later, Yuri was done. He took his time, giving the guard extra minutes to recover.

They trudged back into the camp, carrying the two-meter-long birch log on their shoulders. Overhead, the sky grew cold with brooding, engorged snow clouds. Yuri saw Anna step onto the porch. He stopped abruptly, causing the guard to take the full weight of the log. Yuri turned to Anna and hastily pulled off his gloves. "I will be in the camp medical clinic tonight. Come there alone and unnoticed."

"Why?"

"Freedom from this place; freedom from your brother; freedom from this frozen hole of hell."

"Freedom," she returned.

"Come to me tonight. I will not leave without you."

Anna smiled, then let her lips curl down in worry as she signed, "How will this be done?"

"Do you trust me?"

"I do."

"Good, then dress for the cold and long travel in the forest. Bring some cuts of meat."

"Meat?" she signed back, her face confused.

The guard swore at Yuri. "Pick up the log. We have only a few more meters to go and we can rest."

Yuri returned his fur gloves to his hands.

Anna signed, "I will do as you say."

Yuri coughed as he again hoisted the log. He coughed again, harder. "I feel sick."

"You were not sick all day, prisoner."

"I want to go to the clinic. I want to see the camp doctor."

"Only the sickest prisoners see the doctor and then they are mostly dead."

"I will make a deal with you, guard. I will not speak of your drinking a full bottle of cognac and passing out in the snow, and you will escort me to the clinic."

The guard glared at Yuri.

"I could have run into the forest and escaped while you were unconscious. I could have killed you with my ax. How would it be if the commandant knew of these things?"

The guard cringed.

"I think it is only fair that you do this thing I ask. I at least deserve a night of warm sleep for my silence."

"Prisoner, you are most clever and are up to something, but I have no choice in the matter. If I do not go along with you, I will be the next prisoner put in this place." He paused a long moment. "I will take you to the clinic when I come to lock the prison doors tonight. You cough convincingly, prisoner, or it will be disastrous for us both."

"Agreed," Yuri said, then hacked a hard cough into his gloved hand.

chapter 20

THE CONVERSATION

JEFFREY STOCK STOOD in a small basement darkroom that felt every bit like a tomb. He raised a hand and groped for the pull chain dangling somewhere near his head. With a slight tug, a ruby monochrome blush replaced the black. The darkroom served as his sanctuary, a quiet place where he could retreat from the harsh light of the sun and inquisitive eyes.

He liked the dark. Long ago, when he was a young man, he took photographs of nature, capturing the inspiring images of hawks in flight, or a thundering wave pounding the shore against the backdrop of a golden sunset. He hoped these new photographs would bring him income. But like most every venture in his life, it failed miserably.

With wood tongs, Stock prodded the paper immersed in a fluid-filled stainless steel pan. After the image slowly materialized, he gently pulled the treated 8x10 paper from its chemical bath and studied it under the red overhead light bulb.

He saw the image of a dark-haired young female, not yet a woman and certainly no longer a little girl, standing in the shade of the Washington Monument. The photo clearly showed her face; a face that belonged to Tanya Novak. The photo would be a card that he would play in a dangerous game of chance in hopes that his miserable chain of life failures would be finally over.

* * *

Accumozzo's Bar was an out-of-the-way place where a man like Victor could drink unnoticed. The seedy, gloomy establishment was wedged in a storefront under a dark freeway overpass at the edge of Georgetown. Broken glass littered the parking lot, and broken dreams littered the bar stools.

Victor took a circuitous route to the bar. He knew FBI agents liked to follow him around the city. He was not a paranoid man, just extremely cautious, knowing that technicians had discovered over twenty radio-transmitting beacons in embassy staff vehicles, most in the cars driven by KGB officials. He also had been informed that someone was passing along secret information.

He looked behind him as soon as he turned his black Plymouth from the embassy compound and turned north on Sixteenth Street. Sure enough, behind him a dark sedan eased onto the road. It had been parked under a drooping elm and behind a parked delivery truck.

Victor made a sharp turn on M Street and headed west. He sped up and made a quick turn on Twenty-fourth, then east on K Street. He did a sudden U-turn. The sedan was nowhere to be seen. Confident he had lost the tail, he made his way to the bar at a leisurely pace.

Victor sat alone at one end of the red painted bar. The surface was scarred with cigarette burns, deep wounds from broken beer glasses and chipped edges from years of service to uncaring patrons. Victor motioned to the lone bartender who showed little concern for his clientele, which consisted of the Russian, a face-planted, snoring drunk at the end of the bar, and a married government accountant and his girlfriend in a dark booth in the back. They were all regulars. The couple was giggling.

The bartender was reading the race results from the previous day and tried to ignore Victor.

"Another whisky for me now!" Alcohol had thickened his Slavic accent.

The irritated bartender lowered the crumpled paper, snatched a bottle of Jack Daniel's from a glass shelf behind him and trundled to the big Russian. He filled Victor's shot glass till it sloshed over the brim, bleeding into a puddle on the bar top.

Victor had developed a taste for American whisky, preferring it over vodka, at least while he lived in America. He was not there to drink for the pleasure, or to savor the smooth taste of the liquor. He had come to get drunk. He clamped his fat hand around the small, freshly filled tumbler and lifted the liquor to his mouth. In a single motion he tossed back the whole drink, feeling the burn of the fluid in his throat. His lips puckered, and his eyes squeezed shut. Once the joyful pain passed, he opened his eyes, locked onto the bartender, slapped his palm on the bar and snarled, "One more." This time the barkeep didn't bother looking up from his reading.

A man stepped from the shadows near the rear entrance and approached the bartender. "No more drinks for the Russian; he seems to have had enough."

The barman grunted. "You sure ain't telling me anything new, pal. I've already lost count of the shots he's knocked back."

The new arrival, dressed in an army fatigue jacket, dark sunglasses and Yankees hat, handed the bartender a new, crisp, folded twenty. "Make us some coffee."

The barkeep grinned and tucked the bill in his shirt pocket. "Will do."

Victor, who now teetered on the threshold between drunk and really drunk, watched the transaction. He didn't know who the stranger was and didn't care. He wanted only one thing. "Where is my drink?"

The barkeep said nothing as he made his way to a can of coffee and flipped off the plastic lid. He grabbed a brown-stained glass pot for the brew.

Victor huffed as he ran his finger over the puddle of spilled whisky and rubbed his tongue with the liquor. A moment later, Victor felt a hand on his shoulder and instinctively flung it away. His angry glare was met with a smile.

"We have business to discuss."

Victor tried to focus on the stranger. His alcohol-clouded mind searched for words to say, but all he could do was gaze in confusion.

"Victor Ivanovich Pochinko. KGB. You once let a girl escape from you. It was at a monastery. You remember that, don't you?"

The comment sobered him some. "I think you are a fool."

"I'm no fool, Victor Ivanovich. I know many things about many people, including you." The man sat on the stool next to Victor. "I am sure you will pay me well for what I have."

"Who are you?" Victor slurred.

He smiled. "I am your new friend."

"I have no friends."

"You've just made one. I have information you want."

"You have nothing I want."

"I have sold the KGB information before. I want to make a deal about the girl you let slip through your fingers. Her name is Tanya Novak."

Victor's mind retreated to a night seven years ago when the girl was in his grasp. He reached up and felt the raised scar on the back of his head—a scar created by a shovel. "I'm listening. Where is she?"

"Ah, she is well and is close to us right now."

Victor's hand clamped around his shot glass. "What do you want?"

The stranger drummed the bar top with his fingertips. "I want you to do something for me, Victor Ivanovich, and then you can have the girl."

"How do you know my name?"

"I know a lot of things about Russia. I know the language. I know the government, and I know that when a KGB agent fails to capture a simple little girl, his superiors consider him unreliable. Are you unreliable or simply not that smart, Victor Ivanovich Pochinko?"

"How is it you know all this?"

"I read a dossier on you obtained by the FBI from one of your old comrades in Leningrad. He's a spy for the CIA now. He has succumbed to the lure of the Western luxuries." He grinned, amused by his own wit. "Anyway, I read about how you were assigned to capture the girl and failed. It is a rare failure on your excellent record. I'm sure you want to clear it up."

Victor turned his stool to face the unwanted guest. "Sometimes people can know too much, and then they end up dead. Besides, I have nothing that proves to me you know where the girl is."

The man removed a silver lighter from his pocket and lit a cigarette he had pulled from a pack of Marlboros tucked in his shirt. He inhaled, and after a few seconds released a lungful of blue smoke. It washed over Victor's face. "Meet me tomorrow—exactly at noon— at Poor Richard's bookstore on Connecticut Avenue. Are you sober enough to remember that?"

Victor started to speak, but was stopped when the bartender appeared and set two cups of steaming coffee on the bar. The barkeep said, "Drink fast." He glowered at Victor. "We close in twenty minutes—sharp."

Victor waited until the bartender left, then turned to the visitor. He was three steps away heading for the rear door, his slightly smoked cigarette smashed in the ashtray.

The woman in the darkened back booth stood quickly and headed in the direction of the ladies' room. Victor saw the man bump into her.

The woman staggered back a step, then said in a thin Slovak accent, "Watch where you're going, mister."

The stranger slipped past the woman and out the back door.

chapter 21

DUPONT CIRCLE
METRO STATION

STOCK WALKED INTO the hall of the ISS offices, an unlit cigarette dangling from his lips. He was uptight, desperately needing a light because his lighter was missing. Sometime after he left the bar and before he reached his apartment, he realized it was gone. The way he lost things, he was surprised he had managed to hang onto it all these years; he had lost almost everything else he carried.

He asked three coworkers for a light, but none smoked. He went into the break room and foraged through the drawers under a coffee pot until he found a small box of wooden matches. He ignited one and set the small yellow flame to the end of his cigarette. He inhaled deeply. The nicotine had an immediate, soothing effect.

The rest of the workday he spent at his desk, reading and shuffling papers. The last hour he immersed himself in Tarle's history of Russia. The reading helped pass the time quickly. A glance at his watch made him realize he was almost late. He grabbed the duffel bag from behind his cluttered desk.

He walked from the ISS building and headed for the Dupont Circle Metro station. Several times he checked to see if he was being followed. From the corner of his eye he caught the sudden appearance of a kite. It swayed in the wind, dodging back and forth, dipping and arching to the whims of a cool spring breeze. It spiraled over the rooftops, and then, tripped by a gust of wind, became ensnared in phone lines.

A boy stood beneath the wires, crying over his torn paper kite with its limp tail of rags. The snared kite reminded Jeffrey of when he was a boy. A homemade kite was the only toy his mother allowed. She believed constant study enriched a child more than time-wasting recreation that could only produce laziness and nonproductive character traits. She only allowed the kite because Stock had to make it himself and she considered that a good way to develop problem-solving skills.

He trotted down the subway stairs and then waited on the platform to see if anyone had taken notice of him. The Metro train appeared out of the round tunnel in a gust of pushed air and screeched to a stop. The coach doors automatically opened, and Stock looked around one more time before stepping aboard. He took the train to Cleveland Park, exited and weaved his way through the rush-hour crowd like a football player slicing through a weak defensive line.

He stepped from the curb and flagged a cab. Once he was seated, the cab edged onto bustling Connecticut Avenue. Stock told the driver to circle the block. As they drove, he turned his head back several times to see if anyone was following. Once satisfied he was in the clear, he reached inside the duffel, pulled out a Yankees baseball cap and army coat, and donned both items. The coat was too tight.

He slipped a few bills through a slot in the Plexiglas barrier that separated the driver from the passenger area. "Stop here."

The vehicle pulled to a stop. An annoyed driver behind them had to slam on his brakes. He vented his frustration through a long blast of his horn and an angry hand gesture. The driver tilted his head out the window and shouted several obscenities.

Stock hopped out of the cab, paying no attention to the agitated man behind him. The cab sped off.

He stood on the sidewalk for a moment looking up and down the street, then ducked down a narrow alley flanked by three-story, red-brick buildings.

No one was in the alley except for a vagrant sleeping on a flattened cardboard box by a Dumpster. Jeffrey Stock cautiously walked up the alley, then stopped. He returned to the slumbering, homeless man. The man slept under battered cardboard. Stock slowly pulled away the boxes, revealing the curled form of a big man in tattered clothes. He was snoring. An empty bottle of wine lay near his head.

Stock could see the sweat stains that impregnated the cardboard and knew the man had been using this as bedding for several weeks, if not months.

He shook the man awake. The man's deep-set eyes fought to focus on the intruder standing over him. His breath was sour. The smell of tobacco smoke and urine permeated his clothes. The bum blinked a few times. "What the— Whatcha want?" The man sat up.

The vagrant's face was gray, sooty and stained; a spiderweb of broken capillaries reddened his cheeks. His hands trembled— not from fear but from years of alcoholism. Stock continued to study him.

"Got a cigarette, man?" His voice poured from a dry, abused throat.

Stock reached in his coat and handed the bum a five-dollar bill. "Go buy your own, I need mine." Stock paused and took out another five. "Here, buy some wine to wash it all down."

The man's yellowed eyes widened as he grabbed for the gift. He struggled to his feet, and Stock could see the man's joints caused him pain. He watched as the derelict limped to the end of the alley and turned onto the street. He waited several moments to see if the man would return.

Victor breathed a little faster as the man in a Yankees cap and army coat came in the side door of the bookstore. He stepped just inside and slowly looked around the silent people, all with faces buried in books or scanning shelves for a potential purchase.

"Looking for something special?" Victor spoke from behind a row of books. Stock saw the man and walked over. Victor leaned in close and whispered, "I want proof that you have the girl."

Stock removed a large envelope from his bag and handed it to Victor. Victor pulled an eight-by-ten, black-and-white photo from the envelope.

"That is Tanya Novak," Stock said.

"I saw her at night, but she was much younger then."

"She's older, but I think you can see it's the same person."

"Maybe."

"I know all about that night," Stock said.

"How do you know so much about me? You Americans are usually so clueless."

"Let's get down to business. I know that seven years ago you were assigned to capture the girl in that picture. It was near Leningrad. She was to be interrogated, but she escaped. You were shamed because of your failure and demoted for incompetence. Man, that had to hurt."

Victor said nothing.

Stock went on. "Now I'm sure you would appreciate an opportunity to redeem yourself by getting the girl and taking her back to the U.S.S.R. Am I right?"

"It is difficult to do that."

"Don't tell me the Soviets have never taken a defector back to Moscow. I know of several being smuggled out via Cuba or Mexico."

"You know much for an American." Victor rubbed the photo between his thumb and forefinger. "I will need to see the girl's eyes, and then I will know if she is the one. I will negotiate only after I see the girl in person, and that is not negotiable."

Stock thought a minute. "I can arrange that. I will have the girl at Big Al's Liquor Store tomorrow at ten o'clock. We will make our deal then. I assume you know all the liquor stores."

"Big Al's. I'll find it."

"Good. I must ask one more question of you, my new friend. I have access to a great deal of information about the Soviet Union's workings and secrets, but I cannot find one reason you want this girl. What makes her so valuable to you?"

"You will find the truth soon enough."

chapter 22

BIG AL'S
LIQUOR STORE

THE FOLLOWING NIGHT'S rain came in torrents. Victor stood hidden in the shadow of the alley next to the defunct Faraj's Dry Cleaning. Across the street was Big Al's Liquor Store. Victor laid his rifle across the top of a gray gas meter box that was mounted on the alley's graffiti-painted brick wall. The wind and rain could be trouble, he thought, but he couldn't wait for perfect conditions. He could control many things, but weather wasn't one of them.

He focused one eye through the 9X power scope mounted on his Remington 308 rifle that had the sleek cylinder of a silencer screwed to the barrel. He had a clear line of sight to the glass double-entry doors of the liquor store. As the scope moved about, he saw the magnified image of the red and white striped canopy over the entryway. He eased the scope's crosshairs to the center of a man's back as he walked to the liquor store's doors. He was dressed in his army coat and Yankees hat. His coat collar was pulled up high to ward off the pelting rain; the small form of a teenage girl walked by his side. She wore a tattered yellow rain slicker and a wool naval cap pulled low on her face.

Victor knew it would be an easy kill; he would drop the man like a deer with one shot. He would then take the girl and not have to pay a dime to the brazen American. *How stupid of the man. He stands right in the open.*

Victor lowered the rifle when the man entered the liquor store with the girl. He would not risk taking his shot through the plate glass: A bullet does strange things when it passes through thick glass. His plan was to drop the American in the street, then run over and take the girl away into the rain-soaked night.

He would force himself to be patient now. Patience was a frustrating requirement of his work. The brass casing with the copper-jacketed bullet rested in the rifle's chamber.

Patience.

The firing pin would strike primer, and the gunpowder would ignite, sending the projectile down the long barrel at supersonic speed.

Patience. It would then puncture the man's flesh and rip open his body. The girl would be his and all for the simple price of a single bullet. How stupid of the man to think he could threaten a Soviet KGB agent and live.

Patience.

His victim would soon reappear on the rain-splattered sidewalk and just stand there with the girl looking up and down the drenched street, waiting for Victor's arrival.

Victor smiled at the man's naiveté. He didn't know it, but he would soon be facedown in the rain, never knowing what killed him.

"Wait," he whispered. "Breathe slow; breathe deep." His lungs needed air to feed oxygen to his brain, to his muscles; everything in his body needed to be alert and responsive. "Breathe in slow. Take your time."

His prey was hard to see in the liquor store, hidden as he was by a beer advertisement pasted on the window. The rain came harder, falling like lead pellets hurtling from a dark sky. He saw the man purchase cigarettes and a bottle of something that looked like wine. The girl was inside the door, facing the man.

His target turned and started for the door. Again Victor propped the rifle on the gas meter. The thin crosshairs fell steady on the man's neck. The under rim of his baseball cap glowed as the red tip of the cigarette brightened. The man stood under the darkened entry of the liquor store. Why would he go out into the rain? He would wait there with the girl.

The sights slowly migrated to the middle of the man's spine. A head shot was too difficult in the dark rain, but the trunk of a man was easy to hit in any condition.

Victor argued with himself. *Take the shot now. The man will not come out in the rain; he will stand there and wait.* A second later: *Not in the dark, not now in the rain. A skilled hunter needs patience.* He had learned this in the KGB, learned this from other assassinations. *Wait out the kill shot; don't ever be rushed.*

Victor didn't listen to his own advice. The man was going to die. He was going to die now, die here, die in that doorway. Victor's finger slowly snaked over the knurled edge of the trigger's tongue and he made slight pressure. His tendons and muscles needed to obey him. Tightening too fast now, expanding his lungs too much, he would miss his shot. Every ounce of his body needed to be in control at the crucial moment. The here and now seemed surreal. He felt exhilarated; he felt confident; he felt power in it all. The life was his for the taking. All doubt had now passed.

"Squeeze and keep the scope floating steady on the man's back," he whispered. His finger eased back on the wet trigger. The magnified image of the army coat exploded as the rifle lurched when the bullet touched off. Victor knew that it was a perfect shot, a dead-on kill.

When the violent lurch of the rifle had settled, and Victor peered over the barrel, he saw the man curled on the wet sidewalk, an extinguished wet cigarette stuck to his lower lip, his broken bottle of wine bleeding from inside a wet paper sack. The girl screamed maniacally.

Victor ran across the street still holding his rifle in one hand. He grabbed the girl's hand. She was convulsing in fear, her movements restricted to muscle memory; her mind had entered another place. Victor had seen it all before. He felt empowered. He controlled life, controlled death. He controlled the girl and the entire situation. It seemed too easy; a skilled shot in the rain, to be sure. The rush of adrenaline made him chuckle like a giddy child.

He paused long enough to use the rifle to flick off the dead man's baseball cap.

Victor's breath caught. The man on the ground was not the man in the bar, not the man in the bookstore. He immediately yanked on the girl's wrist, flinging her around. She wasn't the right girl. In fact, she wasn't a girl at all, but a small, older woman—small and thin. Her face flared with fear. "You . . . shot my Charlie. You killed him. Murder! Help!"

A bright flash went off in Victor's face. He looked at the sudden burst of light and another flash seared his eyes, then another flared like lightning flashing across his naked retina. With each flash came the click of a camera shutter.

Blinking furiously, he tried to force his eyes to focus. Seconds passed like hours as he tried to blink away the momentary sting of blindness. When his sight returned, he stared into a silver sheet of rain where the flash had come from. He turned his gaze to the dead man at his feet, his blood being washed away by rivulets of water. The man had a scruffy beard and a sunken face. He had the dirty appearance of a homeless man.

The distant sound of sirens coming his way brought Victor around. He looked at the woman, who continued to scream hysterically as she bent over the body. "Who are you? How did you get here?"

"Let me go!"

Victor relaxed his hold, and the woman pulled free. She wheezed, trying to catch her breath. She backed away, then turned and ran. Victor raised the rifle and shot. The woman fell to the street, spitting up dancing raindrops.

He had no time to think; no time to plan. What were those bright bursts of light that had blinded him? A thought occurred to him. Victor seized the dead man by the collar and dragged him across the street and into the dark alley. Sweat joined the rain on his face as he strained to move the corpse. If Victor had been a small man, he would never be able to accomplish the task.

Moments later, Victor had loaded the dead man in the trunk of his car.

chapter 23

BED-AND-
BREAKFAST

PETERSBURG, VIRGINIA, THE BELL BED-AND-BREAKFAST
WHITE OAK ROAD

SHANNON AND TANYA walked beneath a wide, white arbor and inside the Bell Bed-and-Breakfast Inn, and were greeted with the pleasant but musty odor typical of old antebellum buildings and furniture. Shannon thought of it as the "museum smell." The floors bore scars and wear marks from nearly a century and a half of foot traffic, boots and shoes wearing away the oak since before the Civil War. The planks creaked beneath their feet as they walked to the front desk. Even though it was well beyond the century mark, Shannon could see that someone had taken great care to restore the two-story red-brick home. The windows were dressed in fine handwoven German lace drapes, and the floors wore intricate Persian wool throw rugs.

The lobby was once a parlor or greeting room with a small round maple table resting between two wingback chairs, each covered with blue upholstery and trimmed with a gold tasseled fringe. The walls were dressed with red crushed-velvet wallpaper, and an old oak flat desk was topped with a yellow-domed glass oil lamp that welcomed arriving guests. The lamps were dry of oil, unneeded since the arrival of electric lights. Regardless of the encroachment of technology, the ambience remained that of an old Civil War-era home.

Shannon thought it a suitable place for her and Tanya to stay,

since the girl was afraid of the hustle of D.C. The wail of police sirens had kept Tanya awake through most of the night. She was glad
to be out of D.C. for another reason: she had developed a fear of Jeffrey Stock. Stock had said nothing to trigger Shannon's concern, but
Tanya picked up something that made her very uneasy. During dinner at the Old Ebbitt Grill, Stock said he wanted to help. To Shannon he sounded honest, but Tanya heard the opposite in a way only
she could. It was a lie. Shannon believed her when the girl said, "He
is a man with a dark soul. He is evil."

On the drive from the restaurant to the bed-and-breakfast,
Tanya asked, "Why wouldn't he tell us the truth?"

"If the snuff box truly contains a vial of manna," Shannon explained, "then it becomes very valuable. The fact that it was used to
murder the czar makes it a valuable historical object, but the manna
inside makes it more than priceless. A greedy person might do anything to possess it."

The sign over the lobby desk read: BED-AND-BREAKFAST—OUR
MORNING MEAL IS SERVED BETWEEN SEVEN AND NINE O'CLOCK.

It was a simple, quaint place and Shannon could see Tanya felt
more at home. Shannon craned her neck to peek around the corner
to see if anyone was there. She coughed politely to announce their
presence. While she waited, she studied an old-looking photo on the
wall: a picture of a rundown home with a leaning porch. It took a
moment for her to make the connection. The photo was of the inn
when it was the residence long ago. Below the photo was a caption
on a small brass plaque: HOME OF THE WIDOW EMMA BELL AND HER
YOUNG SON ELIJAH, 1859.

The sepia image showed a blurry carriage kicking dust off the
dirt road that had once passed in front of the home. While the present structure differed in some ways, it remained true to the style of
the original house. Trees that seemed small and anemic in the photo
were tall and full now. She had no doubt the trees in the front yard
had stood sentinel over the building for more than a century.

Shannon impatiently tapped the pin of a brass-domed an-
nouncement bell. The ping echoed down the dark hall, but there
was no answer.

As Shannon waited, she rubbed her tired eyes. When she refocused, she saw a small sign by the front desk: FOR THE INTEREST OF OUR GUESTS—A YANKEE CANNONBALL LEFT A HOLE IN A BRICK WALL ON THE REAR PORCH OF THIS HOUSE DURING THE SIEGE OF PETERSBURG. IT REMAINS TO THIS DAY AS A MEMORIAL TO THE NORTHERN AGGRESSION INTO VIRGINIA.

A Southerner must have written the sentence, Shannon thought. To most people the Civil War was just that—a civil war. To a Southerner, however, it was the time of hatred, a time of the "Northern aggression." People of the South had long memories and many still held a grudge about those horrible years.

Shannon looked at the desk bell again, and this time brought the palm of her hand down hard on the bell's pin.

"Can I help you?" The voice was frail. A thin, elderly woman dressed in a pink flower-print cotton dress emerged from the hall.

"We have a phone reservation under the name of Shannon Reed."

"Yes, of course. I'm sorry you had to wait. I've spent the last two hours baking breads and Danish pastries. It is a bit of demanding work, especially in such a small kitchen." A grease-stained apron hung from her neck and a streak of baking powder graced her sunken cheeks. A residue of dough clung to her hands. She noticed it, and hurriedly wiped it away on her apron. "Let's see. Shannon Reed, you said."

"Yes, R-E-E-D."

She pulled a large registry book from the desk and set it on the table. "You asked for a two-bedroom suite. We only have one of those, you know, but it's available. Most of our rooms are singles. Since we're not in our busy season, I'll give it to you for our winter rate."

"Thank you. We may need it for as much as a week." Shannon retrieved her wallet from her purse and removed an American Express card.

"I'm sorry, but I only accept cash or a check drawn on a local bank."

"Who doesn't take credit cards these days?" Shannon put the card back in her wallet. "I can write a check, but we're from out of state." Tanya motioned for Shannon to come close. Shannon bent, and Tanya whispered in her ear, "She is not telling the truth."

Shannon nodded. "Are you sure you can't take a credit card?"

"I can, but they charge me a percentage, you know."

"I know," Shannon said, as she handed the woman her card.

"I just hate filling out those little forms, and my hands can't slide the machine across the carbon copies—arthritis you know, such a bother."

"I'd be happy to help."

The woman pulled a credit card machine from the desk, and said, "I hate this knuckle buster." With Shannon's help, she took the impression of the card. It was then that Shannon noticed the crooked fingers of the old woman's hands.

Shannon signed the registry. "Sorry to make you go through all this fuss."

The woman massaged her afflicted arthritic fingers. "Welcome to my humble inn, Ms. Reed. My name is Emma Bell, and I hope you enjoy your stay."

"Emma Bell?" Shannon's eyes darted to the photo she had studied a few minutes before.

Emma noticed. "Yes, it's the same name of the first owner of this house. We're related. Lived most of her life here. She died here. A remarkable woman with a remarkable story, both her and her son, Elijah. Now, let me show you to your room."

Emma closed the guest book, handed the credit card receipt to Shannon, then gave her the key to the room. The woman lifted the corner of her apron and wiped the flour from her hands one more time. "We'll have fluffy Danish and buttermilk biscuits for the morning meal, so you don't want to be late. I serve between seven and nine in the morning."

Shannon sniffed the aromatic air wafting with oven-baked bread. "We'll be here."

chapter 24

BLACKMAIL

WHEN VICTOR TOOK his usual seat in Accumozzo's Bar, he was handed a sealed manila envelope. The bartender stood there a long moment.

Victor snapped, "What's this?"

The bartender shrugged. "Some guy left it for you; told me to give it when you came in."

"Get me a drink."

The bartender rubbed his hands with the bar towel, then tossed the rag onto the counter and turned to grab a bottle of Jack Daniel's off the shelf behind him.

Victor slid his thumb under the lip of the envelope and broke the Scotch tape the sender had used to seal the package. It contained a letter.

My new friend, the second mouse always gets the cheese.
Now, I have a proposal, and I think you are smart enough
to accept it, as I am sure that Party officials in the Kremlin
do not want an international incident, especially one
where it can be proven that a KGB agent masquerading
as a cultural attaché in the Soviet Embassy killed two
innocent American citizens. I'm sure such news would
upset your superiors. It might cost you your job. It might
cost your pension. Let's be honest, it will cost you your

*life. I'm certain they have a bullet with your name
on it.*

*Now to my proposal. I possess the negatives of the
photos taken of you with rifle in hand, standing over that
poor dead American. I think my negatives would be worth
a lot of money to you and your country, but I don't seek
money from you. I suspect under the circumstances you
would be worth more dead than alive to your comrades in
Moscow. So I propose this: I want a prisoner who is now
rotting away in one of your prisons. His name is Yuri
Novak, and he is in Work Camp C-23, located somewhere
in Northern Russia.*

*I'm sure you remember this man. You should—you shot
him in the leg the night you tried to capture the girl. Now here
is where you will be pleased with our bargain.*

*I will show you where the girl Tanya can be found, and
all for the simple task of you getting that man out of prison
and making him tell you where he hid a golden box he
received from the grave of a monk.*

*I'm sure your well-known interrogation techniques will
bring forth the answer I seek. When the gold box and its
contents are in my hands, I will reveal where you can find the
girl. I will also, out of the goodness of my heart, hand over the
negatives.*

*You should know that I have put copies of the photos
in the hands of a trusted friend, so killing me is ill-advised.
If I end up dead, then my friend will send the photographs
to the police, to my and your governments, and to the world
press.*

*I am sure you will agree that we will all benefit from
such an arrangement, but if you think this bargain is unfair,
then I want you to use your small brain and ask how you'll
fare if every television and the front page of every newspaper in
the world has your face looking into a camera as you stand
next to a dead American citizen.*

So, my new friend, I will give you thirty days to get me

*that gold snuff box and its contents, before the rat trap is
sprung on your neck. The snuff box will have the seal of the
Romanovs on its face. Be sure you succeed. Don't fail as you
have in the past.*

Victor crumpled the letter in his massive fist. A moment later, he
smiled.

chapter 25

REVERSAL

JEFFREY STOCK WALKED to the ISS building; his usual mundane life now had a jolt of adrenaline. For the first time in his life, he felt alive, and that he too could be a part of making history instead of reading about the past. If he could force the Russian to get Yuri out of that prison, he would then be able to find where the gold snuff box was hidden. Inside the box was a message from Czar Alexander, and with it a precious sample of the manna that rained down on the wandering Hebrews thirty-five hundred years ago.

A thin woman wearing a scarf that covered her cheaply dyed red hair tapped her path with a red-tipped white cane along the sidewalk just a few feet from Stock. Her dress was worn, her shoes old and scuffed. She wore wire-frame glasses with thick round lenses that sat awkwardly on her face.

Stock stepped around her, but she veered into his path. They collided. Stock took a step back. The woman fell on the hard concrete sidewalk and lay still, her cane and glasses by her side. He didn't think he had hit her hard enough to knock her down.

The woman tried to push herself up. Stock helped her to her feet. As soon as she gained her balance, she asked, "Would you please be so kind as to pick up my cane and glasses for me?" She had a Slavic accent. For a moment, Stock thought he had met the woman before, although he couldn't remember where.

He gathered the woman's things. Something about the thick-lensed glasses seemed unusual. *She is very poor of sight,* he surmised quickly.

The woman held out her hand. "My glasses, please."

"Yes, I'm sorry," Stock muttered as he handed them to her.

She walked off. It took a moment for Stock to realize the woman didn't put the glasses on. Then he realized that she wasn't using the cane as she had before. Just as Stock began to wonder why the woman no longer needed the glasses and cane, a hand landed on his shoulder. He turned and saw a large man with an unfriendly silver-toothed smile—Victor.

"This gets complicated now, especially since we both have incriminating evidence against the other that proves we shot a man last night."

Stock felt as if all his blood drained to his feet. Beads of sweat formed on his upper lip. He pulled at his collar. "This . . . this is not the place to discuss this."

"Agreed. Let's walk. It is always better for the health if one walks."

Victor slipped his hand into his coat pocket. Stock got the intent.

They walked two blocks before Victor said, "If you do not bring me the negatives—all the negatives—then an anonymous caller will telephone the police and tell them where they can find a poor, homeless man in a shallow grave in the woods. In the grave next to the corpse will be your Yankees hat and army jacket. I am sure they will find some hairs in the hat that probably will be very similar to yours. And I am sure they will find a silver lighter in the pocket of that army coat—a silver lighter that has your name engraved on it and your fingerprints."

"You stole my lighter in that bar, didn't you?" Stock did nothing to hide his anger.

"Let me explain. The woman in the bar, the one you bumped into on your way out, stole your lighter from your coat. I found it convenient that your name was inscribed on the face of the lighter. It made finding you easy."

"What if I tell the police my lighter was stolen, or maybe I lost it someplace? Everyone who knows me will testify that I misplace things all the time."

"That may be a sufficient alibi, but your fingerprints are on the scope of the rifle that shot the man buried in that shallow grave. All they have to do is get another anonymous tip where the rifle can be found; and when the authorities find it, they will conduct a ballistics test and see it is the same rifle used to kill the man."

"My prints aren't on any rifle. I never touched—"

"Dr. Stock, the eyeglasses you picked up from the sidewalk only a few minutes ago have your fingerprints on the lenses. I saw you touch them. I assumed an intelligent man like you would have noticed the unusual nature of the lenses."

"They were thick."

"And round—like the lenses on a rifle scope."

Stock moaned.

"I removed the lenses from the scope earlier today and fitted them in the woman's glasses. Now that the glass has your prints on them, all I have to do is place them back into the scope. I am sure you will have a difficult time explaining why your prints are on that rifle. And even if you show them the photos of me, they will think you set me up. Which, of course, you did."

"Preposterous."

"Is it? Since the bartender saw you approach me in the bar while I sat alone, the authorities will think you tried to get me to help you shoot the homeless man, and you, my friend, will appear to have set this whole thing up: the shooting, the photos, everything. They will even suspect that you tried to get rid of your own clothing and lighter by throwing them in the grave. Remember, the bartender saw you wear those clothes and saw the lighter as well."

Stock took a moment to think. "Still, my photo shows you holding the rifle."

"Yes, it does. So what?" Victor gloated. "I can come up with a dozen explanations: I seized the rifle from you, fearing you'd kill others and someone took my picture. For that matter, the bartender on my payroll will testify that I was in the bar when the shooting took place, as will several other people. The man in the photo just looks similar. Difficult to make out images in such a rain, don't you think? Shall I go on?"

"No. The police might not believe you."

"Perhaps, but I carry diplomatic immunity. In the worse case, your government could expel me from this country; with such a flimsy case they would do very little more."

"Is that all?"

"Just one more thing for now. You paid the bartender with a crisp, new twenty-dollar bill to make coffee. He kept that bill, and it is now in the dead man's coat as well. I am sure they will find your prints on it."

"Okay, okay," Stock said. "I'm just a researcher and not well-suited to matters like this." He lowered his head. "It seems that you have me real good."

Victor looked smug. "The mouse that taunts the cat should have the sense to have a hole in the wall very close by. You, my friend, have no hole to run to, so you must now go where I say or be swallowed whole."

Stock licked his dry lips but said nothing.

Victor scratched the top of his head. "It seems we are facing personal mutually assured destruction. I believe you Americans call it a Mexican standoff. When you think of it, such fear of mutual destruction is the reason our two countries have not blown each other up in a nuclear war. Both fear unleashing hell upon each other. If someone sends the first missile, then nothing would be left of either of our countries. I think we are in the same position."

"Now what?" Stock asked weakly.

"If you tell me what is so important about that gold snuff box that you would have a man killed, then I will tell you why I seek the girl."

Stock thought for a moment. He didn't trust Victor, not for a minute, but he saw no other way out. "Okay, I'll tell you, but whatever happens from now on, we're equal partners."

"Partners? I have no need of partners; I am a Communist."

"I make very little money as a researcher of Soviet behavior; I'm sure you make even less. I propose a deal that will make us both more money than we could ever dream of."

"How much?"

"So much that you will want to be a capitalist."

"First you tell me about the gold snuff box. Why is it so important that you would kill to get it?"

Stock nodded. "I assume the girl is important to the Soviet government. Am I right?"

"Yes."

"And you know why she is of such importance?"

"I do. Tell me about the box first. Then I will tell you why the girl is important."

Stock sighed. "Stalin once said that he who has food to feed the masses can rule the world. It was back in 1935 that several of Stalin's senior KGB and general staff officers were on a parade ground to hear him give a speech. Joseph Stalin carried a chicken in the crook of his left arm onto the stage. Stalin walked back and forth on the platform as he shouted orders that multitudes more should be sent to the Siberian gulags. All the while Stalin's right hand plucked handfuls of feathers. The bird squirmed from the pain. Bloody feathers fell at his side as he continued to denude the bird. Soon the bird was plucked clean, naked and shaking. He dropped the creature on the ground. It hobbled about in pain. Stalin then reached in his coat pocket and removed a handful of corn, which he let trickle through his fingers.

"The chicken ran to the corn at Stalin's feet and calmly pecked away. Stalin said, 'People are just like chickens—treat them nice and they will revolt at every opportunity. Give an inch and they will want a mile. Treat them tough, real tough; pluck all their feathers, take everything from them, leave them naked in the snow, and like this grazing chicken at my feet the people will love you forever, they will never forsake you. Just feed them a little now and then.'"

Stock continued. "I know how we can find this secret to feeding the masses. It is hidden in the gold snuff box, and Tanya's father is the only one who knows where it's hidden."

"The girl does not know where it is?"

"No, only the father does."

Victor nodded. "He is a man willing to die before he betrays his daughter, before he betrays his God. It is a fool that dies for a God that does not exist."

"I believe God gave manna to feed His people as they fled from Pharaoh. If we have what God gave them, then maybe we can have the world eating out of our hands and we will both gain wealth and power."

"I do not know many Bible stories, but didn't Adam and Eve say a similar thing in the Garden of Eden?"

"Listen, if we have the girl, and threaten to harm her, the father will tell us all we want to know." Stock looked at the ground. "Now, my new friend, why are the Soviets so interested in Tanya?"

"We had big plans for her. She has a gift. It is called the Pravda."

"Truth?"

"Yes, Pravda is a gift of truth. She knows when someone is lying."

Stock thought for a moment, dredging through his memory, examining facts he had learned in a lifetime of research in Russian history. "I have heard of the gift. It is said that a girl is born with it every fourth or fifth generation from the far north country of Russia."

"Yes, and we think Tanya has that same gift . . . this Pravda."

"That would explain a few things, such as why she is so cold to me. She knew I was lying about wanting to help her. Yes, I can see why you want the girl so badly. Think of it: a natural gift in her ears, the genetic ability to tell when a person lies. She could give an unbelievable advantage in international security; traitors and spies could be ferreted out in minutes. Negotiations with world leaders could be maneuvered at will; every treaty and contract could be assured or rejected. In short, they could stack the deck so much that they could rule the world."

"Yes." Victor gave a silver-toothed grin. "She can help us control everything. With more like her the Soviet Union would have an unparalleled advantage. If this manna is what you say, it would make for a Soviet Union that has the world eating out of its hand."

"What do you mean by 'More like her?'"

"That, Dr. Stock, is not any interest of yours—or part of our bargain."

chapter 26

BELL'S STORY

SHANNON COULD SMELL the bacon before she and Tanya arrived downstairs for breakfast. The aroma mingled with the rich scent of coffee.

Downstairs, Tanya and Shannon found a table lined with steaming trays of creamy grits, plump pork sausages shimmering with grease, spinach omelets, potato casserole, corn muffins drizzled with wild berry sauce and a plate of Danish pastries.

Emma, bent and wearing the same apron draped around her neck that she had worn the day before, ambled to the table with a coffeepot in hand. "Sleep well?"

"Yes, thank you," Shannon said. "We slept soundly. The room is very comfortable."

Tanya brought the Bible to the table with her. She had asked Shannon for permission, and Shannon reminded her that she owned the Bible. "You can do whatever you want with it. Just remember that it's very valuable."

"That's an old Bible, young lady," Emma said. "It looks older than me and I'm ancient. How'd you come by it?"

"It fell from the sky," Tanya said.

"What?"

Shannon sipped her coffee. "It's a long story."

"I'm never too busy to hear a good story. There are only two other couples staying in the inn at the moment, and both ate early and left. It's just me and dirty dishes, so if you feel free to tell it, I'm free to hear it."

Shannon and Tanya took a sample of everything.

"What is this?" Tanya pointed to the white grainy material in a large bowl.

"It's grits. It's made from corn. You never had grits?"

"No, ma'am. Is it good?"

Emma smiled. "Most folk like it. Put some butter in it. I like a little pepper on mine, but I suggest a dash of sugar for you."

Shannon watched Tanya lift a fork full of grits to her mouth. A moment later she smiled. "It's different, but I like it."

"Do you want to tell her about the Bible, or shall I?" Shannon asked.

"You can," Tanya said as she scooped another spoonful of grits. "I'm hungry."

Shannon told as much of the tale as she felt comfortable relating. She mentioned the jet crash, but nothing about the Pravda or of Tanya's special skills.

When she finished the story, Tanya offered the Bible for Emma to examine. The old woman took the leather-bound volume and rotated it in her hands before placing it on the table. Slowly, reverently, she thumbed the pages. Shannon watched her carefully and grew concerned when the woman stopped at the front piece. Her thin hand began to shake.

"Are you all right, Mrs. Bell?"

"This . . . I don't . . . I don't know." She brought an arthritic finger to the page. "This name . . ."

"The Bible has many names in it. Which one—"

Emma didn't wait for Shannon to finish. She handed the Bible back. Shannon looked at the name that had startled the old woman. The page had a reddish-brown inscription: *Elijah Bell.* Shannon had not gone page by page through the Bible. Sir Richard Cooper had considered it so valuable that he had sent a special courier case to hold it. It was the only reason the Bible survived the jet crash. She had opened it in Colorado to examine its condition after it had been stolen from the crash site. Jeffrey Stock had examined the monk's inscription, but nothing else.

"Elijah Bell . . ." The name was familiar. The photo near the check-in desk mentioned Emma and Elijah Bell. "You think this may be the signature of your relative?"

She paled. "Oh my Lord, could it be? Could the Bible have made its way back to the old house from where it started?" She leaned on the table as if she needed the extra support. "The Bible of the Bell Messenger." She pointed at the russet stains on the edge of the pages. "The stains . . . what are they?"

"I don't know," Shannon admitted.

"Blood," Emma whispered. "Blood of the boy prophet from when he was shot in that cornfield in 1865."

"I don't understand," Shannon said.

Tanya had stopped eating. Shannon wondered if she were hearing something in the old woman's voice that no one else could hear.

"The Good Lord moves in mysterious ways." Emma poured coffee into a cup and took a sip. The cup rattled on the saucer as she lifted it.

"You know things about this Bible," Tanya said. It was a statement, not a question.

"Yes, young lady, I do believe I know a good bit." She set the cup down. "I think it is Elijah Bell's Bible from the Civil War days. It must be his Bible. It's old enough to be, that's for sure. It can't be anything else."

Tanya said, "I found two folded letters in the Bible, I have them in my room. I didn't want them to fall out and get damaged. They're so brittle and yellow. Some of the edges are crumbling off."

"Did you read them?" Shannon asked.

"Yes, but I don't understand them. I can get them if you like."

Emma brightened. "Go, child."

Tanya scurried upstairs and returned with the two letters.

Emma took them gently, as if she were handling a sun-dried butterfly's wing. She read,

To the man who kilt me.

The wind blows where it wishes and you hear the sound of it, but cannot tell where it comes from and where it goes.

So it will be with your own life.

You will surely come to find my ma's picture and try to return the Bible to her, but I want you to have the Holy Book

and be the wind that carries forth the word of our Lord and
be God's messenger as I have been.

It shall be a blessing for all that come to have this book
and read its words, for in that day they will surely save lives
and give life. But if anyone who has this book and does not
follow the Lord then I fear a dry rain cometh.

Elijah Bell
April 13, 1865

For a long while Emma sat in silence. When she did speak, she kept her eyes on the old, worn letter in her quivering hand. "Elijah Bell was just a boy, no more than fourteen, but he was reported as doing many courageous things during battles. I've heard the story many times from my mother and grandmother. My young relative carried twenty canteens slung over his shoulder to the many wounded and dying soldiers. It happened at Marye's Hill. They were believed to be unreachable, and anyone foolhardy enough to try would be mowed down in an instant, from a fusillade of shots from the lines of Yankee soldiers crouching behind a nearby stone wall. Young Elijah held this Bible to his chest and ran down the hill. The shots peppered the ground all around him, but he made it to a cannon crater without a scratch. When the Union soldiers saw that he was just a boy tossing canteens to the wounded, the Yankees stopped their shooting, and some even let out a cheer of admiration for young Elijah."

Shannon watched Emma warm with pride.

"Elijah, he never held a rifle the whole conflict with the North; all he carried was this here Bible. He was holding it the day he was shot. It was such a pity that he was shot on the last day of the Civil War." She pointed to brown stains that were once red blood. "They called him the Bell Messenger, because of his battlefield sermons and continuous shouts of prayers to the men as he ran alongside them every time they charged into battle. Many times he was seen kneeling next to a mortally wounded soul, praying over them as they breathed their last."

"The other letter," Emma asked, "what does it say?"

Tanya handed the second letter to Emma, who read it aloud.

Dearest Mother.

I will not see the morrow. My wounds received three days ago are the cause of my demise. They will send me to a better place. A man will assuredly bring my Bible to you. He is the man who kilt me, but Mother, please find the grace to forgive him. I received a whisper from my Redeemer at the very moment the man stood over me. He was to have the book. Mother, I love . . .

Emma lifted her eyes from the document. "He could not finish the letter; those were the boy's final words." She lowered the shaking page and whispered, "I was named after the woman in this letter." She handed the yellowed letter back to Tanya. "Thank you for letting me hold these, dear."

Tanya said, "They are not mine to take back. They have come back to you. The Bible is yours too."

"No, child. I will accept the letters with deepest gratitude. When I am dead and gone, our family's future children will learn of their relative Elijah Bell, and the knowledge of his story will make them proud. The Bible, however, is a different matter. Elijah gave it to the soldier who shot him. The Yankee was named Jeremiah Tate, and became the messenger when he took it. You are the messenger now, Tanya."

"Emma is right, Tanya," Shannon said. I don't know everything about the Bible, but my client briefed me on a few things. I also learned a few more things from the previous owner, Gary Brandon. From long ago, the book has been passed from person to person, and each person receives it for some unique reason known only to God. I know Tate gave it to a Chinese immigrant, who later gave it to a woman who took it to Egypt. From there, it became the possession of my client and was carried into battle during the First World War."

"Does your client lay claim to the Bible?" Emma asked.

"No, ma'am, not any longer. He died a short time ago. The family spokesman told me to give it to Tanya."

Emma touched her coffee cup but didn't lift it from the saucer. "It shall surely save lives," she whispered. "It surely gives life. Those prophetic words are from Elijah's letter."

Tanya said, "I am a little scared about owning this Bible."

"You will never own that Bible, young lady. It's only lent to you as a divine gift, as it has been lent to others in the past."

Tanya looked saddened.

"What's the matter?" Shannon asked.

"I'm confused about all that is happening. I only want one thing, and that is to see my father again. This book has done amazing things, and I now can see that, but will it . . . can the book do that for me?"

Emma answered before Shannon could speak. "The Bible is God's words breathed upon its pages. It is God's revelation of Himself to man. The book itself has no power, but the words printed inside are the most powerful force on Earth. Read the words, girl; let them seep into your soul and then call upon the One who sits upon the throne in Heaven. The answer will come. Isn't it a wonderful thing that we small creatures can petition in prayer the same God that laid the foundations of the universe?"

"I don't know if I have that kind of faith."

"You must, my dear, because it is faith that brings Heaven down to earth. Now pray and read the Bible you have been given; it is yours for a reason." Emma looked out the window as if searching for answers among the dogwoods laden with early spring buds. "Take the Bible, and take a walk. There's a park down this road. It's called Bell Park. They named it after Elijah shortly after the war. It has a message there chiseled in stone about the boy Elijah. I think you might enjoy reading it."

Tanya thought for a moment, thanked Emma for the breakfast, and walked out the front door, the Bible secure in the crook of her arm.

BELL PARK

Tanya crossed the park's patchy carpet of spring grass and sat on a bench. In front of her rested a large rock with an inscription on its smooth face. The monument was overgrown with vines, but she could still read the words. It seemed someone had recently pulled the vines away to read its stone face:

ELIJAH BELL FELL SILENT UPON THE SOD
AS ANOTHER NOW CARRIES HIS SACRED ROD.
IT WAS THE WORDS OF HIS FINAL WILL
THAT JEREMIAH TATE BE HIS MESSENGER STILL.
MOTHER, JULY 1865

Tanya had just heard about Elijah Bell being shot on the last day of the Civil War. Seeing his name on the monument, she thought of Jeremiah Tate being given the book she held and becoming the messenger. Her eyes followed the final words, *Mother, July 1865*, and found warmth in the cold, chiseled words. She opened the Bible and read a verse: "The very stones will cry out."

She wondered why all of this was happening. Even though it was all disconcerting, it was also comforting to think this was part of a divine plan, albeit a plan she didn't understand.

She was lost in tumbling thought when she heard a man's voice behind her say, "Tanya, can we talk? I have some important information about the golden snuff box."

She recognized Jeffrey Stock's voice. Before he had finished speaking, Tanya knew the man's words were a callous lie. "You're not telling the truth to me, are you?"

"Maybe you really do have a gift. Come with me now." His tone turned as hard as the stone monument.

Tanya stood and started to run, but a man stepped in her path—a large man.

"You have grown, little one."

She looked up and saw the man's silver teeth. A flood of horrible memories washed through her brain. She remembered seeing the same teeth seven years ago as she knelt next to her wounded father. "You shot my father," she said. She backed away, the Bible shielding her wildly pounding heart.

"I did, and I will shoot him again if you do not help us." He flashed his metal smile. "I might even shoot you."

She heard the truth in his words and it terrified her. She backed away. "What do you—" Before she finished the sentence, Stock covered her head with a black sack. A second later she felt herself lifted from the ground. One of the men carried her, her feet dangling a foot above the ground.

She struggled but couldn't free herself. She assumed the KGB man who was much larger than Stock was the one carrying her. She started to scream, but a large hand clamped across her mouth.

Tanya kicked, thrashed and screamed against the hand that held her mute. Tears ran down her cheeks.

She heard the creaking of a car door hinge. The large hand grabbed her skull and pushed her forward—pushed hard. She crumpled onto a vinyl seat, the hand still on her head. The sound of a car engine rumbled in her ears.

She felt the car speed off.

chapter 27

FREEDOM'S FIRST STEP

FROM HIS HARD-PLANKED bunk bed, Yuri looked at the thin band of his silver wedding ring. It was the only jewelry the commandant allowed the incarcerated to own. He slipped off his ring and removed a piece of sandpaper he had folded into his pocket, working it against the tarnished ring until he had reduced much of it to small granules. Years ago, another prisoner told him that if someone mixed silver dust with tobacco and smoked it, then was x-rayed, the film would show a shadow in the lungs that looked as if the patient had silicosis, a severe lung disease. Yuri sprinkled the silver particles onto the small pile of tobacco that he was given as his monthly ration of three cigarettes. He rolled it in thin white paper. He lit the cigarette and inhaled deeply. He felt no effect, but hoped the metallic residue had done its job.

When done, Yuri stepped from the bunkhouse and found the guard waiting in the dark as promised. He knew he'd be there since Yuri could easily let slip the truth about how much of the Yakut's cognac the guard had consumed on duty.

They didn't speak as Yuri walked slowly beneath a sky void of stars. Dark, snow-gorged clouds hid the heavens from view. Beams of light from the watchtowers sprinted along the ground. The three guard dogs barked as a flashlight beam guided Yuri and the guard across the camp. Yuri coughed again, stopping to bend over, placing his hands on his knees. It was a good act.

The warmth of the infirmary enfolded Yuri as the guard opened the door. The camp doctor sat at a small wooden desk next to one of the log sides of the medical facility. Several clean beds lined one of the walls. All but one of the beds was empty. Only the severely ill were brought here. The other patient was a man who had cut off all his fingers with an ax to avoid going into the forest to log. It didn't matter to the commandant that his fingers were gone; they told him he would have a day to recover before being sent back to the forest to cut trees with his one good hand. His quota would remain the same.

The camp was filled with men who were dying and needed medical care, but a man in bed could not work, so only the most extreme cases were admitted to the hospital. They would be forced out of bed if they could manage to walk, and if a man could walk he was expected to return to his assigned work and fill his full quotas.

The doctor looked up as Yuri and the guard entered the room. Again Yuri bent and coughed as hard as he could. He could taste the silver in his mouth. He straightened and labored to catch his breath. The doctor rose and seemed pleased to be needed. He was not like the guards who enjoyed watching prisoners suffer.

The doctor approached and did a brief exam. "He needs an X-ray. I will know better then."

"I should stay," the guard said.

"If you wish, but I may need to keep him overnight. The cough sounds serious. He may have pneumonia, or silicosis, or maybe something else . . . a disease you might catch, perhaps. There is no need for you to be here. He will be watched tonight, and if he is able to work at all, I will release him."

The guard protested. "The commandant wants this man to make a gun cabinet. He wants him to start in the morning."

"Fine," the doctor said. "He is mine tonight and yours tomorrow."

The guard glanced at Yuri and sneered.

The doctor said, "If he is to do special work for the commandant, then I must do a thorough exam. I do not wish to explain to him how I let a prisoner with a communicable disease infect him, his sister or even you."

"I will expect to retrieve him in the morning." The guard spat, then spun and stomped off.

"Take off your coat and shirt, prisoner."

Yuri did as he was told. The doctor stepped to a box of medical masks and donned one, then returned. He stopped.

"Why is it you do not reek like the other prisoners?"

"I was washed so I could work in the commandant's home."

"That explains it. What is your name?"

"Yuri. I am from Leningrad."

"Why are you here?"

"They tell me I am an enemy of the state."

"And are you?"

"No. I am a simple carpenter who needs to see his daughter again someday."

The doctor chuckled. "The KGB may have other ideas." The physician donned a stethoscope and placed the cold end on Yuri's chest. He listened for a moment. "Take a deep breath . . . let it out." He placed the metal end on Yuri's back and repeated the command. A minute later, he stepped away.

"I am here as a prisoner like you, and for a similar reason," the doctor said. "A high-ranking official was drinking and fell at his mistress's house. He hit his head on the corner of a table and died. I was the doctor who treated him. I refused to rewrite my report to say the Communist party official had died in his own home of heart problems, so they sent me here."

"You are a prisoner?" Yuri asked.

"Yes. It was a convenient and cheap way to get a doctor to camp."

The doctor led Yuri to an X-ray machine. "I'm allowed to live in the infirmary. My food is better than yours, and I'm warm most of the time. They want to keep me healthy." He set up the machine and took several images. "Take that bed over there. I must develop these."

Yuri moved to the bed and sat. It had been seven years since he'd felt a mattress beneath him; seven years since his skin had touched a clean sheet. He lay down and for a moment felt like he was hovering above the floor. He lay quietly as the other patient snored softly in his bed.

The moments moved too quickly. Yuri wanted them to last forever, but reality returned with the doctor. "You are a carpenter, a logger in the taiga, aren't you?"

"Yes." Yuri coughed hard, placing a hand to his ribs. He winced.

"Then why is it you have dark images on your lungs? Did you serve in the coal mines?"

"Yes, but most of my work has been logging."

The doctor looked at Yuri's hand. He took hold of it and ran his thumb over the area of skin discoloration where the ring had been only a short time ago.

"You ground that ring into powder filings and inhaled it with a cigarette. It is an old trick, and I have seen most all of them. Your lungs are clouded with what would appear to be grinder's disease—silicosis." He raised a finger. "Except silicosis stems from the inhalation of silica dust. We don't have much of that around here. I admire a man with a creative mind, but I am afraid all I can offer you is some fresh bread, a bowl of hot soup and a clean bed to sleep the night."

A soft tapping came from the front door. The doctor answered and Anna stood on the stoop. She wore heavy clothes, thick padded boots that were too large and the commandant's heavy goose down jacket with a fur collar. On her head rested a wool black hat with the red Soviet hammer and sickle on it. In her hand was some cubed red meat.

"What is this?" the doctor said. "More headaches?"

Yuri assumed the doctor had treated Anna before and needed no introduction.

Yuri rose and approached the doctor. He was blunt. "We are going to escape this place."

The doctor's jaw dropped. "Escape? You and the commandant's sister? No. I cannot let you do this. It is madness. Do you know what they will do to me?"

"We must, Doctor, and we have to act quickly."

Anna signed to Yuri.

"What does she say to you?" the doctor asked.

"She wants to leave this place." A second later, Yuri said, "Give us sedatives for the dogs."

"You have lost your mind, prisoner. Do you know how much danger you put this woman in?"

"The infirmary is near the entrance gates. If I had sedatives in some meat for the dogs, they would be quiet in only a few minutes. The sedatives will work on the dogs, yes?"

"Yes, and the dogs will be down for an hour or more. It is a workable plan, but for one thing, prisoner. I have to tell the authorities, or they will shoot me for collaborating."

"You can come with us."

"Then who will tend to the patients? Who will help these men in their illness?"

Yuri scratched his chin. "Doctor, I will bind your hands and feet. Someone will find you, or the man with the missing fingers will awake and yell for help."

"You are a fool. You will both die in the forest. It is deep with snow; there is a storm starting. Think of the wind, the additional snow. How will Anna survive?"

Anna tugged Yuri's arm and signed.

"What is she saying?"

Yuri translated.

She signed again. "We may live if we cross the taiga, but we are already dead in here."

Yuri could see the doctor was torn by his duty to the commandant and commitment to help others. Yuri gave him a few moments to think.

The doctor went to his closet and pulled out some rope. "Here, tie me up and do a good job. Why did you come to the infirmary? You are in the woods every day cutting wood; you could have easily escaped then."

"There are things I need," Yuri said, taking the rope.

"Yes, the sedatives. I know, but—"

"The less you know, Doctor, the better for all of us." Yuri bound the man to a chair. "Where are the pills?"

"In the cabinet behind me."

Yuri felt guilty about binding a man who was so willing to stay behind to treat prisoners who had no hope. But he had Anna to think about. Once he bound the doctor, Yuri retrieved the sedatives and placed them in the meat Anna had brought. At Yuri's direction, Anna gathered three folded white bed sheets and tucked them under her arm. He retrieved his shirt and coat. The coat was heavier than normal, made that way by the wire cutters he had stolen when he returned his ax to the toolshed.

They would have only one chance at this. They had to sneak from the infirmary, feed the dogs the drug-laced meat, wait for it to take effect, cut their way into the kennel and make their escape through the gate that led from the dog pens to the forest.

"I would appreciate some time before you call for help." Yuri motioned to the man sleeping on the bed.

"I gave him medication for pain. He will be asleep for hours."

Yuri nodded, opened the door a crack and slipped from the infirmary. Anna followed close behind.

chapter 28

GEORGIA

RAIN.

The noon Georgia rain tapped a steady drumbeat on the metal roof of the van. Victor sat behind the wheel of the old Chevy. He had been driving all night, and his weary eyes felt dry and swollen. Now he had to drive in the rain over unfamiliar territory in an old delivery van that Stock had purchased from his brother-in-law.

Stock was in the passenger seat scanning an unfolded map. Tanya sat on an oily tarp in the back of the van. Her ankle was chained to a support strut that braced the side wall of the van. Her wrists were bound with silver-colored duct tape.

Using his contacts in the Soviet embassy, Victor had arranged a meeting with a man named Carlos Avila at a marina in Miami that evening. Carlos would sail them across the Florida Straits to Havana.

The KGB had used him for several small covert operations. As long as he was paid well, he could be trusted.

Victor glanced to the cargo area of the van. Tanya sat still, staring at the van's floor. Ten military style five-gallon jerry cans of gasoline shared the space with her, as did a large cooler stuffed with ice, beer, bologna and bread. A spare tire with lug wrench rattled on the floor by the rear doors. No doubt she would like to get her hands on that lug wrench and pound her abductors with it, but the chain around her raw, red ankle was too short. An empty Folgers coffee can with a plastic lid was her only bathroom facility.

They had no intention of stopping at gas stations along their way. They wanted to avoid any place or situation where a passerby might hear a girl cry for help. They ate and drank, and when they needed to fill up on gasoline from the cans they carried, or relieve themselves, they would drive down one of the many side roads.

If they could get Tanya to Miami, they would be able to leave American waters by sailboat and after spanning a mere ninety miles, they would be safe on Cuban soil. It was an island closely allied with the U.S.S.R., a place where the girl would fetch a high reward.

For Victor, it was not only the money that motivated him. He hoped that Leonid Brezhnev, the Soviet General Secretary of the Communist Party, would bestow accolades upon him. He wanted men toasting vodka to his name; he wanted the Order of Lenin; wanted pink-faced Soviet schoolchildren to call out his name; and maybe have his name written in a history book. The politicians, the military leaders, the workers in the wheat fields would laud the man who did so much for the U.S.S.R. Perhaps then the stigma that had followed his family would be finally erased.

All this would be for giving Tanya to the Motherland. Her strange power could accurately cull out spies and dissidents in mere minutes. She would save millions of dollars in defense spending and scare the free world half to death with her abilities. No country could offer false or misleading testimony in treaty negotiations. With Tanya, Cuban and Soviet officials could hold all their cards concealed close to the vest in any negotiations venue while everyone else had to lay their naked cards face up.

Victor caught Stock staring at him. They exchanged no words. Victor's pressing desire was to direct the van down some side road, yank Stock from the passenger seat and beat him to death. He didn't consider Stock a human being but a malignant life form. Victor would do it if it weren't for those photos and negatives. If Stock turned up dead, the photos would be released, and, for now, that would be bad. Sooner or later he would be traced back to the Soviet Embassy in D.C., causing a media disaster and making their job more difficult than it already was. So, for the time being, they were in a standoff—the quintessential odd couple that formed an alliance out of fear that each could, and would, destroy the other.

Their distrust mirrored the animosity and dread shared by their countries; each survived because they feared mutual assured destruction. The thought of being swallowed in a brilliant flash of light and of having your skin vaporized in an instant had been deterrent enough for their respective governments to forgo a preemptive nuclear first strike. So it was with Stock and Victor; each man had everything to lose by attacking the other and everything to gain by forging the awkward alliance.

Stock sat with his back pressed against the torn vinyl upholstery and lit a cigarette. He seemed nervous. "We're close to the Florida border." He took another drag. "According to the map, we should arrive in Miami in five or six hours if we're lucky."

Victor curled his lip. "Luck has nothing to do with it. I have it all arranged. When we get the girl on the boat, we will soon be with my good Soviet friends in Havana." He reached to his waistband and felt the cool barrel of his Smith and Wesson .357 magnum.

"How large do you think the reward will be for bringing the girl?"

"Enough to live the rest of our lives as czars," Victor said. "Don't worry; you will soon be a very rich man. The deal has been made with the Soviet Union officials that the girl's father will be brought from his prison to Leningrad. At the same time you will take an Aeroflot flight from Havana to Moscow and then a connecting flight to Leningrad. You will show the father photos of Tanya bound and gagged with Cuban and KGB officers standing around her . . . it will be most effective, I think."

Stock smiled. "That should make the man talk. What's a snuff box compared to the love a father has for his daughter?" Stock crushed his cigarette in the already filled ashtray and lit another.

Tanya was tired and scared as she sat on the gas-splattered tarp in the back of the van, but she had some comfort knowing that the men would not kill her. She was worth nothing dead—and everything alive.

Tanya held the old Bible to her chest. It was awkward to grasp because of her bound wrists. Still she clung to it as a drowning man clings to a life preserver. For what had to be the hundredth time she told herself that she would not cooperate with these evil men no matter what, but it was a weak proclamation. She wondered what

Shannon was thinking. She must be frantic by now. Tanya had come to like and respect the woman, and considered her a friend, despite knowing her such a short time. At least she had never lied to Tanya.

Tanya felt the weathered edge of the Bible and remembered the words of Emma Bell at the bed-and-breakfast, "It shall surely save lives," she had whispered. "It surely gives life." The Bible had changed so many lives in the past. Its history was saturated with those who had been saved because of it. She closed her eyes and prayed for God to help her and let the book save her life as it had done for others.

A minute after she had said a silent "Amen," she heard a bang, a rattling and then felt the van jerk left. Something was striking the undercarriage. It took several seconds for her to realize a tire had blown out.

The car shuddered as it slowed and pulled to the side of the road.

The big man plucked the keys from the steering column. Tanya had heard Dr. Stock call him Victor.

"I will change the damaged tire." Victor looked at Stock. "Watch the girl."

Tanya noticed that the man took the keys with him, a sign that he didn't trust Stock.

Victor exited the driver's door and disappeared into the rain. A moment later, the rear doors swung open and moist air, laden with the smell of wet ground and asphalt, filled the cargo area.

Tanya stared at the man who had shot her father. Victor saw the gaze and raised his large, meaty right hand. "You make a sound, and I will crush your head like a walnut." He clenched his fist for effect, then pulled out the lug wrench and jack. He put them under his arm, then slid out the spare tire with his free hand. He shut the van doors with the swing of his hip. Tanya pressed herself to the side of the van, clinging tighter to the Bible. She quaked with fear that she had not known since the last time she was with Victor; she was seven years old then.

Stock turned in the passenger seat. "Don't move or else." She saw him lean to the side to watch Victor in the side mirror. The back of the van began to tilt with each ratchet of the jack.

Tanya moved the chain that was clamped on her ankle and winced as it grated against her raw flesh.

Stock's head swiveled back. "I told you to keep still. I don't want you to move a muscle."

Tanya said in a hushed voice, "The Russian lied when he said you will have wealth. He is planning to kill you when we get to Miami."

"Stop talking," Stock snapped.

Tanya lowered her voice to a faint whisper. "Do you really think he wants to help you? Why would he? Once he is out of America, you will be of no use to him. You are headed for a trap. I can hear it in the voice of others when they lie. The Russian is betraying you. You are being fooled and will be dead soon."

The next ten minutes passed in eerie silence, but Tanya could see her words worried Stock.

The driver's door opened suddenly. Stock jumped, startled by the Russian's sudden appearance. Victor hopped back onto the front seat, wiped the rain from his face with his plump left hand and inserted the keys into the ignition with his right.

"Wait," Stock said. "Aren't you forgetting the spare tire and jack?"

Victor said, "We won't need them anymore. They are only extra weight."

Tanya wondered if Stock would be the next item left by the road for being extra weight.

Victor cranked the engine over and stomped on the accelerator. Tanya felt the tires slip on the wet shoulder, then grab asphalt. She heard the squeal of tires. There was a violent bang and the van lurched violently to the left.

The jerry cans of gasoline and the cooler careened inside the cargo area. So did Tanya. Ice and food sloshed from the cooler. Gas fumes mingled with the humid air. Less than a second later all was silent, except for a hissing coming from the stalled engine.

Stock touched a knot on his forehead. "That was a stupid thing to do."

Victor turned the key over and over, but the engine wouldn't restart. "I could not see out the windows from all the rain." He jammed his foot on the accelerator; the van's engine struggled to start once again. The van rattled and coughed to life as Victor gunned the engine twice and then dropped it into drive. The tires spun furiously and the van fishtailed in the mud. Tanya strained to look back in one of the side mirrors. She caught a glimpse of the underside of a car as it rested on its side, its wheels still slowly rotating.

chapter 29

SCRAP MAN

MELVIN CRAMPTON, WHO had lived his entire sixty-eight years in Waverly, Georgia, was a junk man who sold mostly scrap metal. He was as stout and as hard as the steel he scavenged. He wore a flattop haircut that was trimmed once a week and always wore junkyard-stained blue jean bib overalls with *Jesus Saves* embroidered over his chest in deep crimson thread.

On Saturdays, he loaded his old Dodge pickup truck with the week's salvaged metal and covered it with a green canvas tarp. He would then drive to Brunswick and sell it to the salvage yard. On Sundays, however, he was the preacher at Christ's Church in Waverly. It was a small, faithful congregation of six people who met in a turn-of-the-century church building pieced together by salvaged wood from an old cotton warehouse outside of Savannah. The church's only two male members had painted the humble church white, and the four women members had planted flowers along the crushed stone walkway. On Sunday Melvin stood and preached like a man on fire. The people often said that on cold Georgia winter mornings they never needed heat from the potbellied stove in the corner because old Melvin's preaching was heat enough.

As Melvin drove up Interstate 95, from behind his slapping windshield wipers he saw a green Ford Fairlane 500 resting on its side near the shoulder of the road. A crowd of about ten people had already stopped to help. Cars lined the side of the road. Melvin steered his truck over to the weedy shoulder. A police car coming from the opposite direction cut across the wet, grassy median and slid to a stop next to the crashed car. The car's siren faded to silence, but the red and blue lights continued to twirl.

Melvin climbed from his truck and trotted to the upended vehicle, arriving at the same time as the trooper. Both bent down and looked at the driver through the spiderweb cracks in the windshield.

"Are you hurt?" the policeman asked.

Blood smeared the man's face. "I'm pinned in. I can't feel my legs."

"Hold on," the young cop shouted. "I'll call for an ambulance."

Melvin returned to his truck, pulled a half-inch piece of galvanized pipe from the truck bed, and returned to the Ford. "Cover your face."

The injured man put his hands over his eyes. Melvin swung the pipe into the windshield. It splintered but did not break free. Melvin hit it two more times.

Melvin tossed the pipe aside and leaned into the vehicle. He unbuckled the man's seatbelt. The officer returned. "What are you doing? You can't—"

"I'm gonna pull back on the steering wheel," Melvin said. "It's got his legs pinned to the seat. I won't be able to move it much, but it should budge some. When I do, you help the guy out. Got it?"

"Maybe we should wait for the ambulance—"

"Got it?" Melvin didn't raise his voice, but he managed to put more weight in the two words.

Melvin took hold of the wheel, placed his shoulder at the spot where windshield met the car's hood and pulled. He managed to pull the wheel back two inches, freeing the trapped man. A minute later, with the help of the officer and two bystanders, the man was free. He was able to stand, but looked pale and moments away from passing out.

"I'm a nurse." A woman with a blanket brushed past Melvin. Melvin stepped back, wiping blood on his overalls.

The officer stood and shouted over the rain peppering his yellow rain slicker, "Anyone see this accident?" His words were shaky, and Melvin guessed the man had to be fairly fresh from the police academy.

A young female witness pointed down the road. "A white van pulled right in front of this man's car and they hit real hard. The van split, going that way."

"You get a license number?" the cop asked.

The young woman said, "Well, it all happened so fast, it's hard to see much from your car when a thing like that happens."

"Did you see the driver?"

"Yes, but only for a second or two. He was a big man. That's all I could see. Oh, and I think another guy was in the passenger seat."

The officer stepped back to his police car, got in and grabbed the radio's microphone. Melvin couldn't hear what he was saying, but he could guess. He picked up the galvanized pipe he had tossed aside.

Melvin could see the muddy tire trench where the van had clawed its way onto the Interstate. He could see a discarded hubcap, a car jack and lug wrench next to it. "Who changes a tire and leaves the hub and jack?" He knew he could get at least ten bucks for them at the salvage yard.

The cop hollered at Melvin, "Get away from there; that's evidence."

Melvin nodded, and stepped to the edge of the asphalt. He could see where the muddy trail had left the road, where the clods of undercarriage gunk had dislodged from beneath both cars as they smacked into each other.

Melvin waited for two eighteen-wheeler rigs to pass, then stepped a few feet onto the highway. He saw bits of metal strewn about and could see where the Fairlane's driver had slammed on its brakes before striking the other vehicle. There was a mosaic of white paint particles, busted headlight glass and the light green film of antifreeze mingling with the rain. The antifreeze trailed off to the south. He heard a truck's shrill blast and shuffled off to the safety of the road's shoulder. The passing trucker sizzled through the wet road and shouted something through his window.

Melvin walked to the officer who stood outside the patrol car's driver's door. He looked as much in shock as the victim. He stood motionless, holding the microphone at the end of a stretched coil of black wire.

"If you got just a minute, I think I can help in this, young man."

The frazzled officer stammered, "Do I look like I have any time for you asking questions?" He turned and rattled off something in the mike about a tow truck.

Melvin walked back to his truck, getting in with the intent to head up the 95 to the scrap yard in Brunswick, but instead he turned the pickup around and followed a line of radiator fluid.

The green trail thinned to just the occasional streaks nearly washed into oblivion by the rain. Of course, the van had a limited amount of fluid in the radiator and was sure to bleed out soon. But that was the beauty of it. Once the coolant was gone, the van's engine would overheat and die. It couldn't be very far from the last drops of antifreeze. The thin trailing line veered from the highway and onto the side road. Melvin followed on the dirt—now mud—lane. He didn't need a trail of coolant here; the tire tracks in the mud would do the job. It was a winding road, dotted with large patches of weeds indicating that few people used it. Around the bend, Melvin saw a white van billowing steam from under the hood. Two men were inspecting the badly damaged right side. Melvin could see the wheel with the missing hubcap. The men turned to face him.

Melvin stopped the truck, picked up the pipe he used to break the windshield of the Fairlane from his front seat, exited and studied the two men in front of him. He kept his hands behind his back. They seemed an odd pair. One was large and brutish; the other reminded Melvin of a schoolteacher. The large one fidgeted with something under his belt. "You boys ain't from around here, are ya?"

Neither man answered.

Melvin motioned with his head to the plates on the van. "Those plates you all have were taken from another vehicle, weren't they?"

Again the men said nothing.

"You boys don't say much, do ya? Well, I have a bucket mouth and am fine with doing all the talking." Melvin clasped his hands behind his back and rocked his torso like he was about to let go with one of his fiery sermons. "It seems you boys ought to know that it's a crime here in Georgia to hit someone and then just up and drive on off. That ol' boy in the Ford is hurt, and I must insist you boys stay put till the police can get a proper accounting of what went on back there."

The large man pulled a gun from beneath his coat, pointed it at Melvin and stepped close. Melvin felt the barrel in his ribs. "We want your truck."

"That a fact?" Melvin twisted quickly and brought his hand around. The half-inch pipe hit its mark, breaking the big man's thumb. Melvin heard the bone snap like a dried cottonwood twig. The gun fell at Melvin's feet. He kicked it across the slimy mud and down the side of a drainage ditch that ran next to the road. The ditch was choked with moss, tangled vines, and tall grass.

"Now the way I look at it, boys, I'm no match for you two, but then again, I had me a little training from Uncle Sam. I was in Company A of the 116th Regiment in World War Two. I was in the first wave on Omaha Beach. Ninety percent of our boys died that day, and I am not ashamed to admit I killed a parcel of German boys. That was the way of war, that's the way with all evil—it must be killed. In the end God always vanquishes the evil ones, so I have little to fear from the pair of you." Melvin gripped the pipe tighter; his eyes scanned the situation.

Victor stared down at his broken thumb that looked like a bent nail pulled by a claw hammer from an old board. He growled and lunged at Melvin. Melvin stepped to the side and brought the pipe came down even harder on Victor's collarbone, shattering it like a dropped clay pot. The man fell to the ground, moaning in pain. Melvin shook his head. "It's a bad trait to be so stubborn as to not learn a lesson the first time around."

The other man bent over and threw up. Melvin chuckled. "God got your attention, didn't He, boy?" He moved closer to the van. "Normally I would not be so harsh with visitors, and the good Lord will surely be disappointed that I didn't turn the other cheek, but I am sure the Lord will forgive me."

The man fainted.

He heard a muffled cry from the back of the van and took a step to the rear curtained windows, and peeked through a gap in the cloth. He saw a girl, her ankle shackled and her wrists bound. She held a Bible. "Holy Moses!"

Melvin flung the rear doors open. The girl yelped.

"I am here to help you, child."

Tanya reached out with her bound arms, and said, "They're taking me to Havana."

Melvin took the Bible, his mind whirring with confusion. Melvin slipped the old black book into the front of his bibbed overalls. It slid down and rested on his pouching stomach. He started to lift a knee to get in the van and free the girl when he heard the sound of shoes squishing in the mud behind him. He then felt the weight of the large man as he fell hard on him. A hand clamped around Melvin's throat and closed like a vise. Melvin shoved an elbow into the man's face. He screamed with the pain and released his grip.

Melvin spun, looked and saw the man's face twist in pain. An ear-splitting explosion rang in Melvin's ears as the white orb of his attacker's eyeball turned into pink mist. The big man fell to the muddy ground, an empty cavity draining a stream of blood where his eye used to be.

The smaller man stood swaying in the downpour. He loosely held a muddy gun that trailed a wisp of thin white smoke. His hands shook. He raised the weapon and pointed it at Melvin. The mud-swathed gun recoiled, and the scrap man felt a driving force knock him backward. A horrible pain spread in his chest. He staggered, dropped to his knees then fell to the cold ground.

chapter 30

CARLOS

CARLOS READIED THE yacht for the KGB officer's arrival. This would be easy money. The G2, the Cuban special police, would be waiting with a fifty-thousand-peso pay-off.

Carlos knew why they didn't hire a sleek boat with musclebound engines that could fly across the ocean. The U.S. Coast Guard took an unhealthy interest in such craft. They seldom showed interest in such an innocuous-looking, small pleasure boat as his. The ocean was filled with sailboats, most every one manned by owners seeking the joys of the sea and smuggling nothing more than a few boxes of Cuban cigars. Some, however, carried more valuable items than a few boxes. Carlos had just made the passage with a hundred boxes of Holo de Monterrey double coronas and three hundred boxes of Partagas Lonsdales. Not a great living for anyone, but a handsome profit for only a couple of days' work.

Carlos also used the *Teresa Ann* to smuggle fleeing emigrants. Many a night he waited in the inky blackness off the Cuban coast as would-be escapees walked across the lonely beach littered with the debris coughed up by the sea: plastic bottles, coconuts and old Styrofoam floats bearded with green sea growth on one side. They would enter the dark waters, cross jagged coral reefs and make their way to a waiting black rubber Zodiac manned by Carlos. If all went well, he would row them to his anchored sailboat.

Peasants wanting to flee Castro were usually dirt farmers trying to eke out a living on a small patch of land. The property was often owned by another. These desperate souls sought freedom and opportunity across the ninety-mile stretch of ocean to Key West, Florida, choosing the only means available to them. Some floated across the Florida Straits on rickety woven-palm rafts, or inner tubes lashed together, or anything else that would carry the weight of a human being. The makeshift boats were floating death traps, tracked by hungry sharks looking for an easy meal. Many never made it to America, but thousands did.

Once in Florida, the refugees would have a welcoming family member or friend to stay with. For most, it was well worth their entire savings to get to the land of the free. But most of the older men and women preferred to stay in Cuba; they didn't have the strength or the will to make a living in America. In Castro's Cuba they would get their *libreta*, a ration book that entitled them to a certain amount of meat and fish each month. But in Cuba entitlements were not the same as guarantees, and many went hungry. For these the short span of the Straits of Florida was too much of a temptation, even if it meant risking prison or execution.

Carlos had emigrated from Cuba twenty years before and was now a U.S. citizen. He hated Castro for destroying his homeland, but hated the Americans just as much for letting his brother die on a beach during the Bay of Pigs operation in 1961. Most of his business involved smuggling cigars, rum, humans and anything else except drugs. Drug smuggling was done by dirty, unprincipled men, and drug dealers were executed, or went to jail never to be seen again.

Carlos had contacts in the highest levels of the Soviet Embassy in Havana and also in G2. He brought them American liquors, fine clothes, even family members who had emigrated to the U.S. and wanted a return surreptitious visit. For these services and others, he was rewarded with a blind eye from port authorities when he entered Hemingway Marina in Cuba.

For Carlos, the job would be simple. He was to transport the girl across the sea and deliver her to a Dr. Pablo Ramirez, head of the Cloning, Trans-Genetics and Biotechnology Research Center in Havana. Dr. Ramirez sent a return message to Carlos saying that he was eager to examine the girl that had this "special gift in her ears."

Stock walked down the dock at Dinner Key with the gun barrel shoved hard into Tanya's side.

"Be a good girl; be a smart girl." He released some pressure on the barrel when he saw a sailboat named *Teresa Ann* tied to the dock.

A Hispanic man stood on the deck holding a motor-oil-smeared rag. His hairy belly slung below his shrunken grease-stained tank top. His shaggy side hair stuck out clownlike as it clung to a balding sun-browned head. "Are you Victor?"

"No, Victor had an unfortunate accident and is no longer with us."

"Do you mean he's dead?"

"Sadly so."

Carlos looked at the gun against Tanya's ribs, and said, "I am Carlos, and I expect to be paid the same amount of pesos, even though I now have one fewer passenger to take to Cuba."

"You will."

"*Bueno.* Let's go."

Stock nudged Tanya to the edge of the dock, and the girl let out a shrill scream. In a blur Stock raised his free hand and clamped the girl's windpipe closed and shoved the barrel into her back. "I will kill you if you make another sound." The girl bit down hard on his hand and inhaled to scream again, but Carlos grabbed her shirt collar and pulled her onboard. A second later he stuffed the greasy rag in her mouth. Her eyes went wide, her back arched and her nostrils flared to take in oxygen. Carlos barked, "Manny, vamoose."

A black-haired teenager, whom Stock guessed to be sixteen years old, bounded from the cabin and untied the ropes tethering the boat to dock-mounted cleats. He wore only cut-off blue jeans and frayed deck shoes. After he hopped back onboard, he quickly stepped to the stern and tugged the thin rope from the top of the twenty-horse-power Evinrude mounted to the back of the boat. The small engine coughed out white puffs of exhaust, then rattled to life.

The engine's throttle vibrated in the boy's brown hand and the dark bay water frothed, churned to life by the propeller. The craft moved slowly away from the dock, passing rows of luxury yachts and motored into the darkness of the bay.

Manny took the *Teresa Ann* across Biscayne Bay and far from the outer coral reef, then took a southern tack. Once clear of the bay, the sails were set and filled with a balmy wind. The sleek hull slipped effortlessly through the inky waters under a moonless and star-clustered night sky.

Carlos removed the dirty rag from the girl's mouth and stripped off the tape around her wrists. "No one will hear you out here, and I would guess you're smart enough not to try and swim away."

Tanya pulled free from the man and grabbed the rope lifeline that ran the perimeter of the boat. "I will jump if you come close."

Carlos laughed. "Jump, if you must; it will only make the sharks happy."

"Sharks in the water; sharks on the boat. What difference does it make?"

"You are a clever girl." He walked to her and gently ran his knuckles under her chin. "You will soon be in Cuba, where women obey men and show proper respect."

Tanya spat in his face.

Carlos cocked his hand to slap her, but stopped when he heard Stock shout, "Don't do it. I want to deliver her unharmed." He still held the gun.

"Manny, take the girl below and lock her up."

"*Sí*," Manny said, then set the wheel to maintain course, rose and approached Tanya. He took a different tack. "This way, please."

"I assume your deckhand can be trusted," Stock said.

"He wouldn't be on the boat if he couldn't. He's worked for me for four years. He's loyal and does his duties without complaint. He never gets drunk, is always alert and he's very smart."

Carlos stepped to the ship's wheel and placed his hands on it. "Four years ago, Manny was a student in the Lenin School for the very bright. He excelled in biology, math, chemistry and physics. One day he came home from school and his father told him that he, his mother, two sisters and the family dog were to escape Cuba on a raft that his father had made out of rope-lashed Styrofoam and inner tubes. His father had assured them it was safe. His father made a poor forecast. After seven hours on the sea, the sky darkened."

"A storm?" Stock fingered the gun.

"A bad storm, with squalls of fifty knots or more and swells ten of feet. Makeshift rafts are no match for an angry sea."

"Sounds like a lousy way to die."

"Do you know of a pleasant way? Death is death. Hunger makes men risk their lives."

"It seems an extreme act for just being hungry."

Carlos paused, then said, "All change comes only when one's pain supersedes the will to resist. I'm sure you have never known such pain, have you?"

Stock didn't answer.

Carlos went on, "The craft was capsized. Manny held onto an inner tube, but the waves separated him from his family. I came by and plucked Manny from the sea. The kid had spent two days floating alone in the water. He's been with me ever since."

"A touching story." Stock saw Carlos staring at his pistol.

"A gun in the hands of a nervous man is a very dangerous thing."

"I'm not nervous at all."

"If you say so," Carlos said. He didn't sound convinced.

Manny took Tanya down narrow steps that were in front of the mast to a lower cabin.

"Do you speak English?" she asked him.

"Yes, a little." He opened a varnished, louvered teak door and pointed to a wedge-shaped V-berth that had two bunks. One was covered in engine parts and a small barnacle-crusted anchor. The other bunk had a filthy blanket over a thin vinyl cushion absent of any pillow. The cramped space stank of fuel and oil.

Tanya stepped in and slowly climbed on the bunk, pushing away a rusted wrench. "Where are we going?" She knew the answer but wanted to test the boy's knowledge and English skills.

"I think you already know. You heard the captain say he was taking you to Cuba. It is not far." The boy paused. "I will make sure you are safe."

"You tell the truth, but I doubt you will be much help to me."

Her words seemed to wound him. Manny turned and closed the door behind him. She heard him lock it. She began to sob.

Manny returned to the helm and Carlos told him to set a heading for Hemingway Marina. The boy took the stainless-steel wheel and followed a heading on the compass. They were running dark, the only lights being the twinkling stars above and the green glow of the compass mounted on the console in front of Manny. The one other light was the intermittently bright red tip of Stock's smoldering cigarette.

Carlos sat on a hatch and motioned for Stock to join him. He held up a bottle of Pribluda rum. "This is Cuban rum, my friend. It's not as sweet as a woman's lips, but it is much more sincere."

Stock took the bottle, unscrewed the cap and took a long swig. It burned from his sinuses to the bottom of his belly.

Carlos took his turn at the bottle, then looked up. "All these stars—aren't they magnificent?"

"They are nothing of consequence, only faraway burning balls of gas."

"Ah, I see you are not a romantic." Carlos returned his gaze to Stock. "It is sad to not see the worth of what God has given us as a gift."

"I am about to show the world the greatest of gifts from God."

"And what is that?"

Stock took another drink of rum. "Manna."

"Manna?"

"Yes, Food from Heaven."

Carlos chuckled. "I see you are a man who believes in God but also lives like the devil."

"If I am the devil, then who are you?"

"Ah, a fine question. I am a rogue by family tradition. My grandfather was good friends with Al Capone. It was the 1920s, when Prohibition brought many thirsty tourists to Havana. My grandfather helped Capone with illegal molasses and Cuban rum, but when Capone got too old for such a life, my father took over the family business and worked with several Mafia dons in America. After the Second World War there was much sin in Havana; gambling houses brought narcotics and prostitution. All made possible by the support of our ex-president Fulgencio Batista, who turned blind eyes to organized crime."

Carlos stared over the dark ocean, then drew another mouthful of rum. "The Mafia had free rein in Havana and anything could be bought. No one believed it could end."

"Until 1959," Stock said.

Carlos said, "You know about our history."

"I know about the Soviet Union and that means I know something about Cuba. Go on."

"In 1959 the shabbily attired *barbudas* rolled into town, led by Fidel Castro, who was sitting triumphantly upon a rumbling tank. Eventually he closed the casinos, shut down five hundred years of our island's prosperity, and left us with only rumba music and cigars." Carlos spat on the deck. "My family lost everything, and my father was shot. Many of his friends were rounded up and killed. It is the way Communists work when they come into any country. The hopes and dreams of all become nothing but shadows."

Stock passed the time drinking with Carlos. Halfway through the second bottle, he began to feel the full effect of the alcohol. The boat rolled in a way that had nothing to do with the sea. "You tell . . . a good story . . . I'm . . . tired." The bottle slipped from his hand and rolled onto the deck. Stock's last memory of that moment was falling and the taste of salt as his face met the damp deck.

Carlos bounded down the stairs and unlocked the cabin door. Tanya sat up from the grimy vinyl-covered mattress and wiped away some trailing tears.

"The fool that brought you here is unconscious. What do you know of this man?"

"I know he lies all the time."

"That I already know. Tell me something else of the man."

"He intends to do harm to me."

Carlos said, "He has already done you great harm," then locked the door.

chapter 31

HOSPITAL

A TALL, UNIFORMED POLICE officer stood at the threshold of Brunswick Hospital room 223. His arms were crossed, and his feet spread, striking a commanding, don't-mess-with-me pose. He spoke with a voice that sounded as if he gargled with gravel. "Only medical personnel are allowed in."

Shannon said, "I understand that, Officer, but we were told to meet Special Agent Frank Smith here."

A voice came from behind the room's curtain just inside the door. "Let them in, Officer."

The policeman stepped aside, and Shannon and Murk entered as the curtain slid open. Reclining in the bed was a large man in his late sixties. He was naked from the waist up and an oxygen tube rested beneath a nose that looked like a sun-dried tomato. The man's eyes were narrow slits and the skin on his face hung in pale folds.

"Hello, and welcome to the party," he said. His voice was weak.

Shannon said hello back. Murk just offered an obligatory smile in return.

A man in a gray suit lifted his hand, holding a black leather identification holder. "I am Special Agent Smith out of the Savannah office. Thank you for coming." After shaking hands, Smith glanced down at Melvin. "This is Melvin Crampton. He took a pretty hard jolt to the chest, but the docs say he should be fine in no time."

"What happened?" Shannon asked.

"I was shot," Melvin said.

"Maybe you should let me do most of the talking, Mr. Crampton." Smith returned his attention to Shannon and Murk. "The assailant used a hollow-nose thirty-eight-caliber slug, which embedded in Mr. Crampton's sternum. Fortunately it didn't go any farther. He's a pretty lucky fellow."

"Luck had nothing to do with it. I'm protected by mighty angels; abundantly blessed by our Lord and Savior Jesus Christ." He looked at the ceiling as if he could see through it and into Heaven. "God knew I had more to do, so He kept me in this mortal state a little longer."

Shannon looked at the red-stained gauze covering the middle of Melvin's chest. It made her queasy.

Agent Smith continued. "Here's the interesting part: he had an old weathered Bible in his bib overalls and the book took the round, slowing it enough that it couldn't push through the man's chest bone. If not for that Bible, we would be having this discussion in the morgue." He looked at Melvin. "Sorry about that last comment, but it's a miracle you weren't killed."

"The Bible is my shield; I shall not be vanquished by mine enemy's arrows that are slung against me."

"Is it possible to see the Bible?" Shannon asked.

Agent Smith lifted a briefcase from the floor, set it on the empty bed in the two-bed room and removed a clear plastic evidence bag containing a book. He handed it to Shannon.

Shannon gasped and her legs went weak. She had no doubts that the Bible in the evidence bag was the same one she had handled over the previous days. She fought back tears as she thought of Tanya. She was frantic at her disappearance—had thought of nothing else since she went missing. "That's the Bible, that's . . ." Her eyes then fixed on the upper right edge of the book, where she saw a small hole that pierced both covers and pages.

"That book slowed a bullet that would have killed me for sure."

"Mr. Crampton . . ." Shannon was having trouble speaking. "A girl, a young teenager, had this Bible just yesterday. Did you . . . I mean . . ."

"That vermin has the girl. I saw her. I was just about to free her when I took the shot in the chest. I don't remember anything after that."

"But she was alive?" Shannon pressed.

"Yes, she was alive all right. She was in a van that was involved in a hit-and-run up the interstate."

Agent Smith spoke up. "After Mr. Crampton was shot yesterday afternoon, he lay unconscious for about six hours until a cotton farmer came by. He brought Melvin here. From the vehicle identification number on the engine and dash, we think we have a suspect: Jeffrey Stock. The plates didn't belong to the VIN number. We tracked them to a car owner who reported them stolen from a shopping center near where Stock lives. The van was sold to Stock by his brother-in-law."

"We know him, all right," Murk said. "I didn't think he would do such a crazy thing as abduct a girl."

"What can you tell me about him?"

Murk cocked his head. "He works for—maybe I should say worked for—the Institute for Soviet Studies. He has a lot of classified information about the U.S.S.R. and U.S. counterintelligence."

"Could he be a risk to American security if he goes over to the Soviets?"

"I believe so. His superiors at the ISS would know better," Murk said.

Shannon felt ready to explode. "What about the girl? What about Tanya? Do you know where they're taking her?"

"We think he and a Russian embassy worker were headed for Florida."

Murk raised an eyebrow. "Embassy worker? How do you know that?"

"We have his body, all two hundred sixty pounds of him, less an eye and some brain matter. He had a diplomatic ID that gave us his name: Victor Ivanovich Pochinko, a KGB agent working under the guise of cultural attaché at the Soviet Embassy in D.C."

"Hey, I just remembered," Melvin interrupted. "When that girl handed me the Bible, she said something about being taken to Havana. I guess she thought saying that and giving me the Bible would help in identifying her or something."

"Havana." The agent rubbed his chin. "I guess they went from Key West . . . or maybe Miami, if they wanted to get to Cuba. It's only ninety miles from Key West to Havana. A slow boat can get them there in a night's travel; a fast one in just hours." He looked at his watch. "They could be there by now."

"Oh dear Lord," Shannon said. "I should never have let her go to the park by herself. I shouldn't have let her out of my sight, not for a second. This is all my fault."

Murk put an arm around her. "Take it easy, Shannon. This isn't over yet. Have a little of that faith you always talk about."

The words didn't help. Shannon had been condemning herself ever since she realized Tanya had gone missing. She had searched the park, called the police and even called David Murk. "We need to tell you about Tanya."

"What is it?" Agent Smith said.

"First, I need the Bible. Can you take it out of the bag?"

"You know I can't do that. This is evidence in an abduction, murder and attempted murder case."

"Don't forget they stole my truck," Melvin said.

"I'm an attorney. I know about the rules of evidence; in fact, that book has been evidence before this. If you don't want it to be evidence in the girl's death, then let me have it now."

"What are you saying?"

"I can't explain it all now, but the Bible seems to help the one who has it."

"I don't understand," Smith said.

"You will," Shannon said. "You certainly will. The Bible—please give it to me. It is the only way to get her back."

"How can a Bible do that?"

"I've been asking that question since I first learned about it." She held out her hand.

Smith gave her the Bible.

chapter 32

HAVANA

HEMINGWAY MARINA

THE MORNING BROUGHT a salmon-colored sunrise, with shards of orange light fanning out behind a bank of tropical clouds. Stock had slept on cushions in the back of the boat, an empty rum bottle next to him. His eyes struggled to focus. He rubbed his throbbing head as the bottle rolled back and forth on the deck in the rhythm of each swell. His dry tongue made its way across teeth that felt moss-covered. Rum had its pleasures, but they came with a price.

Struggling to his feet, he took a moment to get his footing. He gazed over the bow, and for the first time in his life saw the shoreline of a Communist country. He had read much about Cuba, read of the wars, the ebb and flow of power, the greed and disarray of its several ruling governments.

When the small sailboat finally reached the marina's white entrance markers, Carlos started up the auxiliary outboard engine while Manny lowered the mainsail. Carlos picked up the hand-held VHF radio. Although not fluent, Stock knew enough Spanish to get the gist of the message. "Hemingway Marina, this is the *Teresa Ann*."

"Proceed in, *Teresa Ann*, and stop at customs dock. Special Police are waiting for you. You have papers waiting for your passengers."

Ten minutes later, Carlos eased the sailboat to the dock, where the bow gently bumped the rough wood pier. Manny jumped off with a bowline in hand and looped it around a rusted cleat. He then stepped quickly to the stern, where Carlos tossed him another rope. Once the craft was tied off, several men who waited at the dock helped the two passengers and crew disembark.

Before Tanya and Stock were escorted to an old '48 Studebaker, a man in green military fatigues handed a white envelope to Carlos. He lifted the envelope's flap. Inside was a stack of ragged-edged bills. He thumbed the pesos. "I can buy a whole shipment of cigars with this. In three days I will be in Miami once again and will have doubled my money."

"Capitalist pig," the soldier said. He spat on the ground.

Carlos laughed and taunted the soldier by waving the envelope back and forth. "Yes, a well-fed pig, at that."

Stock sat in the back of the battered Studebaker. Tanya was wedged between him and a KGB agent. The prerevolution American car had been poorly painted with a brush: bright red with yellow trim. A red star was painted on the sun-cracked dashboard. The car's metal skin was dimpled in a crude attempt at some body-and-fender work with the aid of a ball-peen hammer. The liner overhead was torn and ragged, as were the side panels. The seat springs did their best to escape.

At the marina, the KGB agent introduced himself as Arkady Fooks. He had unruly eyebrows and a shaved head with ever-present beads of sweat. The driver, a young man, wore a Che Guevara T-shirt and drove adroitly around potholes in the ill-repaired asphalt road. Manny and Carlos were crammed in the front seat.

Stock's head continued hurting from being saturated with rum the night before, and a jarring ride in a car packed with adults wasn't making him feel any better.

Trees along Fifth Avenue abated the heat somewhat, but not enough to make traveling comfortable. They were entering old Havana, passing mansions that once housed wealthy owners, but they had all fled, died in prison or been shot. Jungle growth had taken over untended lawns. The sidewalks were crumbling and the buildings sported soot-blackened roof tiles.

Arkady turned his head. "What happened to my good comrade Victor Ivanovich?"

Stock's chest tightened. "He died in a car accident. It was most unfortunate."

Arkady looked at Tanya. "Is that true?"

"No. He's lying."

Arkady placed his hand on her knee and gently squeezed. "Yes, you will be most useful to us, and as far as Victor is concerned, he was seldom useful. It is better for all that he is dead—it is of no concern to me how he died."

The Studebaker belched a trail of black smoke as it moved along Malecón, Havana's seaside drive. A high seawall buttressed crashing waves that rolled in from the Florida Straits. As they drove along up the six-lane boulevard, Stock could hear the sucking sounds of approaching waves, followed by the rumbling slap of the ocean's swells against the sea wall. The surf hit with a pounding fury, and the bludgeoning waves sent up a high frothy plume of spray. The swirling mist of salt water speckled the windshield as they drove past.

There were few cars on the wide oceanfront, and what cars did use the boulevard were a mix of Russian Ladas and old pre-revolution American-made classics.

Dark-skinned old men fished from the wall with long cane poles. Boys sat under a cluster of banana trees, selling homemade fishing lures and hooks that they filed and hammered out of scrap metal. Three women, wearing yellow, blue and red scarves on their heads and plastic sandals on their black feet, sat on a bench and waved to the car as it passed. The women clenched big cigars in their teeth.

Under a royal palm, young girls made shaved ice and held up bottles of red and green syrup for potential customers to inspect. Stock's throat constricted when he saw a hammer and sickle painted on the side of a building. The red paint was peeling, but it was nonetheless imposing.

Stock said, "I can't wait to smoke a Cuban cigar," as he placed his last American-made cigarette between his lips. The buildings in the area had been assaulted by the relentless sea winds. The once-proud cement façades had become nothing but dull, crumbling exteriors. The only bright colors visible came from laundry draped over rusting ornate wrought-iron balconies or from the many scarlet bougainvillea plants that tumbled over the lips of clay pots resting in the many apartment porticos.

Where there was a rare painted cement surface to be found, it was a hodgepodge patchwork of colors drawn from leftover paint cans. One building's color scheme combined lime and a forest green, much of which bled into a light turquoise.

Arkady turned to Tanya. "You will be taken to a good hotel with running water that is heated. You will rest there, and then we will go talk to some people who want to help you."

She shook her head and said dispassionately, "Your words are completely false—nothing but lies."

Arkady smiled. "Good! Victor could be an incompetent fool at times, but he seems right about you and your gift."

They turned at the end of the sea wall and entered Havana Harbor. As they did, they passed a man in a small boat pulling a fish from the bay with his cane pole.

"I have read," Stock said, "that the bay is polluted from Castro's oil refineries dumping crude oil in the water; I wouldn't eat those fish if I were them."

"The bay has been cleaned of all the oil by Castro, with the help of Soviet engineers." Arkady said. He pointed to the many people in small boats fishing. "See, the waters are clean now; the people, they are all fishing."

"The water is not cleaner, my Soviet friend; I think it may be that the people are just hungrier," Stock said.

Despite his criticism, Stock marveled at the thick verdant foliage that passed by. He had never seen such a fertile land as this. The mangroves along the water's edge, the wide fanning ferns, the tall belly palms and the graceful butterfly jasmine belied the harsh conditions in the city. Three egrets lifted from their nest along the bay, their ivory-colored wings contrasting with the dark smoke spewing from a distant sugar refinery.

The car turned right on a street lined with plain buildings that looked like little more than concrete boxes with dirty and cracked glass fronts. The car pulled to a stop, and a man in a green uniform bounded down the tilting stone steps. At the top of the steps, a man in a white medical coat waited.

He greeted the group with a hearty "*Hola*." He shook hands with Arkady first, then with Stock. "I am Dr. Ramirez. I've been looking forward to meeting you, especially you, Tanya. I have heard about you from Victor Pochinko—"

"He's dead," Arkady said bluntly.

"Oh, really. Such a shame," Ramirez said, then changed subjects as if the news held no importance. "I apologize for the smell. Unfortunately our refrigeration is not working. It's been three days now." He looked at the sun. "It always stops working during hot spells as this. We have over ten animals ready for autopsies and this heat . . . well, I'm sure you noticed." He looked at Tanya. "I am sorry to speak of such disagreeable matters. Please come to my office and enjoy real coffee from the good earth of our Cuba."

Dr. Ramirez led Tanya to his office. Stock followed close behind. They passed through a room lined on one wall with wood shelves holding clear jars of animal organs. There was a white enamel cabinet on the other wall, along with a sink, refrigerator and freezer. And in the middle of the room sat a stainless steel table with a dead lamb on its surface, its eyes dull, its extruding tongue gray and crawling with black flies.

The smell made Tanya nauseous. The doctor gave no indication he noticed the repugnant odor. He spoke in fast but stilted English. "I have good news: we will accept help here in return for a good life for you in our beautiful Cuba."

Tanya frowned. She was growing weary of the lies and the way everyone tested her. "You're lying."

The doctor stopped and placed his hands on his hips. "I do not lie. I am head of the head of the Cloning, Trans Genetics and Biotechnology Research Center here in Havana."

Tanya rolled her eyes.

Dr. Ramirez pursed his lips. "Maybe you are just more clever than we think, or maybe you really do not have this gift as Victor said."

Tanya remained silent.

"What will you do with the girl?" Stock asked.

"We have been working secretly for years to clone a sheep, and we now have successfully done it."

"A sheep? No one has ever cloned anything. It simply is not possible."

"It *is* possible, or we would not have done it. Now that we have cloned a sheep, we will be able to clone a human soon, maybe in as few as ten or twenty years at the most. The Soviets are funding us with all that we need."

"I follow Soviet matters very closely," Stock said. "I've never heard of this."

"Let me explain in my office." He led them through the office entrance. The space was large but lacked any decoration, with only anatomical charts of pigs, cows, sheep and humans hanging from dull walls. He motioned to a pair of chairs opposite his desk. Arkady stood next to the wall by the door.

Ramirez sat behind the desk, which was stacked neatly with files and reports. He interlaced his fingers and gently rested his hands on his desk. "I can see you doubt my claims." He smiled. "You are not the first and you will not be the last." He leaned forward. "Be honest with me, Dr. Stock—the real problem is that you can't believe that such cutting-edge research could be done in a backward country like Cuba. Am I right?"

"It's just that such technology hasn't been achieved in . . ."

"More advanced countries?"

"Yes."

Dr. Ramirez explained. "The Germans had created fission in 1938, a couple of years before World War Two. Fission, as we know, is the basic advancement necessary to the making of an atomic bomb. The Nazis had many scientists working on creating the nuclear device, and took a wide lead on the Americans. Fearing Hitler would be the first with such a bomb and knowing he would not hesitate to use it, the Americans put unlimited resources in creating an atomic bomb first."

Tanya sensed Stock's discomfort. She also knew Ramirez was telling the truth.

"How do you know about all this?"

"At the end of the war, an Allied science intelligence unit captured several German nuclear scientists, along with equipment and top secret research papers. For ten months, ten German scientists involved in the German nuclear project were kept in Farm Hall, an English country manor near Cambridge. They had many private conversations while staying there; those conversations were recorded. The Soviets came to own those conversations."

"What do those recordings say?"

"The Germans wanted the bomb first, but the Americans had more resources. It's the same reason Americans got to the moon first; they put as much money and as many people behind it to make the impossible happen."

"What does this have to do with cloning?"

"The Soviets want to clone superior cows, goats and other animals. You can imagine how success in that area would change the world. Cloning would be a powerful tool."

"I can understand cloning sheep and cows. Better farm animals mean better food, but what does that have to do with the girl . . ."

"It has come to you, hasn't it, Dr. Stock? It is not a new idea. Humans have been, in a sense, on the path of cloning for centuries, by taking a simple cutting from one tree and grafting it to another. Ranchers and farmers have practiced selective breeding to bring out the best qualities of an animal. Someday soon, animals will be cloned to produce needed medications."

"What is cloning?" Tanya asked, with a shaky voice.

"It is making an exact copy of animal, a replica in every way: hair, teeth, eyes, organs and even ears are all the same. In short, cloning takes the cell from one animal, and puts in it the nucleus of a cell from another animal. That cell then is stimulated to divide, implanted in the womb of the parent animal, and later a replica of the first animal is born. They have the same DNA, you see. Research has been going on for decades and serious cloning research began in the 1950s."

Stock said, "I have read of no such research going on. Cloning is nowhere near replicating an animal, let alone a human."

"There has been ongoing research in cloning for three decades now. Mostly this research has been carried out in silence at small university labs or private institutes with meager private funding. It has been a timid and almost secretive effort at best, because of the moral implications."

The doctor frowned as he continued. "Moral implications have been thorns in the side of science. But we have assembled a top team of researchers at this institute. They have come from around the world. They are the finest of minds and the Soviet Union has funded us with millions of rubles. We are making cloning a reality."

Dr. Ramirez brightened. "But our advances are astounding and are completely unknown to the outside scientific world. You see, here in Cuba, we already have clones of sheep and dogs." The doctor proudly looked at Tanya. "We believe that a cloned human will follow soon."

Tanya's heart stuttered. "You want to clone me?"

He grinned. "If you truly have the special gift the Soviets think you do, then you are a very valuable resource. You are young and healthy, and will be in the prime of life when we use you as a specimen for cloning. Isn't it a marvelous thing to think of having ten, or twenty, or even a hundred copies of you?"

"You can't be serious?" Stock said, stunned.

"Of course I am. Isn't that why you brought her here?"

Stock didn't answer.

Tanya said, "I won't cooperate!"

The grin on Ramirez's face faded. "I am sorry to say this, young lady, but you have no choice."

"I have gotten to know the girl; she is very strong-willed."

Ramirez waved a dismissive hand. "This is no problem. I have three solutions if necessary. One, we harvest eggs from her ovaries and freeze them. Then, at our leisure, create embryos. Of course, the special gift of the girl may rest in the DNA in the nucleus of her cells, so we will harvest those cells and transfer her nuclei to the eggs of other young women, stimulate them to divide in the proper medium and then implant them in the wombs of volunteers. We have many such volunteers here are in Cuba; many who want to help the cause of Communism."

"I would rather die first," Tanya shouted.

Ramirez ignored her. "Our second option is to sedate Tanya or to keep her in an induced coma. Of course, there are dangers to her mind and body if we keep her in such a vegetative state for very long. Third, we can place her in an indoctrination program." He glanced at Tanya. "This is my preference. You are young and still impressionable; it will not take long to mold your mind. All it takes is the right mix of drugs and long-term confinement."

"Confinement?" Stock said.

"Of course. We have learned much from the Chinese about such techniques. They have successfully used the program on many male and female prisoners in China. In any event, we will eventually get what we want. If all goes well, we will now have this special gift of the Pravda to pass through future generations. We will create from Tanya generations of good Communists who will easily rule the world. Think of it—we will be able to distinguish friend from foe, truth from lies. Such a power is unimaginable."

"But the Pravda only comes every fourth or fifth generation," Tanya said. "Cloning me won't help."

Ramirez's smile returned. "It will not take several generations as in the past for the Pravda to appear in a descendant of yours. We'll clone you and clone the clones of you." He laughed at the sentence.

Stock said, "Have you thought of the fact that if you make a clone from a human all you will end up with is a fabricated shell, a soulless person?"

Ramirez said with a sniff, "I have no belief in souls. That is a concern for ignorant priests. I am a scientist, and scientists like me have wiped out the scourge of smallpox. God did not do this, men in laboratories did; men who worked uncounted hours. The same is true for polio and for many diseases that ravage the human body. We correct the flaws and cruelties of nature. If there is a God, then we are certainly smarter than He.

"Our scientists are so advanced," Ramirez continued, "that we have already taken genetic material from the udder of a sheep and fused it with an egg from another sheep. Of course, we had to re-move all the genetic material from the egg. The cells grew. The result was a perfect biological copy of the original donor.

"A similar clone of a human is very possible in the near future. Just think—you can create a perfect copy of life: life without the risk that comes from a random genetic lottery. We can produce selected advantageous genes and eventually have a race of perfect healthy and productive people in the years to come. There will be no more infirm to drag our economy down. If someone needs a limb or an organ, then all they have to do is harvest what they need from a perfectly matching clone of themselves kept in stasis. That limb or organ grafted into your body will never be rejected like those from a stranger donor, because your exact mirrored self is the donor. Bone marrow could be gathered from your clone donor if you have leukemia. If you need anything from a skin graft to a kidney, it will be waiting for you. The thought is amazing: we can keep our finest minds from politics, literature, the arts and science alive for much longer, and when they die, another perfect match of them will take their place. We will have a perfect world with perfect people."

Ramirez tilted his head. "Maybe in the future someone would meet a perfect but fifty years' younger match of themselves. I am sure that the older one will want to offer advice to his younger self, unless, of course, he needs the younger's heart." He chuckled. "It is a joke we have around here."

"I think someone may have already taken out your heart, Doctor," Stock said.

"Americans, always with much humor and little intellect."

Arkady moved to the desk and placed a hand on Stock's shoulder. "We must go. It is time to take Dr. Stock to the airport. I'm sure he would like a few hours' rest before his long journey."

"Airport?" Stock said.

"Yes, you have a ticket for a flight. In eight hours you will fly to Moscow, and then to Leningrad aboard an Aeroflot jetliner. From there, you will go to the prison in the taiga where the girl's father awaits. He is safely in our good care, and I am sure after you show him photographs of the girl in this hospital he will talk. Did Victor not tell you this?"

Tanya's breath caught at the mention of her father. A meeting meant her father was still alive, but the words were all a lie.

Stock nodded. "He mentioned some of it. He didn't say anything about going to a remote prison."

"As I said before, Victor could be a fool. Remember, you are just visiting the girl's father. It is what you requested. We are enthused about how much you are helping the U.S.S.R. and wish to waste no time. Seeing the prisoner is what you requested, is it not?"

Stock smiled weakly. "I hope to be paid well for my services."

Arkady nodded. "It is my understanding that you will be paid very well for bringing us the girl. You have my word."

Tanya tipped her head as she listened to the KGB man, hearing what no one else could. She turned to Stock and said with narrowed eyes, "They lie just as much as you."

chapter 33

THE ROOM
ABOVE THE
BANANA TREES

AN OLD WOMAN led Tanya up a set of narrow, creaking, wooden steps to an upper room with a long dark hallway. The old woman smelled of cigar smoke and sweat. Over a small meal in the research institute workers' lounge, she told Tanya her name was Alicia. Since Tanya refused to speak, the woman passed the time by doing the talking for both of them. Tanya learned Alicia was a descendant of early slaves who had brought her relatives to the island in the early 1800s to harvest sugar cane. The slaves were not as oppressed as those in America. They were allowed to stay in tribal groups, even marry, and some eventually bought land and, more importantly, their freedom.

The African slaves often intermarried with the Spanish that controlled Cuba at the time and the amalgamation of the two cultures spawned a people with a lust for life, love and the rumba music they created.

Alicia was stoop-shouldered, her skin leathery, wrinkled, the color of mahogany. Her stubby teeth were a tarry brown from smoking cigars. She stopped at a bare door to the room that she and Tanya would share.

Inside, Alicia drew back a faded floral curtain. The smell of hibiscus and jasmine scented the room as a warm breeze blew in from Havana Harbor. The fragrance filtered through a rusted iron grate. The grate was once used as a stylish ornament meant to keep unwanted intruders out. Now it kept Tanya in. With the sweet aroma came the sounds of rumba music that rode the breeze above the trees. The rhythmic sultry poundings came from a dozen or more radios set in windows or on porches along the sun-shaded street. Overhead a large, in-ceiling fan turned, venting hot air to the outside.

Tanya looked out the window and saw shirtless men in a small park below. They huddled around domino boards on wooden tables spaced around the area. Two women in curlers stood with babies cocked on their hips as they watched three young girls skipping a fast-spinning rope. Tanya gently felt the window bars and then took her hand and rattled it. The old metal flecked rust particles in her hand, but the grate was securely anchored.

Alicia hummed to the Cuban melodies mingling in the hot moist air. "The music you hear is our life. We cut sugar cane in the merciless sun and we sing. Cubans sleep only six hours or less a day because everyone dances all night. I am old, but I still sing and I can dance." She seemed to sadden. "I dance slowly now. My body does not move like it did when I was young like you. But I can still sing all day as I sweep the floors. It is in my blood to sing and dance all the time. When I cannot hear the rumba or move my feet to the beat, I think I will not want to live anymore." The old woman bent and leisurely folded back the frayed sheet on the bed. She started to sing softly.

Tanya moved to the bed and sat on its edge. Its metal springs squawked at her weight. The old canvas mattress had a hole from which white goose feathers protruded. Despite the glow of the sun pouring in through the window, Tanya felt the darkness of despair roll over her.

Alicia said, "We will share this bed; it is comfortable even though it seems even older than me."

A naked electric bulb dangled from the ceiling and bore black carbon scars from shorted wires.

"The lights do not work," Alicia said, and pointed to a book of matches on the chipped black dresser. Other candles were spaced around the room. "A candle is all you will need. We rest now. You will need your strength for the tests tomorrow."

"What tests?"

"That is not for you to question; you are now the property of the bearded one. You belong to the great Castro."

"No one owns me."

"This is Cuba, my young one. Everyone belongs to someone else but is owned by no one." She sat next to Tanya and lit a white candle that rested on the old small table next to the bed. The sagging candle was set in the cup of a large seashell. "I will pray for you, little one. I will pray that Mother Mary will hear my prayer and the men in this building kill you fast so you will not suffer." She sighed. "I have seen many suffer. I think God is angry with me for helping these evil men who experiment on people like they are rats in a cage."

Tanya heard truth in the woman's words and trembled.

The woman rose and lit a row of other candles resting in small containers that were once shot glasses in a casino. Now they were filled with wax and wicks.

"You wonder why I light candles in the day. I would light candles in the church, but I seldom leave the compound, so I light them here to burn to the Holy Mother Mary."

Above the shot-glass candles was a small framed picture of a white-robed Jesus with His red heart exposed. Tanya watched the woman as she mumbled prayers.

Tanya saw the dark skin and wide pink scars on the woman's knees as she knelt on the floorboards. Tanya sat silently as the woman mumbled her prayers. After a few minutes, Alicia opened her eyes and struggled to rise on arthritic legs. She sat again on the edge of the squeaking bed.

Tanya asked, "How did you hurt your knees?"

The women touched her kneecaps. "I take a pilgrimage to Santuario de San Lázaro each year. I walk two kilometers on my knees to the venerated shrine to Lazarus."

"You walk that far on your knees?" Tanya tried to picture it.

"Some who cannot walk on their knees crawl the distance on their stomachs to the place of the saint that helps the poor. San Lázaro will take evil spirits away from the afflicted and grant miracles." The old woman wiped a trickle of sweat away from Tanya's forehead. "I hear from the men that you are a miracle, that you have the power to hear when others tell a lie. Is this so?"

"Yes."

Alicia sighed. "If God has given you the gift, then He will protect you."

The thought comforted Tanya.

"Now rest, little one. I see weariness in you. Rest will bring you strength and hope." Alicia rose from the bed, then patted the mattress. "Sleep for a while."

Tanya lowered herself to the mattress and curled into a fetal position. She closed her eyes and forced the faces of Stock, Victor and Dr. Ramirez from her mind. She tried to focus on home and the fact that her father was still alive.

Tanya had slept only minutes when a knocking woke her. She had been dreaming that she was locked again in the stinking cabin on the sailboat. Although awake, she kept her eyes closed. She heard Alicia walk across the squeaky floorboards, then heard the door open.

"Do you speak English?" She recognized the voice.

"Yes," Alicia answered.

"I need to speak to Tanya."

"She is sleeping."

Tanya sat up, her stomach twisted into a fist at the sound of Stock's voice. He saw her and pushed past the woman.

"I thought the KGB man was taking you somewhere." Tanya tried to sound confident and unafraid.

"We haven't made it out of the building yet. He got a phone call and I slipped away." He moved closer to the bed. "Why did you say they lie just as I do?"

"Go away."

"What did you hear?" He raised the volume of his voice.

"I hate you."

"Answer my question!"

"That KGB agent lied when he said you would be rewarded with wealth. And they lied when they said my father waits for you in that prison."

"You can't know anything about your father. If I understand this right, you *hear* lies—you're not psychic."

"All I know is that your KGB friend lied to you." Her tone quieted. "I think they mean to harm you and also me."

Stock blinked several times but said nothing.

"Do you doubt me?" Tanya asked.

"No. I don't know how or why you do what you do, but I believe you. I'd be foolish not to. Still, you don't know they mean me harm, just that he was lying about my . . . compensation."

"True, I don't know if they mean you harm, but it makes sense."

"I should have known that the KGB would not be honest with me . . . of all people I should have known."

"Greed blinds," Alicia said, as she moved to a wooden chair where she had been sewing a button on an old dress. "I have been here a long time and have seen many people sell their souls to the lowest bidder."

"I don't need an old woman's philosophy," Stock snapped.

"You need many things," Tanya said. "No one can steal from God."

A sound just beyond the door drew Stock's attention. He looked down the hall. "Arkady and three other men. They're armed." His next words surprised Tanya. "I regret what I have done to you and to me."

Her own words surprised her. "I can hear truth in your words."

Arkady appeared in the doorway. Three men with machine guns stood behind him. "I told you to wait for me."

The words came out heavy. Tanya didn't need a special gift to know the KGB man was angry.

"I wanted to see Tanya one more time."

"You have seen her. Now we must go."

Stock faced the KGB agent. "The girl's father is not waiting for me at the prison, is he? Did he escape?"

"He has not escaped," Arkady said.

Stock shot a glance at the girl.

She whispered with a smile, "He lies."

Stock lowered his head. "You're lying to me. I will not be rewarded with wealth as Victor promised me, will I?"

"You of all people should know that, with Soviets, truth is not spoken often. Truth is a habit of the weak."

Arkady turned and nodded down the hall. He then stepped aside. Tanya saw Stock stiffen and retreat into the room several steps. A man dressed in green military fatigues entered the small room, a cigar in his mouth trailing smoke behind him.

He nodded to Arkady but ignored Stock. Tanya scooted toward the headboard, trying to put more distance between her and the man. She didn't like the look in his eyes or the five-inch beard that clung to his weathered face.

"El Presidente," Alicia said, startled, and lowered her head in submission.

He rolled the smoldering cigar in his fingers and turned to Stock. "I know of your plan, but I have no interest in your fabled manna. We Cubans work in the real world. Genetics is our future, not chasing myths from the Bible. In a few years we will be able to make small cows that will provide the same amount of milk as large cows. We will engineer cows to be so small that they will be like family pets. Imagine, a cow so small that he lives in an apartment and feed on grass grown in a dresser drawer with special lighting."

"Yes, El Presidente." Stock lowered his head also. "What will happen to me now?"

"You are not my concern; you belong to this KGB man. You may find yourself in the great Soviet Union being questioned about all you know of the CIA and FBI and how you did research for them. They must be interested in what you told your intelligence agencies about the inner workings of our comrades in the KGB."

Stock turned to Tanya, who said, "I am afraid his words are truth."

Castro smiled. "Good, little one, very good."

Stock slumped for a moment, but straightened when Arkady took him by the elbow. Tanya watched two of the men with machine guns take Stock into custody and lead him down the hall. She had no doubt this would be the last time she saw him.

"Do you know who I am?" the man in fatigues asked.

Tanya slipped off the bed and faced him. "Fidel Castro."

"So they teach about me in your American schools."

"Yes, but you wouldn't like what is said."

He guffawed. The other men joined him. "Capitalist propaganda." She could see he was a man of confidence and power, but his face showed the scars of age and stress. His eyes, however, blazed with the intensity of a much younger man. "So you know that I have great power in my land."

"Yes."

"Good. Then you will help in our cause. You will cooperate and I will give you my word that you will be treated well." He spoke with a finger in the air as if he were giving a speech.

She looked at the floor: a cockroach ran along the edge of the wall. It took a moment to muster the strength to speak. She had been through too much: been abducted, seen death, and been told she would be the center of scientific research. "Your words have no truth. I will not be treated well."

He stroked his beard. "You will be of much use to us. Everything will be much easier if you would agree to cooperate." He turned to the remaining soldier. "Bring the girl shaved ice with cherry syrup." He asked her, "You do like shaved ice with sweet cherry syrup, don't you?"

Every organ within her seemed to quiver as she sat in silence.

Castro said to Alicia, "Get her some sugar treats. Perhaps that will make her more accommodating to us." She bowed and left the room like a cat sneaking out a door. "Castro said you will soon be eating shaved ice, and I hope you will be thinking of how we may work together for the common good of my people, and, of course, our good friends from the Soviet Union." He raised his wiry eyebrows. "Am I speaking the truth now?"

Tanya nodded.

"Good! Very good. I will follow the progress of the research that will go on here." The bearded leader of Cuba sucked on his cigar, then quickly turned and strode from the room, trailing smoke behind him.

Tanya watched his departure, then looked out the window and thought of being in the cold air of Colorado, and of the day she found a Bible in the snow. She did not know if that day was a blessing or a curse.

chapter 34

TESTED

THE MORNING SUN shoved a sliver of brilliant light into the room. Tanya lay awake. The old woman snored next to her. Alicia's mouth hung agape like someone with a dislocated jaw. She gulped air, then rolled over.

A soft knock came through the door. Tanya waited for Alicia to rouse from her sleep, but the woman remained under. Another knock. Tanya slipped quietly from the bed and opened the door.

Dr. Ramirez stood on the other side. "Good morning. We have eggs for you and lots of ham and beans. We were told by Father Fidel to feed you well. Did you enjoy the shaved ice with cherry sauce?" Tanya nodded. She stood with a sheet around her young shape. The doctor cleared his throat. "I am sorry to intrude. You should wear this today." He handed her a cotton gown. It was washed clean but she could see russet stains from the blood of previous patients.

"I'll change."

She started to close the door, but he blocked it with his hand.

"I will wait."

"Turn around," Tanya said.

"I am a doctor; it is no shame for me to see your body."

"Turn around, or I won't put this on."

"You are a difficult child." The doctor turned his back and impatiently tapped his foot. Tanya slipped on the gown and then followed the man down the stairs.

She was led to a table in a room that had several soldiers drinking coffee. They gawked at her. Tanya felt their prying eyes and crossed her arms over her chest. She sat on a wooden chair next to an empty table. A pudgy black woman in a blue, flour-coated apron set a plate of boiled ham and beans and two fried eggs in front of her. She had a pleasant smile and spoke softly. "*Buenos dias, señorita.*" Tanya smiled at her.

One of the soldiers said something in Spanish and the others laughed. The woman retrieved a broom from its resting place in a corner and shooed the soldiers from the room. "*Es bireno para usted,*" she said, and then scattered them from the room like chickens from a coop.

Tanya was hungry. She had eaten very little since breakfast at the small inn where she and Shannon had spent the night. It had been less than two days, but it seemed like forever. As she ate, she thought of her father and about how the KGB man had lied about him still being in prison. She thought of the gold snuff box of Czar Alexander that Stock wanted so badly, and now would never have.

"He was the next victim of that cursed object," she whispered to herself. *Why can't people leave me alone? Why am I such a freak?* She felt she was no longer Tanya, no longer a girl who raised goats on a small farm outside Pueblo, Colorado—she was a specimen.

Tanya felt completely alone.

First there was the mental examination conducted by a Cuban woman who had been educated at Oxford, or so the diploma on the wall read. She even spoke English with the hint of a British accent. She wore her raven hair in a tight bun and spoke through red-painted lips.

"Hello, Tanya, I am a psychiatrist here to evaluate you. Do you know what a psychiatrist is?"

"Yes, a doctor for the mind."

The woman smoothed out the page on the note pad resting on the weathered table between them. "Very good. All right, Tanya, I want to be your friend; I want to know about what you think."

"That's not true. You don't want to be my friend."

"Maybe I should have said, 'I hope we become friends.' "

"That's not true either."

"Well, maybe I will stick with 'I want to know what you think.' Am I on safe ground there?"

"You're getting close."

"I can live with that. Okay, Tanya, how about some small talk? Do you have a boyfriend in America?"

"I can hear when someone tells a lie. I hear it in their voice. It never fails. Now, do you really think I would ever have a boyfriend?"

The woman shifted in her chair and offered a disingenuous smile. "I would guess that any woman who could hear every lie in a man's voice would be always disappointed." She lifted up her notepad. "Am I correct in assuming you are offering to help the Cuban and Soviet governments with your special gift? Is that correct?"

"No, that's not correct." Tanya slouched in her wobbly metal chair.

"Well, I assure you they have ways of making you contribute your medical attributes even if you refuse. It is a simple choice between pain and cooperation."

"More lies. I will experience pain no matter which way I choose."

"I can see that you are different than I originally thought."

"That statement is true."

The woman pursed her lips. "My report will reflect a total lack of cooperation and reason on your part, and that methods other than psychiatry are required here." The woman stood, gathered her notepad and clicked her pen closed. "I fear that you are not making proper choices under the circumstances."

Tanya remained stoic. She didn't bother watching the woman leave.

A minute later, old Alicia appeared. They walked from the room with Alicia's hand on Tanya's shoulder.

"What now?" Tanya asked.

Alicia hesitated, then said, "First a physical exam by one of the doctors, then they will test your ears."

Tanya didn't respond. There was nothing more to say.

They took her blood.

They took a urine sample.

They x-rayed her head.

They swabbed her mouth and nose.

By the end of the day she had been poked and prodded by a dozen people. Only the blood draw hurt, although the inside of her cheeks burned from the dozen times they scraped cells from the tender tissue.

The day of tests ended with her being taken back to the sanctuary of her room. But her fear remained.

chapter **35**

UP

THE ORANGE DISK of the sun dissolved into the green western horizon as Tanya tore off the hospital gown she had worn all day and donned her Levi's, blue blouse and red tennis shoes. The familiar clothes made her feel better, and Alicia had washed them clean of the smells from the van and sailboat.

Alicia had brought Tanya to the room, showed her the clean clothes, then returned to work. Tanya heard her lock the door from the outside. Nonetheless, she tried the doorknob. It refused to turn.

She moved to the window barricaded with the rusting iron bars. She thought of the Bible, and lowered her eyelids and whispered a prayer. "Oh Father God, I pray for a miracle. I pray You hear my prayer. Help me. Please, dear God, help me now. I am so alone."

She opened her eyes and saw the old Bible floating in the balmy evening breeze in front of the rusted bars. She blinked several times. She told herself it couldn't be the same Bible. How could it be? She had left it with the old man who had tried to rescue her from the van, but Stock had shot him in the chest and killed him.

Tanya closed her eyes and then snapped them open, as if doing so would prove she was dreaming. She rubbed her eyes and refocused on the strange apparition. Was it really there? Was the strange Bible just outside her window? Tanya reached through the bars and pulled it into the room. Her heart pounded.

As she pulled the Bible near, she discovered fishing line snaked through a hole in the upper edge of the black book. Dried blood was crusted on the cover. *The big man in the overalls,* she thought.

She snapped the fishing line and opened the Bible. A crisp,

folded note was tucked inside. She read in the fading light of the setting sun.

> *Look up, for your redemption draws near.*
> *Love, Shannon*

The phrase confused her; the sight of Shannon's name paralyzed her mind. Tanya thought for a moment, reread the note and then looked at the ceiling. The only thing she could see was the ventilator fan that slowly rotated from a soft wind. It squeaked with every rotation. Tanya heard a slight grinding sound from the fan. The outside rain cap was removed, and then the dark face of someone appeared, framed by the small opening. The person took a crowbar and bent the fan's blades off the frame. With the blades removed, it made for a foot-and-a-half by a foot-and-a-half square opening in the ceiling. Tanya saw the dark, smiling face of Manny, who whispered, "We go now."

A rope dropped through the throat of the opening and dangled a few inches from the floor. Tanya looked at the burning row of candles under the painting of Jesus. Tanya took two candles, then set one under the curtain and one beneath the bed. Smoke choked the room as Tanya shoved the Bible under the belt of her Levi's and took a tight hold of the rope.

"Ready."

She began to rise.

Her last view of the room was of smoke and belching flames that crawled up the curtain and licked at the bed. She struggled through the opening, thankful for her small frame. Manny helped her onto the tarred roof. "We go now."

She asked, "Why are you doing this for me?"

"I do it for Carlos, and Carlos does it for the money that your American friends paid him."

"Shannon?"

"Yes, and the man named David Murk."

Smoke billowed through the vent opening and the window.

"There is fire," Manny said.

"I know. I set it."

"Why?"

"This place is evil. Very evil."

A long rope with knots tied in increments dangled over the side of the building, reaching to the green bushes below. "We hurry," Manny said. "The fire will draw attention."

She shinnied over the edge, clinging to the rope and using the knots to keep her from sliding.

Just before her feet reached the ground, someone grabbed her—someone with strong hands. She struggled to free herself but stopped when she saw it was Carlos. He set her down.

Carlos steadied Manny as he descended the last few feet of rope. He turned to the girl.

"I don't understand," Tanya said.

"I am making ten times the money to take you back as when I brought you. It seems you have become my very best contraband." He looked about, then put a straw hat on Tanya's head. "We must go!"

"But—"

"Don't argue, girl. David Murk and Shannon Reed are waiting for you. We go now, or we all get caught."

Tanya clutched the Bible. It felt good to hear truth.

Carlos led them a short distance to a tall, shirtless black man with a machete. "Follow me."

"Who are you?"

"No more questions, girl," Carlos said. "Just do as we say."

Tanya resented being told to shut up, but saw the wisdom in it. The tall man walked the small group to the edge of the park. Most of the park was clear and neat, but one edge ended in thick brush. Like the neglected buildings that slowly crumbled, the park was losing a battle with wild foliage that wanted to reclaim its own.

Three feet into the burgeoning jungle, the tall man began swinging his machete. The long blade sliced down on limb and leaf. Tanya felt disoriented in the thick green foliage. Plants slapped her face as she clawed at branches and broad leaves. Lancing barbs cut her arms. She tasted the salty sweat that rolled down her face and seeped into her panting mouth.

Not enough time had passed for them to have traveled very far, but it felt like miles to Tanya. Finally she caught sight of an open grass area. She also saw ash floating down from the sky like a hot, dry rain.

They pushed their way past a final thicket of pink hibiscus and found themselves in front of a rusty corrugated hut. The family that lived there sat on a rickety front porch, trying to escape the evening heat. A radio resting on the windowsill sent out the throbbing beat of a rumba. No one said a word at their appearance. No one called out, no one followed them. Thankfully, no one cared.

"Will they report us?" Tanya asked.

Carlos waited until they had moved well beyond the family. "In Castro's Cuba, only a fool dares get involved in someone else's business. Everyone knows a friend or a father or a cousin who has been taken away by Cuban authorities and never heard from again."

At the edge of an eroded road dotted with asphalt chunks was an old, rusty, white sedan. The man with the machete opened the back door and motioned the three in the back seat. He then hopped in the front. "Keep your heads down."

A fire truck rolled past, its siren screeching. Six men hung on the vintage truck as its diesel exhaust mingled with soot from the burning building. Rolled-up hoses were coiled on the hood and a stack of ladders, axes and shovels was piled in the back.

The fire truck hit a pothole and the driver overcompensated. The truck slid into a parked car and the men hanging on the truck flew like pins in a bowling alley.

The tall man started the car, pressed the accelerator and drove slowly down the road, the car bouncing over broken slabs of asphalt. Tanya looked back and saw the orange glow of the raging fire dance above the banana trees and coconut palms.

"Looks like it will burn to the ground," Carlos said. "They have many chemicals, and fuel for generators. The whole place will be ashes soon."

"The girl started the fire," Manny said.

When Carlos looked at her, she thought she saw admiration in his eyes. "It looks to me like you have put a dagger in the heart of Castro's work."

"That place never had a heart."

In ten minutes they were at the water's edge of the darkening harbor. The only lights were from the rotating white beam of the lighthouse and the buildings rimming the big bay. In the dark waters, some boat lanterns bobbed in the gathering wind.

Adrenaline and fear began to take its toll on Tanya. Her body shook.

"Don't worry," Manny said as he took her hand. "I will be here."

"Well, I worry," Carlos said. "A storm is coming this way, a tempest." He ran his tongue over his lips. "I can taste it in the wind."

The car parked in an empty lot. Carlos and the others exited. Carlos reached inside his shirt and removed a wad of money. He handed it to the tall man and said something in Spanish. The man laughed and waved the money. As soon as they stepped away from the vehicle, the man drove away.

Manny led Tanya to a small boat. The word ZODIAC was printed on the side. Bay water lapped at the rocky shore with each break of a swell. Manny held the rope as Tanya crawled into the boat. In the middle of the craft Tanya saw a pile of fish nets with cork floats. They smelled of dead fish and were spotted with slime from fish scales. Even so, she thought it a better smell than the building she had just escaped.

Carlos pushed the boat into deeper water and climbed in. The boat was soon sputtering over the dark waters of Havana Bay as shards of lightning split sullen clouds, followed by loud thunderclaps.

"The sea is angry this night," Carlos shouted over the gathering wind. "I think this is good for us."

chapter 36

AFTERMATH

ARKADY FOOKS WALKED over dead mangrove roots that clung to a rocky shore, strewn with regurgitated debris, remnants of the fierce storm that had passed over Havana the previous night. An hour earlier eight soldiers had pulled the *Teresa Ann* onto the rocks. Storm-driven waves had bashed the sailboat somewhere in the Florida Straits and vomited it onto the jaws of the jagged reef. The craft looked like a chew toy for a sea monster. The hull had been nearly halved like a cleaved melon. Its shredded sails flapped eerily in the morning sun, and the lanyards slapped an irritating, rhythmic ping on the bent aluminum mast. The storm had hit hard, displaying a violence only the sea can commit. Nature had unleashed its fury, and the *Teresa Ann* paid the price for being in the way.

A search revealed the life vests were gone from the boat, as were the life preservers. A Zodiac, half filled with water and nearly clawed into strips by the reef, bobbed next to the jetty. A quarter-inch umbilical rope was still tied to a boat cleat. Since the aft cleat of the *Teresa Ann* was missing, Arkady assumed the dinghy was associated with the sailboat.

Arkady squinted against the sun and scanned the sea. A steel-hulled Russian-made patrol boat jammed with Cuban soldiers searched for anything that remained from the damaged *Teresa Ann*.

One of the soldiers shouted something as he extended a pole into the sea and snagged a tennis shoe. Arkady saw it was a red tennis shoe; a tennis shoe like those worn by Tanya. He spoke to himself in Russian. "Dead, they are all dead." He thought of the report he would have to file. He wondered how best to report that the priceless girl was gone. He shook his head. It would not be well received.

The nose of the small jet dipped as it descended through dark rain clouds on approach to Bembridge airport in England. It was a spit of an island, connected to the Isle of Wight by a short bridge. Its landing gear lowered from the bowels of the plane as the jet banked above a slate-colored sea. Slowly it dropped toward a wide stretch of chalky coastal cliffs crowned with a patchwork of farms and country homes. A wave of spray swirled behind the wheels when the craft set down on the wet runway. The jet's engines roared as if protesting the pilot's attempt to slow its inertia. When the jet stopped at the far end of the runway, it pivoted about and made its way toward a lone black limousine waiting on the tarmac.

Seated in a leather seat, Yuri gnawed at a small bit of dry skin on his lower lip. It was all so surreal to him; all so unbelievable. The crisp new cotton shirt and pleated pants he wore felt odd against his recently bathed skin. As he gazed at the gentle green hills rolling down to the sea, he felt the warm, smooth hand of Anna caress his own. He looked at her and smiled. He mouthed the words "I love you" in Russian. She smiled from moist eyes and held a hand over her heart.

His shrunken stomach now extended in a slight curve. He had stuffed himself with baked veal smothered in cream sauce, served a short time ago on the flight from Helsinki. He had almost forgotten there was such a thing as meat marbled with fat, malleable and tasty, and the ill effects it could bring to a body not used to such food.

The loud roar of the jet's engines ebbed from a loud roar to a gentle whir. The sky brooded as the air thickened with cold rain. Yuri thought, *How is this all possible?* His greatest fear was that he would awake in bunk number fourteen, his lice-infested bed in prison C-23. The thought made him shudder.

He replayed the amazing events of the last few days. He had escaped with Anna from prison with the help of a Yakut man. After traversing over many craggy ice-crusted mountain ranges, he was taken down a trail into a birch-filled valley, and came to a waiting car parked by the side of a remote logging road. The car door opened, and Sergey, the one-armed caretaker, emerged and embraced Yuri, kissing him on the cheeks. Yuri had not seen the man since the night he saw him shoveling snow at the monastery . . . since he had knocked out the KGB man with one swing of his shovel. Yuri owed his daughter's life to the man.

Yuri began to weep.

"Here is where I leave you," the Yakut said.

What composure Yuri had left melted under the hot realization that he owed this man everything. He had found him, waited for him when Yuri insisted on returning for Anna, then led the two of them through land and weather that would kill anyone without his special knowledge. He hunted their food, and to Yuri's delight, hadn't needed to kill and eat the dog.

"I . . . I . . ."

"No words are necessary, friend. I am well paid for what I have done."

"No payment is enough," Yuri said.

"I did not do it for the money; I did it because we have something in common."

"What—"

"Ask the old priest when you see him," Tengri Boo said.

The men embraced.

"Go with God," Yuri said. "May He make your path straight."

Sergey and Tengri Boo allowed him a few moments before encouraging him and Anna to enter the car.

After a wild ride down icy roads that spilled from the mountains, Sergey drove night and day, stopping only to nap for thirty minutes. In the light of a clear dawn, they arrived at the Monastery of the Holy Martyrs on the Neva River. The old priest greeted Yuri with a wooden cross in one hand and the gold snuff box in the other.

Yuri asked about the Yakut man that had saved him. The priest smiled. "The mountain man is the great-grandson of a woman named Olga. Your daughter Tanya is the great-great-granddaughter of the same woman. Olga was the last woman with the gift of the Pravda."

Yuri was stunned. "How is it possible that I am free? No one will tell me."

"God has provided you with a benefactor. He contacted me to arrange your escape and money was no object."

"But how would he know to contact you . . . Tanya!"

"She is well, my son."

"Who is this benefactor?"

The priest shook his head. "I am not permitted to say, but you will know soon enough. Come, eat. You have more journeys ahead of you."

The priest arranged for Yuri and Anna to be smuggled across the border into Finland by a farmer who crossed the border frequently and was known to the sentries.

In Helsinki they were taken aboard a private jet with Golden Well Drilling Company painted on the side. Yuri had experienced a sequence of unimaginable events that unfolded so fast it seemed to be a dream.

The plane's brakes screeched as the aircraft lurched to a halt. Through the window, Yuri watched two men wearing reflective-trimmed vests carrying rubber wheel chocks. The front door opened, and a rush of cool air invaded the cabin.

Yuri's callused hands struggled with the seat belt. A woman dressed in a stylish red flight attendant's uniform with a dark blue scarf bent over him and deftly flicked the tongue of the clasp open. Yuri reached across his seat and helped Anna unbuckle her seatbelt.

They stood, and the pretty blonde flight attendant escorted them to the plane's lowered stairway. Yuri stepped down the steps and into the dank gloom of the rainy day. His legs quivered and he almost stumbled, but he recovered by holding fast to the aluminum safety rails.

The air smelled clean and felt cool on his skin. As he reached the last step, he reminded himself that he was about to stand on British soil. He paused, then took the step, his eyes glued to the tarmac. Tears welled in his eyes and his breath came in ragged waves.

"Papa?"

The voice—sweet with familiarity—made his heart stop. He raised his head. Ten feet away stood a teenager with dark hair matted by the falling mist.

She smiled.

Yuri's hands began to shake. "Tanya? Tanya!" He ran to her and took his daughter into his arms. Sobs came in waves. "Tanya, my Tanya." He heard her weeping in his ear. Behind Tanya stood a woman holding an umbrella; a man was at her side.

Yuri was aware of the presence of others, but he had no room in his mind for them. Tanya in his arms consumed every bit of his consciousness.

After long moments, Yuri pulled back to look at his daughter. "You have grown so much. You are so beautiful."

"I have missed you, Father. I never forgot you. Not for a minute."

"The thought of you kept me alive. Every day, every week, every year, I stayed alive for this moment." He laughed. "You are the mirror of your mother."

Someone stepped to his side. He glanced at Anna. She held the gold snuff box. "Thank you." He straightened and took the box from her hands, then returned his attention to Tanya. "This is yours, along with the message that awaits inside. At long last, it is yours." He raised his hands and signed so Anna could understand. "This is the woman who helped me escape, who helped me see a tomorrow where there was none."

Tanya stepped to the woman and hugged her. After the embrace Tanya said in English, "Papa, this is Shannon Reed and David Murk. They saved my life."

"An honor to meet you," Murk said. He shook Yuri's hand. Shannon did the same.

The limousine pulled close to the group and a man in a black uniform got out. "Excuse me, but someone very important awaits you all at Cooper Hall." He opened the back door and the group entered the stretch limo. A minute later, they drove from the airport under slate-gray skies. Inside the limo, however, there existed nothing but a glow of joy.

chapter 37

LAZARUS

TANYA FOUND THE room intimidating.

The cavernous main hall was arched above and supported by curved, stout trusses. The aged walls bore thick plaster between hand-hewn Tudor beams. The floors were polished granite, covered with century-old ornate carpets from the Middle East. At the end of the big room, soaring leaded-glass windows set against polished dark wood paneling bracketed a massive red-brick fireplace. The fireplace looked more like a red-bricked garage door opening than a place to burn logs. A black-suited butler prodded at the burning logs with a heavy black iron poker. Around the room's high walls were a dozen mounted animal head trophies. In each of the four corners, like silent sentinels, stood vacant suits of armor. Their empty black eyes set in hollow masks seemed to intently watch over the waiting group seated below.

The group of guests sat in a semicircle on Elizabethan carved oak chairs with red pillows edged with orange tassels. Tanya's chair was nearest the front of the fire. She held the gold box as she gazed at her father with a smile that outglowed the flames. She heard a sound across the room and saw a wheelchair with an elderly occupant being pushed slowly through a doorway flanked by two massive bull elephant tusks. Its occupant was bent over with a clear plastic oxygen tube fixed under his nose. A young woman in a crisp white uniform wheeled the chair next to Tanya, and then stepped back a few paces.

"Who's that?" Shannon asked. Tanya wondered the same thing.

"The woman is Nancy Jiles," Murk whispered as he leaned over.

"She's a nurse. I've met her a few times when I've been here on other business. She dotes on the old man. I've been impressed with her compassion. She's one of those rare people who knows how to show mercy and comfort even if the patient is a crotchety old cuss."

Shannon stared at Murk. "You don't mean—"

Murk raised a finger to his lips. "You'll know everything in a minute."

The man in the wheelchair had red, watery eyes and breathed in slow inhalations. He was gaunt, with shriveled, grayish pale skin. He made Tanya uncomfortable.

The words were raspy. "I am R. C. Cooper. I paid for this little gathering."

"R. C. Cooper?" Shannon said. "I . . . I was told you were dead. I spoke to your son."

"I know. It had to be. Mr. Murk? If you would please explain. I am too shallow in the lungs."

David Murk turned to Shannon. "I'm sorry, but I couldn't tell you about this."

Shannon said nothing. She pulled her mouth into a tight, straight line.

Murk explained. "I work for Sir Richard, and have for many years. Once he knew about the Bible coming into the hands of someone who had knowledge of Feodor Kuzmich, he felt that a divine wind had blown the Bible to her for a distinct purpose. He felt it wrong to interfere with such a holy set of circumstances. The Bible and girl would find a way to Feodor Kuzmich's manna. We tried to facilitate Tanya's every move."

"I pretended to die just as Czar Alexander did," Cooper said. "I knew in my heart that after Tanya found the briefcase with the Bible safe inside, she could be allowed to carry out her heavenly purpose."

Shannon erupted. "This is the life of a very special girl you're toying with. She is a girl, not a pawn to be played with. Did you really think that God would allow you to pull strings like she was some sort of a marionette?"

Cooper rubbed his bony fingers across weary, baggy eyes. "You know the Bible's history. You know it gives life and saves life. It holds an amazing power that is far beyond what we will ever know."

Shannon looked down and scanned the face of that tattered Bible, seeing the bullet hole in its face. "Yes, I know its history, but it is God who uses us for His bidding and not the other way around. We should never use Him for our wants."

"How do you know that what we have done isn't what has been ordained to be?"

Shannon shifted in her seat. "This is either a careless stunt or madness."

"Life is often madness intertwined with the sublime," Cooper said.

Murk stood and paced for a few seconds. "I purchased the log-book of Captain Wilber Purdue, which told of the czar's escape and of his trip to Palestine in 1825. It was at a great price paid by Sir Richard, I might add. We were amazed that the pages spoke of the lost jar of manna. It was all so amazing, so remarkable, that the Bible seemed to be somehow pointing to some lost morsels of manna that the czar obtained long ago. To think we could have some of the very bread from Heaven that rained down on the Hebrews thirty-five hundred years ago was absolutely intoxicating."

Shannon furrowed her brow. "Wait a minute, David. The only interest you've shown in the Bible is its value as a historical artifact."

"True, but as things progressed I could see something amazing was happening. A blind man could see it. Like the Apostle Paul when the scales fell from his eyes, I could also see something incredible was unfolding. I could see Tanya had a very special gift, and that the gift was real. If you had told me about her before all this happened, I would have called you insane. Then the events began to unfold, and I began to have doubts about my doubts."

"You lied to us," Shannon snapped. She turned to Tanya. Tanya could see the anger in her eyes. "Why didn't you hear the lies in his voice?"

"He never lied to me or to you," Tanya said. "And he's not lying now."

Murk explained, "I never lied; I just didn't tell you all that I was doing."

Tanya nodded. "I cannot tell if someone is thinking a lie—only when they speak."

Shannon's frown grew into a hardened scowl. "Then it was a silent lie, and that's no better." She crossed her arms in a huff. "How did you know whom to even contact to free a man from a Russian prison or Tanya from Havana?"

Murk smiled and looked at Shannon. "A good attorney knows the law, but a great attorney knows the judge. He has the upper hand, wouldn't you agree? We are no different than that great attorney; we have the money to obtain an edge, to get what we want."

Murk continued, "Smugglers have a very reliable network around the world, and even in Havana. We know the officials, and with money it was easy to get Tanya on a speedboat. All we had to do was fork over the cash for Carlos to buy one. It was easy to get him to take the girl to the Grand Cayman Islands, which by the way are British-controlled, and it just so happens that Sir Richard owns much of the island's real estate."

"And judges," Shannon interjected.

"Yes, judges, customs officials, banking centers, and—"

"I get the picture," Shannon said. "But what about getting a man out of a Russian prison?"

"Sir Richard has connections there as well. His company is funding oil exploration with the Soviets in the north part of the country. Once Tanya told us about the monastery and the events that happened there, we made contact with a priest at the monastery. It turns out it was the same priest who gave the snuff box to Tanya years before. He arranged for a man, a Yakut outdoorsman, to bring about the first part of the rescue. It's amazing what you can do with unlimited funds."

Shannon looked at Cooper. "You have risked a lot of lives just so you could have some kind of a heavenly elixir."

Tanya held the snuff box tighter.

"I did what I had to do, woman—it was what any man would do in my situation. Besides, your opinion in the matter is of no concern to me. All I care about is what lies in that gold snuff box."

Tanya grew weary of the arguing. She held up the snuff box.

Sir Richard turned his head to face Tanya. "In that box is a message from a dead monk who may or may not be the real Czar Alexander; a message meant for you. In that box lies the answer to one of the most baffling mysteries of all time. The prize you hold will make you a fortune, and may just hold some lifesaving morsels from Heaven for me."

Tanya's hands, eager to open the gold box, were moist with sweat. She tugged on the lid, but the long-ago wax seal had hardened and the lid held fast. She reset her fingers more tightly on the gold object and tugged harder. The wax crackled as the seal split apart for the first time in well over 120 years.

Tanya saw a yellowed scroll of fine parchment rolled up inside, and resting next to it was a glass vial holding granules of what looked like dried seeds. The vial had a wax stopper that plugged its small opening.

Tanya removed the parchment. The decayed string tied around it disintegrated at her gentle touch. She removed the parchment scroll and gingerly rolled it open. Her eyes darted across the fading letters written in old, faded Cyrillic, obviously written by a learned mind. The scratchy appearance of the letters indicated they were inscribed by a hand that shook.

She translated as she read it aloud.

Seed of Olga,
I am an old man who has only a few hours more to reside in
this corrupted mortal vessel. Old men know when death is
near—they can feel it tug on their soul. It is like wandering
lost in the cold of night and then finding a cottage lit from
within by a red ember fire, and then the door opens suddenly
and a kindly greeter waves you safe inside.

I willingly let go of this dark life as my Lord now opens
the door of heavenly light and greets me with a welcoming
wave into eternal rest. I will, however, enter God's throne
room with shaking knees, for I have done the most heinous of
crimes. I long ago participated in the death of my own father.
The instrument of death—a gold snuff box—will be found by
you in my decaying hand. I leave this vessel of death to you
and this message and glass vial of manna sealed inside.

Tanya stared at the gold snuff box; she rubbed her thumb on its dented corner, thinking that it was damaged when the assassins of Czar Paul bludgeoned his skull that night in 1801. She shivered to think that the very object she held was a weapon of murderers.

"Tanya," Shannon said. "Is there more?"

"Yes. I'm sorry. I was just thinking." She read on.

> *My interpreter in the royal court was a woman named Olga. She bore a child, and that child now carries in her blood a great gift that will one day, far into the distant days to come, produce a girl with the gift of the Pravda. If you are reading this message, then you are likely that girl with the gift in her ears, and Olga was your distant mother.*
>
> *Olga was a good, kindly woman, wise beyond her years, who warned me of a plot against my life. Her ears heard the lies of those I trusted when I was Czar Alexander. I was to have certain death, just as my father was assassinated before me. My imminent death, foretold by Olga, was my deserved punishment for killing my own father, Czar Paul.*
>
> *So it was then that I fabricated my own death and became a religious hermit living in Siberia. It is a life of reading God's word daily, of prayer, meditation and purity. It is my penance and blessing to lead a life as the poorest of all peasants in this cold wasteland for what I have done.*

Tanya stopped reading aloud and read on in silence, not wanting to reveal what might follow.

> *Seed of Olga, I warn you to keep your special gift of the Pravda a secret from all, as I keep the secret of who I once was. Hide it always, for there are those who will surely kill you because of the Pravda you have in your ears.*
>
> *Seed of Olga, listen well to my final words. I find myself unworthy to have ever owned the manna hiding inside the gold snuff box. It is not for man to own, and I fear that in the hands of the evil ones it will not give life but cause much death. So as I leave the mortal bounds of human flesh and*

enter God's throne room, I leave the few grains of manna to
you, the girl with the gift of hearing truth in her ears.
Hopefully, you and you alone will be able to hear God's words
and do with the manna as the Divine Redeemer instructs.
Remember always that Heaven is never far away.
                                   Czar Alexander by Heritage
                                   Feodor Kuzmich by God

Tanya rolled up the letter and sat still, her eyes fixed on the objects in her lap. A log in the huge fireplace crumbled through the grate, startling her and sending spiraling sparks up the throat of the chimney. Her eyes lifted slowly and she scanned the room, resting her gaze on each person in turn.

The full force of the moment gathered in Tanya's mind. This one object was a touchstone that had changed a nation, changed an emperor, and now was changing her. Being involved in his own father's death was too much of a weight on the czar's heart, a horrid blemish that could never be fully cleansed, even though Alexander had given up everything he owned in this world.

Cooper pleaded, "Give me the manna, girl." He reached for it with frail arms. "I know it must be in there. It must be in the gold box."

Tanya raised the vial from Czar Paul's gold snuff box. She shook it and the small seeds rattled inside. She raised the vial to her eyes, the small granules that had fallen from Heaven's own kitchen dancing in the fire's glow.

She then looked at Cooper, the old man now teetering forward in his wheelchair with his fluttering fingers clawing at the air in front of him. He strained with the last of his strength to hold the manna, to pour the bread of angels into his mouth. He ran his tongue across his parched lips. The vial in Tanya's hand was only a few feet from his grasp.

"Give it to me. Give it to me now, girl!"

"I do not think it right for anyone to have such an object as this. People will only corrupt what God has made holy." She looked at Murk. He looked puzzled. "In Cuba I saw men trying to counterfeit God's handiwork in a laboratory. It was an evil place. I could smell the stench of death all around it. The only right thing for me to do was to try and burn it all to the ground."

She looked deep into R. C. Cooper's eyes with a strength that went beyond her youth. She thought of the words she had read from the czar, that answers would be heard from God. She closed her eyes and prayed. Then she looked up and spoke forcefully. "It felt good to me to see that building consumed in flames, and I am sure it gave God much pleasure as well." She lifted her hand, holding the vial of manna, and faced the fireplace. "People are dead because they tried to get this for their own gain and not for God's glory. The manna was intended for good and now man has turned it to bad."

"The manna, girl, give me the manna. It's mine. Stop talking foolishness. I own the manna. I paid a lot of my money for it."

Tanya stood with her hand lifted over her head as she held the glass vial. "The Bible says in the book of Matthew that the deceitfulness of riches and the lust for other things will choke out the life of God in us."

She threw the vial in the flames. The glass broke and seeds crackled as the fire quickly consumed it to ash. No one should own what God has made.

"Noooo!" Cooper slumped in his wheelchair, his face pale and awash with grief.

Tanya stepped to Shannon and took the Bible from her. She then walked to the front of Cooper's wheelchair. His weepy eyes stared despondently into the flames. She handed him the Bible. "This is all the manna you will ever need. It is as powerful today as when God first revealed it to man. You should have known this when you had in it in your possession many years ago, but many like you cannot see that, because you have choked out God from your own life."

Cooper took the Bible in trembling hands and gazed at it. He then looked at all the silent faces that were staring at him. The only sounds were the log sap popping in the fire and his own wheezing. He forced out his words in a tone barely above a murmur. "I am so very tired."

He paused to gather a gulp of air, and looked up as he held the

Bible over his heart. "This Bible once saved me. In the Great War, a German soldier saw this Bible in my tunic and refused to send his cold steel bayonet deep into my chest. He said he was a Christian and couldn't end my life as this Bible stared up at him. I didn't understand why he didn't kill me then. I only carried the Bible at the request of someone I loved." He rubbed the old, weathered face of the black cover. "It is my time to die now. I fear this book that saved me then will not save me now. Maybe if I had read what it says long ago, maybe I would have . . . have . . ."

R. C. Cooper gasped one final breath as the Bible slid from his slackened hand and toppled to the floor.

No one moved; no one spoke a word. Tanya gazed at the Bible as it rested on the finely woven threads of a red Persian carpet. Nurse Jiles looked pale as she stepped forward and laid two fingers on the old man's neck. Tears began to flow. "He's . . . dead." She drew a hand over her eyes.

"Shouldn't we do something?" Shannon said.

The nurse shook her head. "I am afraid the time for doing has passed."

A shroud of silence fell upon the room for a long minute. Tanya broke the silence. "That Bible is not for me to have anymore. It has brought me together again with my father. It has saved my life and his life and Anna's, and has given us all a new life together. The Bible belongs to someone else, someone God has purposefully brought to this place, at this time."

Murk stood and walked slowly over to the Bible that lay on the floor next to Cooper's wheelchair. He bent down and lifted the Bible. He then tapped his fingers on the Bible's edge. "I have come to know enough of the history of the book to know that it is very special. It seems this book has been on a very special journey, and for a purpose. It also seems to me that the Bible is never owned but lent to whomever God has chosen. That person has always been known as the Messenger." He looked into each face, glowing back in the flickering light of the fire. "I am not to be the Messenger—that I know for sure. But who in this room will be?"

Tanya spoke up. "I know who the person should be. The answer is clear. All who have the book will give life and save life." She looked at Nancy Jiles, the nurse, tears trickling down her cheeks as she stood over the lifeless form of the man she had cared for and comforted for so many years. "You are now to have the Bible and be the Messenger."

Nurse Jiles stood with cheeks glistening and her hand resting on the shoulder of the dead man. "People saw him as an evil man, but I saw him only as an ill and fearful man, a man in pain. I'm only a nurse. I am sorry, but I have no want of the Bible."

Tanya smiled. "But the Bible wants you."

WORK CAMP C-23, NORTHERN SIBERIA

Across the globe, deep in the dark taiga of the far north country of Russia, Jeffrey Stock awoke to a loud shout from a prison guard. "Get up, you lazy dogs!"

He rolled over in the scarce straw that covered the slats of bunk number fourteen. His eyes struggled to adjust to the small flame dancing atop a nub of a candle resting on a wooden table in the middle of the room. A bitter cold gust had invaded the prison ward.

As the flame sputtered to life, Stock could see words that had been carved into the wooden post next to where his head lay:

> BE OF STRONG HEART, AND REMEMBER, HEAVEN IS
> NEVER FAR AWAY.

The carved words were followed by the name *Yuri Novak*.

The jet's doors clamped shut with a thud. The whirring engines were muted now, and they all could talk. Across the aisle were Anna and Yuri; they held hands. Tanya was next to Shannon, and David Murk was seated behind them. He said, "Hey, Tanya, what are you going to do with that old snuff box and parchment scroll?"

"I don't know."

Murk seemed eager. "Maybe I can sell it for a good price . . . after all, it is one of the great finds in history."

"How good a price?" Shannon asked, as she turned around in her seat.

Murk grinned. "I'll do this one for free. I'll sell the gold box and parchment to some sucker for a ton of dough and I will give it all to Tanya and her family. It will certainly be enough for a good life for them all."

"You are quite the man, David Murk," Shannon said softly. "There might be hope yet for a handsome pirate like you."

Tanya cinched her seat belt, and turned to look at Shannon and Murk. "I need to tell you something. In Cuba they did experiments on my ears. I no longer have the Pravda."

Shannon eyed her for a moment. "Is that really true, or does your voice speak a lie?"

Tanya shrugged and winked. "Remember the elephants."

THE
Authors, Book & Conversation

ROBERT CORNUKE

A few years ago, I went on a walk through some tall pines by my home in Colorado and was thinking of a way to tell a story that somehow makes the Bible the main character. I sort of saw the start of a story play out in my mind as a Confederate boy was carrying his Bible across a muddy field on the last day of the Civil War. It was as if a movie projector was flickering images and I was viewing what played out on the screen of my thoughts. I never experienced such a thing before. I saw the vivid portrayal of it all as white smoke spit from a hidden rifle, the boy then crumpled onto the fallowed cornfield. A Union soldier soon appeared standing over the mortally wounded lad as he lay in the decayed stalks of corn splashed with blood. The Union officer stared down with numbing sadness that it was only a boy that now oozed out blood and life. The boy's pale face looked up at the man who shot him and exhaled weakly, "Be the messenger." He then slowly lifted his Bible to his killer. It was a moving scene which I had to write down. I hurried back to my computer desk at home and began to write, just as I saw it, or imagined I saw it.

The continued story spilled out through my fingers as they tapped as fast as I could go on the keyboard. Scene after scene seemed to emerge in a fluid form as if it was really happening. The days that followed became a delight to see what would happen to the characters that became so real to me. As new characters developed I actually cared so much for those that were good and noble and distained those that were evil. I had little planning or outline, it all just sort of flowed past me, like watching the path of a leaf in a stream as it swirls and dances in the water's serendipitous current.

That first novel was called *The Bell Messenger* and the sequel is this book, *The Pravda Messenger*. It was the continuance of the story of that old Bible changing hands and changing the lives of those who possessed it. Good clashes with bad, loves and lives are birthed and destroyed in a saga that always contains the Bible as the centerpiece. It is a story involving Russia, which is my heritage of lineage, and it also involves Washington, D.C., where I once worked and even starts out in Colorado close to where I live now.

I am asked often, how do you get your stories, how does one write as you do? I tell them that it all comes from the deep well of personal experience. I also say that no matter how dull you think your life is, everyone has a fascinating tapestry of experience, which they can weave onto the pages of a book. It is sad for me to think that the characters I created may never have lived, loved or died unless I sat down and typed them into the existence out of my imagination. In a strange way I am glad to have known them all, for they, like many of the relationships in my life, have made me a much richer man for having known them.

ALTON GANSKY

- When not writing, Alton likes to read magazines, novels, and nonfiction books.

- In the warmer months, he spends time in his workshop making furniture that always seems to move into someone else's house.

- He enjoys movies, preferring to go to theaters on Tuesday nights when the place is nearly empty.

- While writing *A Ship Possessed*, Alton developed a deep interest in World War II submarines. To date, he has toured three WWII subs, one Russian cold war Kilo sub and an active duty nuclear attack sub.

- Alton has three grown children and, at last count, six grandchildren whom he loves dearly but thinks he's still too young to have.

- Alton married his wife when he was just shy of his twentieth birthday and his bride was just nineteen. After thirty-six years, Becky's parents still haven't decided if it will work out. Alton remains confident.

From Robert Cornuke

1) How did you get started in writing?

Growing up in Southern California, I never liked English as a subject in school. I felt that any school assignment that I happened to stumble to completion was always something of little value or interest to anyone. Based on my less than adroit skills in English class, I never even considered that someday I would ever get a book published. I preferred sports, going to the beach and yes, those California girls! Yet here I am, a writer. Also when I was a kid, I stuttered out my words with embracing frequency. Yet here I am, a public speaker, often speaking to arenas and churches filled with thousands of people. The irony of this serendipitous journey is beyond any script I could possibly write. So how did I ever get started in writing? I owe a lot to David Halbrook, a wonderful man and talented author. We co-authored my first three books together. I had the stories, having looked for Noah's Ark, the Real Mount Sinai and the Ark of the Covenant and he was a wordsmith with extraordinary writing skills. David helped me discover a latent talent that I had for telling stories and the methodology of disseminating those stories to paper. Once I found the joy in writing, I was able to let my thoughts be set free into the wondrous venue of books.

2) Do you like writing.

Yes, I love writing, most of the time, that is, but I am a social creature and writing is a solitary venture, often resulting in a case of loneliness. But then I begin to have literary interaction with the characters in my books and they seem to make for great company. Those characters that I birth are usually very interesting to me because they are filled with a myriad of human traits that run the gamut of human personalities, resulting in a variety of potential plot scenarios.

3) The idea in this book of a Russian child with the ability to distinguish between lies and truth simply by hearing someone speak is unique. How did you come up with that idea?

I once listened to a woman testify in court and even though she once held a high government position in her past, I knew for a fact that her testimony was unfortunately false. Her words were damaging to someone's reputation and I wondered then, how wonderful it would be if someone ever had the physical gift in their ears to hear a false statement in the voice of others. I then thought of how that person with such a gift as hearing that truth would hold a power unimagined.

4) In the first book, *The Bell Messenger,* and in this book, the Bible travels the world, including Virginia, San Francisco, Egypt, the Sinai Peninsula and now Cuba. Additional action takes place in the cold war USSR. How have your world travels affected your writing?

I write from personal experiences, the people I have known and the places where I have traveled. If you read of a character in my writing he or she is, in some part, a real-life person I have, in some way, come to know.

5) What drives you to write?

I love to take something as simple as consonants and vowels and arrange them on a page, hoping that it all may be powerful enough that it changes and encourages others. I also like being creative, it is a very satisfying thing.

ROBERT CORNUKE
ALTON GANSKY
THE CONVERSATION

ABC

THE
Authors, Book & Conversation

1. Tanya has a special gift that allows her to tell when someone is lying or telling the truth. Is that a gift you would like to have?

2. Tanya's gift causes a great deal of trouble for her and ultimately endangers her life. Apart from the high intrigue of the story, do you think Tanya's gift would make her life better or worse?

3. Shannon Reed becomes Tanya's companion and life guide. How difficult do you think it would be to forge a relationship with someone who could judge the truthfulness of everything you say?

4. R. C. Cooper is a carryover character from *The Bell Messenger*. He has almost everything: money, a mansion, power and influence. Still he is unhappy. What do you think he is missing?

5. In many ways, the Bible in the story is a catalyst, revealing the character of those who come in contact with it. In what ways does the Bible function like a character in the book?

6. Do you think the story would be as powerful if some book other than the Bible were used?

7. David Murk is an unusual character. He has a mysterious history and may be more than he seems. What was your feeling about him when he first came onstage?

8. The book has a powerful, historical backstory about a mysterious monk. The monk is unusual in many ways. What feelings did he bring up as you read the story?

9. A substance from a biblical artifact is a key to the plot. R. C. Cooper hopes it will return him to life. Why was Cooper wrong?

10. If you had possession of the material that comes to Tanya centuries later, what would you do with it?

11. Tanya's father, Yuri, endures great hardship, yet somehow keeps his mind and body together. How do you suppose he was able to do that?

12. When faced with the opportunity of freedom and seeing his daughter again, Yuri hesitates then takes action that makes his escape less likely. Do you think you would do the same?

about the authors

Robert Cornuke is a former police investigator and SWAT team member who has traveled extensively overseas, leading and participating in expeditions to find verifiable historic sites and artifacts from biblical history. Bob is founder and president of the Bible Archeology Search and Exploration (BASE) Institute located in Colorado Springs.

An internationally known author and speaker, Bob has lectured on Bible history in the U.S. and overseas more than a thousand times and conducted a Bible study at the White House under special request from the White House staff.

He has led dozens of international Bible research expeditions, including travels to Ethiopia, Israel, Egypt, Arabia, Turkey, Iran and Malta. His research into the archaeology of biblical times has resulted in appearances on the History Channel, National Geographic Television, CBS, MSNBC, CBN, Fox and TBN's *Ripley's Believe It or Not.*

He holds a PhD in Bible and theology from Louisiana Baptist University and serves as special advisor for the National Council on Bible Curriculum in Public Schools. Bob lives in Colorado with his wife and children.

Alton L. Gansky is the author of twenty published novels and six nonfiction works. He has been a Christy Award finalist (*A Ship Possessed*) and an Angel Award winner (*Terminal Justice*). He holds a BA and MA in biblical studies. He is a frequent speaker at writers' conferences and other speaking engagements.

Alton brings an eclectic background to his writing, having been a firefighter, and spending ten years in architecture and twenty-two years in pulpit ministry. He now writes full-time from his home in Southern California, where he lives with his wife.

*An exciting collaboration between a real-life
archaeologist and a bestselling suspense novelist
that is sure to leave readers breathless...
and wanting more.*

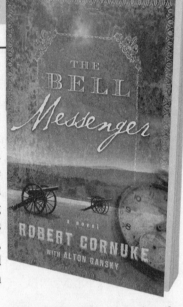

A suspenseful yet touching story of a Civil
War Bible that pops up again and again
over a century and shapes the very history
of the nation.

This rich and involving historical
and archeological thriller begins as a
Union soldier, Tate, shoots a Confederate
preacher known as the Bell Messenger and
is bequeathed a worn Bible by the dying
man. Tate's historical narrative parallels
the contemporary story of John Brandon,
who has just graduated college in 2000 and
received the very same Bible, unearthed in
a Saudi Arabian cave, as a gift.

The potent history of this book is revealed as Brandon searches for
previous owners, along the way uncovering the existence of a mysterio
cache of gold hidden during Old Testament times—which brings shadov
figures hot on Brandon's heels, hungry for the gold and desperate to learn t
new clues he possesses.

As the past and present intertwine, the reader learns that this Bible h
passed through many hands over the years. From the Civil War to the buildi
of the Central Pacific Railroad, to the gang wars and the holding of Chine
slaves in nineteenth-century California, to the trenches of World War I, Brand
learns of the lives this Bible has saved, the deaths it has caused, and the histc
it has changed forever.